To Pips

Enjoy.

TALES OF BLOOD AND SULPHUR

APOCALYPSE MINOR

J.G. CLAY

28/10/...

This story is a work of fiction. Names, characters, places and incidents are either the product of the author's imagination or are used fictitiously. Any resemblance to actual persons, living or dead, is entirely coincidental.

SHADOW WORK PUBLISHING

Editor: Christopher Nelson
Cover: Ashley Ruggirello

For more visit
jgclayhorror.com

CONTENTS

For my late grandparents, both paternal and maternal. The courage of the immigrant is always underestimated by those who have no soul. I know better than that.

PROLOGUE: TALES

"**THEY TELL ME** that you've touched the face of God. How did this happen?"

"An explanation would require time from myself and for you to possess the ability to understand such concepts. I do not have the time. You clearly do not have the intelligence."

Cameron bristled with anger at the arrogant tone. How dare this man--this illegal immigrant, no less—question his intelligence? They didn't just hand out degrees to any loser. His qualifications were well earned, obtained from the finest educational establishments in the land. Mother and Father had put their money to good use. He swallowed his anger, smoothing the lines of tension in his face. Rule number one of interrogation—never let the bastards see your weaknesses. He smiled, ensuring his highly polished and prized teeth were on display. Cameron wanted this undocumented lowlife to see the standards that he epitomised. The man before him didn't have the same high standards. That much was clear. Cameron cleared his throat before speaking again.

"Shall we move on? There's much to discuss and time is pressing."

The sallow faced man nodded, his gaze clear and level. He wore a half smile, his air one of studied indifference. He wasn't intimidated by interrogation rooms, or at least, that seemed to be the impression he tried to project. Cameron had met his type—all bull and bluster at first. Waterboarding and electric shocks soon changed attitudes. If those measures didn't work, there were always pliers and cigarettes, effective tools that made even the hardest case sing.

Cameron cleared his throat, stealing a sideways glance at his superior. Darrow, as ever, was ice cold, a solid bulky counterpoint to Cameron's thin frame and perversely innocent face. They must have looked odd to the detainee—an unlikely looking partnership. Looks were deceiving. The pair were amongst the most vicious and hardened interrogators in the land. Their reputation amongst their peers had been enhanced by some high profile wins—bomb plots, threats of beheading, attempted assassinations of right wing politicians. Their methods, however, left the others wary and a little afraid. These were not men to be messed with. A very vocal left wing journalist had learned this at a high cost. He was only recently able to take in solid food after a month long liquid diet, the consequence of being force fed a cocktail of bleach and paint stripper.

"Let's start with your name," Darrow said. Cameron looked at the younger man in surprise. It was unusual for Darrow to step into the interrogation so early. He was the muscle. If Darrow noticed Cameron's reaction, he didn't register it. He merely lowered his temperature to permafrost, his voice sounding like razors being dragged across a frozen pond. The detainee, unfazed, smiled wider and crossed his legs.

"My name? My name is Null. I believe I have already told you this. I furnished my previous interlocutors with that information before we met."

"Null", an alias if ever there was one. He rubbed his left knee slowly. Darrow clenched his jaw.

"Null isn't a name. It's an—"

"Adjective," the detainee said. "Meaning nothing, nil, void. It is also my name. Really, Mr Darrow. I thought time was pressing. Surely we would be better served discussing weightier subjects than the meaning of my name?"

Darrow ground his teeth. Cameron knew him well enough to know that the anger was boiling. Violence would not be far behind.

"You listen to me, you little shit stain. Firstly, never interrupt *me* when I speak! Secondly, we discuss whatever me and my partner here want to discuss." Null smiled and held his hand up in a pacifying gesture. Cameron stepped in. He could see his partner's ears becoming redder by the second. A bad sign.

"Ok, Null. Let's move on. Swiftly. No beating around the bush. Where are you from and what is the purpose of your visit to the United Kingdom?"

Null laughed softly. It was a pleasant sound, one that put Cameron at ease. The man himself seemed pleasant enough. His age was hard to determine. He had that unknowable quality that Eastern people managed to carry off, an ageless demeanour. Only his eyes, rich, dark brown almonds, spoke of age. There's was a haunted look about them that spoke of horrors and tragedies unimaginable, to those whose only worry was the price of milk and petrol. The lines of sorrow, etched so deeply around his eyes, were nowhere to be seen on the rest of his face. In fact, his skin was so smooth, so flawless, that it didn't seem real at all. Null had the appearance of a shop window mannequin brought to life. Even his lush black hair, swept back into a ponytail, had an artificial look about it.

Null considered the question. "These are questions that I have no adequate answer for. The place I originate from is now closed to me. The doors of that heavenly abode have long been sealed shut. I remain here as a guest at your convenience."

Hah! So he was an asylum seeker. Cameron felt triumphant. He had known, or at least sensed, that truth. The only question that remained was who he was running from and how useful his knowledge would be to His Majesty's Government.

"As to my purpose here—" Null paused. He looked up at the featureless grey ceiling, his eyes fixed on a point in the centre. He dropped his gaze, abruptly. The sudden movement startled Cameron. Darrow sat still. He wasn't bothered.

"What is your purpose, Mr Vale?" Null asked.

Cameron squirmed, unaccustomed to being on the spot like this.

"And you, Mr Darrow? Other than being my torturer, what is your purpose?"

The heavy-set man glowered, saying nothing.

"You have no answers for your own purpose. You both find it difficult to articulate your exact reason for being in this universe. I share your lack of self-awareness. I do not know why I am here." Cameron noted the sadness in the man's voice. Despite his training and his professionalism, he felt a small pang of sympathy. Null seemed genuinely helpless and stateless.

"If it helps the situation, I can tell you this. In my previous life, long before I became an itinerant wanderer, I had a talent, an occupation.

I would roam from place to place, realm to realm, zone to zone, collecting tales of a specific variety. There was no prerequisite, no vetting procedure, and no criteria, save one. They had to pique my interest."

"This is wasting our fucking time! Total bullshit!" Darrow growled from the back of his throat. His patience was wearing thin. Cameron placed a hand on his colleague's shoulder. He was hooked now. He wanted to hear what this man had to say. Something in his voice aroused his curiosity.

"Thank you, Mr Vale. As I was saying, I collected these stories. So many tales to tell. I still remember them all. It would take me a thousand years to tell you even a quarter of them. That was my occupation. I was. I am...a curator of tales and the media to convey them." Cameron's curiosity burned in him. This man had gone from being a failed illegal immigrant, to the most interesting man on the planet.

"You're a story teller?"

Null brightened at the interest. "I am indeed, Mr Vale. In fact, your police picked me up whilst I was gathering. New stories, of course. The fascinating thing about this realm is that there are so many stories waiting to be prised out from their hiding places and shown the light. It's fortunate that I am here to collect them."

Darrow snorted, tapping the table. Cameron turned to him, his eyes narrow with anger. "Problem, Darrow?"

The older man tipped his head toward Null.

"Him, sir. He's just an illegal, spinning us a line. The Chief was wrong about him. Anyone with a half brain can see that we're wasting our time here." Anger burned brightly from his face. He appeared bored, was probably in need of coffee and a cigarette, and he was surely tired.

"Tell you what, Darrow. Go and have your lunch early. I'll carry on here."

Darrow frowned in confusion. "Go on, fuck off. I'll be ok. There's guards outside. Besides, Mr Null here won't do anything stupid. Will you?"

Null nodded his agreement. Darrow looked uncertain and a little mistrusting.

"Honestly. I won't use this against you in a review meeting. Off you pop."

Darrow stood, a mixture of relief and confusion on his face. He took one last dour look at Null before exiting the room.

Cameron turned his attention back to his detainee.

"I'm sorry about that, Mr Null—'

"Null will suffice."

"Ok, Null, then. So, please continue."

"There is not much more I can say. I collect tales and tell them. There is always a fee, modest in some cases, exorbitant in others. But people always pay."

Null's voice, so smooth and soft, wrapped around Cameron. The rational part of his mind, the part that had awakened a few moments ago, told him to stay alert and mindful. He paid it no mind.

"What would be the price?"

Null frowned.

"The price to tell me some of those stories."

Null smiled.

"We can negotiate payment later."

A silence descended on the sparse interrogation room. The air became heavy and warm. Cameron's scalp tingled with excitement and danger. The rational part of him voiced a warning again, the voice sounding older than before. It spoke of barriers being crossed, doors being opened and secrets revealed. Null cocked his head to the left, regarding the interrogator with curiosity. A dreamy look came over his face.

"As settings and circumstances go, this is most agreeable." He cupped his hands, leaning forward, and looked Cameron in the eye. Cameron held the gaze. Null's eyes were of a brown so dark they could have been ebony. There was a smoky enticing quality to them, a suggestion of seduction and mischief. A pleasant thrill emanated through the interrogator's nervous system.

"The *Nass Zubaiders* have a tradition', he said, his tone conversational. "Have had it for well over ten thousand years. Their shamans, the storytellers, take apprentices from a young age. When it is time for the student to take his teacher's place, the elder tells one final tale, the last of his life. As he speaks his final words, the elder is eviscerated slowly. The apprentice opens up his teacher with the sharpest blade, reaches in and begins to pull his guts out slowly. If the elder lives long enough to finish, he is given a quick death. If he doesn't, his soul is cursed, exiled from the realm, doomed to wander forever."

Cameron frowned more from confusion than at the barbarity of the story. Null became alert, the life coming back to his olive skinned countenance. He smiled again, showing a mouthful of teeth that, while serviceable, had seen better days.

"Old traditions, eh? A boon and a curse in all realms of existence. So, you want a story, my dear Mr Vale."

Cameron nodded, his eyes never leaving Null. He felt a growing impatience feeding his desire to hear and to know. "I've said as much."

"And you are willing to bear the cost?" Cameron sighed, a dreadful sound. It was the sigh of a condemned man. Nulls' smile grew wider, a look of triumph on his face. There was something almost gleeful in the sheen of his eyes. The thrill of pleasure Cameron felt was now replaced by unease. He looked once more into the storyteller's eyes. Flecks of red seemed to scuttle across the pupils, flashing briefly before fading into extinction. Something passed between the two men in that brief moment. Cameron's anxiety melted away. He relaxed.

"I've kept you waiting for too long. There are so many tales to tell. Tales of loss, of desperation, of apocalypses minor and major. Tales of blood, shit and sulphur."

He paused.

"What would you like to hear first?"

Cameron waved his hands impatiently. "You decide."

Null lowered his head as if sorting through long-closed files in the dusty recesses of his mind. He looked up. The smile faded, replaced by an earnest seriousness.

"I think I've found just the right one to begin with. Please sit back. Make yourself comfortable. As comfortable as you can." Cameron did as he was instructed with the detached air of a hypnotised man.

"We begin."

Cameron closed his eyes and let the man's voice take him. In the projector screen of his mind, he saw an island set in green inviting waters. An achingly bright sun hung over this forested island paradise, the light eerily focused on the beach. A man sat crossed legged on the white sand. His face was indistinct, blank. It didn't matter. The details did not matter. Only the Tale. The man stared at the sand before him, as if inspecting it.

Null's gentle lilting voice cradled Cameron, guiding him into this place. He hesitated for a moment before letting go, becoming immersed in the Tale.

ON THE BEACH

SOMETHING'S COMING UP from under the sand.

I've been staring at the contorting patch for hours, now. It may even be minutes. I've got no way of knowing. A highly expensive Rolex watch once adorned my wrist, but now it's the property of some nameless Filipino fisherman. The sun hangs in the cobalt blue sky, glaring down at the condemned man below, unmoving and baleful. Hours, minutes or seconds, it doesn't really matter anymore. Something is being born from the heaving piece of beach, as unearthly to me as the half glimpsed forms of my island neighbours. They're not very sociable.

Whatever creatures I share my new home with have long gone, perhaps sensing that something is about to invade their little slice of Earth. In the heavily forested interior of *Ang Isla sa Mangtas*, animals whose shadows stalk me—whose red, green and amber eyes glowed at me from the dark of the bush—are now hunkering down in their nests, waiting for the cataclysmic battle to finish.

I'm ready for this.

In a way, I've been ready for this my whole life.

It's all part of the Game you see.

A Game that's taken me across the world, leaving the corpses of loved ones tossed aside like broken and bleeding dolls, is about to end on this God-forsaken island miles away from civilisation. There's no regret about dying, not from me anyway. That's what gambling's all about. Some you win, some you lose. If I'm still capable of feeling anything at all, it's a slight sense of remorse for not dying sooner, before all Hell broke loose. There would have been people walking around now who deserved to breathe, to feel the sun on their face and hear the gentle lapping of the tide as ocean meets shore.

And yet, a part of me still wants to live. I won't lie to you, not here and now. *I still want to breathe. I still want to feel, to speak, to hear and to listen. I'm still not beaten.* I am human, after all. Even with our backs against the wall, faced with overwhelming odds, our race is still looking for the big win, the easy score, one chance to grab the prize and run for the hills. I've got one more hand to play. Ever the gambler, even in the last moments of my time on Earth. I've made sure that there's a get out clause. If this works, I take the prize and the glory. If it doesn't? I won't think about that just yet. There isn't enough mental space to think of defeat. My mind's too busy going over the shit storm that landed me here in the first place.

It's not a pretty story.

Being stranded on a tropical beach isn't the worst ending I could think of. There are far more debased places on this blue and green orb that we cling to. I've seen a lot of them. For instance, this final hand could have gone down in some filth-filled Mumbai alley, in the basement of a crumbling Eastern European tenement block, or in some seedy Middle Eastern hotel. Here, on this little island in the *Celebes Sea*, I can enjoy the sun on my face one last time before I played the *Familia de Potestas.*

A warm breeze whips off the ocean, carrying the perfume of life and death in equal measure. In the stand of trees behind me, a resident of this Fair Isle cries out. The throaty cackle rides the wind and is thrown into the ocean wilderness. It's an unfamiliar sound. Many of them are. Biologists and cryptid hunters would cream their pants in this place. Or shit them.

I know I did on my first night.

I've grown used to the sounds of the island. The days are filled with the odd little conversations between those creatures who brave the sun. The nights—the nights are something else altogether. It's a cacophony of wailing, howling and screaming. Large bodies crash through the undergrowth, prey and predator playing hide and seek. The rustle of membranous wings fills the sky. Pointed legs grind into tree bark, seeking purchase and stability.

If Hell has a soundtrack, I hear it every hour of every day.

Those sounds scraped at my already raw nerves when I first arrived here. I had visions of eyeless things—hairless, smooth, with a multitude of eyes, teeth and limbs. My dreams were haunted in those early years. Or more haunted than they already were.

Isolation does funny things to you, and here, on the island, I'm as alone as I ever could be. There's no crushing seas of humanity; just seaweed, the odd jittery crab, occasional birds that soon take their leave of the place and of course, my mysterious forest friends.

After a few months I relaxed. The denizens of the jungles of *Ang Isla sa Mangtas* avoided me and I did my best to stay out of the way. On an island as small as this, total avoidance is impossible. I've caught the odd flash of scaly skin, the glint of a tusk in the sun, but that was the extent of our contact. They don't seem to like me much around these parts. Maybe I stink of death.

The ends of my blanket dance in the wind, jarring loose the memory of another time, another place; my wife and I, sitting on this very same blanket, as we watched the huge, burnt orange sun sinking slowly into the Indian Ocean. I let a tear fall and find I am surprised at the gentle outpouring of emotion. It's been a long time since tears have fallen. I thought they had all been cried out.

The wind dies. The heat's bearable enough, even without the breeze. Not that I care much. Any discomfort is well deserved, and it's nothing compared to what awaits me on the other side if I've overplayed my hand. The sand begins to contort more vigorously, taking the shape of different, screaming faces. Some I recognise, others are strangers to me—perhaps they are the faces of other gamblers, other unfortunate souls. Maybe they, like me, went for the easy path to power and glory only to find stinking death and pain unending on the other side.

I will know soon enough.

It had been a long torturous road from the late night gaming dens of Birmingham to the gleaming glitz of Monte Carlo. I might have played it all so differently had I truly known what I was up against. I laughed to myself, a soft broken sound. You didn't need to be a gambling man to guess how many other poor misguided fools had said that before taking part in the Game.

I was a gambler even before careening headfirst onto a path straight to Hell. It was the thrill, the triumph, even the semi-sadistic feeling of smugness when some poor bastard had to be ushered out after losing everything, all hope pulled from them as their fragile little lives vanished in a puff of smoke and IOU's. The adrenaline rush was unbeatable but sordid, as nasty as a blowjob from a crack whore, as fine as a fuck from the world's greatest call-girl.

Of course, winning mattered. There was no point in riding the buzz without a win. It amplified the feeling, making your whole body fizz as if a great power was about to explode forth. When I was winning, nothing mattered. I was strong, powerful. My senses were sharper, my appetite for women, drink, drugs and food, insatiable. I wasn't jumping at shadows or running halfway across the globe to escape the dark. I had whatever I needed.

Until Lady Luck deserted me. The good run I had experienced turned into loss after loss after loss. I was haemorrhaging money and confidence as quickly as it had come. The buzz turned sour. I needed help. Even divine intervention would have been welcome, but instead, I got a little man named Felix Kersher, and an intervention less than divine.

It was Kersher who had first told me about secret rites and rituals, pathways to power and glory only travelled by men of courage and conviction. I had heard whispers of such crazy tales and dismissed them. They were told by rambling, broken men whose minds and bodies had been smashed by the love of the Casino, Gambling and The Big Win. These men shambled around in their too-loose clothing, broken and pathetic. Their fortunes plummeted; their lives transformed into colossal train wrecks. Lady Luck had packed her bags and taken the first flight home, deserting these losers. All great gamblers had these moments—the nights where every hand is shit, every roll of the dice, and every spin of the wheel brings you closer and closer to a desperate end. Some rode it out, others sank without trace.

The night I met my benefactor, I'd nearly lost everything. I'd listened to the muse of Lady Luck, convinced that the big win was coming. The win didn't even leave the traps and now I sat in a darkened corner of some nearby bar, the type of place where the air stunk of smoke, vomit and broken dreams. I was drinking away the little money I had left, trying to catch the eye of a slat-thin woman two tables away.

She didn't notice me. Her lank hair clung to her pale skin like a greasy splat of dark. Despite the gloom of the bar, I could see the vacant look in her eyes. She was shattered and as desperate as me. I smiled, mustering all my remaining energy. The woman stared straight through me, gathered up her things and left, a trail of cigarette smoke marking her exit from this seedy little place.

I couldn't even pick up a crack whore. The world had turned its back on me entirely. Searching my pockets, perhaps it was for the better: I had barely enough money with which to drink the world into a brighter and less miserable place, even temporarily.

Kersher came out of the shadows and smoke, a trench-coated angel with slicked back hair, a big smile and a strange twitch in his left eye. I never asked for his company—he just sat himself down, put a bottle of high-end whisky and two glasses in front of me and began to talk about inconsequential things, as if we were old friends catching up after years apart. There were no awkward silences, none of the straining to find topics of interest. We made friends naturally, and quickly.

Despite the grease in his greying hair, his hatchet face and the bad teeth, I began to warm to this odd little man. He was a refugee from the casinos himself, he said. I didn't care. He was as generous with the drinks as he was with the chat. His company came as a welcome distraction from the thoughts of beatings from casino bosses who would want their pound of flesh and bone.

That night rolled along, wheels well-oiled by helpings of fine beer, finer whiskey and the finest drugs known to Mankind, all paid for by the gracious and good natured older man. I was suspicious at first. This man with bottomless pockets arrived as if from the shadows. He implied he knew me and my troubles; he could help.

I had always been good at spotting scam artists and con men. It was a weird sixth sense I had. Something about Kersher struck me as off, but I couldn't put my finger on it. Those feelings were soon washed away in the tidal wave of whiskey and cocaine. It's hard to be objective when you're smashed out of your tree. Besides, the greasy haired little man, with his expensive looking suit and fat money roll, didn't have a care in the world and he was more than generous.

I unburdened myself, rambling on about the losing streak at the tables, the emptiness of the one night stands, the feeling of total disillusionment with life. He never interrupted, just nodded with understanding at the right places, smiled, and made the odd hand gesture in sympathy. My torrent of woe and bitterness came to a dead stop. The grin on my newfound friend's face seemed to grow, his teeth looking as if they had been filed down to cannibal points. He leant across the table, his eyes twinkling with an unpleasant light. I could see every line in that long sallow face, every open pore, even the unsightly sheen of grease that skimmed the surface of his skin. It might have been a combination of fatigue and brain cells frying in a stew of fine Colombian product and alcohol, but at that moment, the world shrunk. It was just me and Kersher's lined, lived-in face. Nothing else mattered. He spoke three words;

"*Speculum De Mysteriis.*"

I sat back, unable to make sense of his uttering. The room spun lazily and my stomach gave a twitch. Deep in the wasteland of my subconscious, something stirred and shivered.

"The what?" I was slurring now. I squeezed my eyes shut for a few seconds and opened them again. He smiled at me and looked at his glass, his eyes losing their lustre. He tossed back the drink.

"I'll explain. But not here."

I followed suit, throwing the fine single malt down my throat. The world greyed around the edges of my vision for a second. I was sure I saw a shape out of the corner of my eye, something huge and dark, like a statue carved from magnetite. The figure seemed to be leaning towards me, beckoning with a long finger.

"Are you coming or not?"

Confused, I turned to Kersher. He looked impatient, maybe even a little afraid. Was he seeing the spectre as well? Mute, I nodded and followed him out, eyes focused straight ahead. The figure vanished into the night air.

It was a book, ancient and enigmatic.

No one knew for sure when it had been written. Some said it pre-dated the Hindu Vedas by six thousand years. Others believed it had been written by a crazed Roman Centurion who had found himself in *Gehenna*, the Judaic valley associated with Hell, and had covered the book with the skin of a new-born before being crucified for his crimes. But of all of the origin stories, its discovery by a Franciscan Monk in Jerusalem left the darkest mark on me. He supposedly had it translated from the ancient and arcane tongue, to Latin.

The monk's fate was lost to the mists of history, but the book continued to exist, making its way into the hands of alchemists, magicians and the insane, before being denounced as heretical and satanic. The Church held bonfires of the book and burned those unfortunate enough to be caught with the awful tome in their possession. And Judeo-Christians were not the only Crusaders to scourge the Earth of the book. Islamic mullahs also purged the volume from their lands of the Crescent Moon, ensuring its darkness would never taint the sand and sacred mounts of Ibrahim's Middle East. Very few copies existed. The Vatican itself refused to harbour the book within the shelves of Rome's secret library.

The book survived nonetheless. Its owners guarded it very carefully, never keeping more than one copy together and keeping both themselves and the book on the move, to evade the cross and the flame of God's heralds.

I never asked him where he had obtained his copy; he never felt the need to tell me. He made some vague mention of an old Rama temple in the Assamese jungle, but that was as far as he went. To be honest, I wasn't really interested in how the old man had acquired it. I just wanted to know how it could give me back the thrill and the buzz that had deserted me, leaving me a hollow, desiccated version of my former self. I could probe Kersher's relationship with the book later. I had work to do.

The beach has begun to bump up in front of me, as if hands are pushing their way to the surface. I shift on the blanket. Not too much though. There are some things best left undisturbed. A buzzing fills the air, like a giant, irritable hornet. The jungle behind me falls silent. I turn for a moment to look at the trees, hoping to catch a glimpse of the local wildlife. Nothing. No gallery of eyes staring back at me. Not even a solitary whimper, or the brush of flesh against bark. The sound begins to transform into a galaxy of whispers. I strain my ears to catch a snippet, but it's just gibberish. I'm not even sure there's a language being spoken here.

I keep my eye on the sand, and begin to hum an old tune from my youth, an appropriate one under the circumstances; "Message in A Bottle" by The Police.

The first time I laid eyes on the *Speculum De Mysteriis*, I felt simultaneously sick and elated. The binding was soft and warm, like the shoulder of a lover. I opened the book to a random page. The vellum was covered in Latin, a long dead language I didn't understand. The faint smell of gangrene and sulphur wafted up from the pages, pricking my nostrils and scouring the back of my throat.

We were a long way from Monte Carlo now.

I became a semi-permanent guest in his villa just outside Marrakesh. His was the only occupied building. The other villas sat empty. Sand piled like golden snowdrift against the walls of these disposable mansions, reducing the splendour of the once beautiful structures to a ghost town for the rich. Very eerie and appropriate, though.

We began my education. I had never been one for formal study. At school I got by, knowing that my intelligence and my knack for last minute revision would carry me through. The gambling reflected my lazy nature. It was all about the quick fix. My teachers would have been surprised at how avidly I took to instruction. Gone was the fidgety, impatient student looking for the easy solution. In his place sat a dedicated, studious being, possessing a tight focus. Kersher showed me only the passages of the book I needed. The other knowledge in that book was strictly off limits. There was too much power, and far too many dangerous ideas in those odd words, to let a mere greedy novice such as I loose with them.

I devoured each lesson, carefully studying the notes and translations. On one unforgettable occasion, he even let me look at the creatures I would be petitioning; The *Fortuna Devorantum* and the *Fortuna Matris*. Latin was never my strong point; and Kersher never told me the meaning of those forbidden names. I found *that* out much later. During one particular lesson, he showed me a painting by an artist, once feted but now so reviled that his name was erased from the annals of art history. As my eyes traced the details, I couldn't help but marvel at the stunning realism of the piece. I shuddered involuntarily. The subject disturbed me with a level of darkness to which I had never succumbed.

It was an unnamed battle field, with bodies strewn about the plain, spears jutting from chests, stomachs ripped open by sword blades, the grey coils of intestine uncoiling from stomach wounds like obscene tongues. Blood pooled on the rocks in a crimson pond at the centre. A rough table sat in the maroon puddle, two silver goblets at each end and a silver carafe between them.

On the left hand side sat a hardened man. He was a soldier, a killer. The scars and the cruel set of his mouth and eyes reflected a troubled, violent soul. I couldn't quite place him, but from the look of the clothing, he might have been a Roman - fuck it, he could have been a Greek for all I knew.

On the right hand side, staring out at me with fierce yellow eyes, sat the *Fortuna Devorantum*. His arm was leant on the table, fanning a spread of playing cards, rendered in exquisite detail by the artist. The deck was obscene, each suite portraying sexual deviance of a kind that became more perverse and extreme with each suit, starting with extreme torture and ending with coprophilia. The creature was carved from solid black muscle; the ripples of it across his bare chest and abdomen would have drawn appreciative murmurs from a body builder. He sat nearly naked, a black loincloth covering his groin, a robe crumpled in a heap behind him. His face was animalistic. Angry.

Large incisors stuck out from the crowded mouth, pulling his lips into a contemptuous sneer. This was the jaw of a monster with the power to slice through flesh and bone effortlessly. His bald head gleamed smooth, not a hair to be seen. The eyes shone from the page in with eerie green luminescence. The painting screamed with life; I dared not touch it for fear of being pulled into its horror.

"I thought there were two," I croaked, out of the need to say something. Kersher pointed to a spot to the right of the *Fortuna Devorantum,*

"Look closely. Just there. Can you see her?"

Following his finger, I studied an outcropping of rock partly hidden by shadow. A figure sat, hunched and painfully thin, with the hint of a swollen stomach. The shape was female, barely recognizable by a gentle swelling of breasts just above her distended stomach.

I could just make out the lace hem of a tattered skirt, rotted, perforated stockings covering oozing, ulcerated legs. So these creatures would be my pathway to glory and fortune. My mentor left me for a few moments, though I barely noticed, all of my attention focused on the painting. The soldier slumped, beaten, resigned to whatever Fate had decided for him, much like I must have appeared only a few weeks before.

Kersher returned, holding a knife with an ornate handle. Gems glittered in the light, a small fortune held in the hands of my newfound compatriot. He looked to me, his demeanour sombre.

"It's time to begin, my friend."

The beach roils and shifts, as if the earth is being pulled into a whirlpool. There is a primal violence to the motion, frightening and intense. Screaming faces form again in the sand, becoming more distinct. I look away, not wanting to see anyone I recognise. That would be too much. The tightrope of sanity I've been treading would give way in an instant. I'd be a sitting duck if my mind was lost. I still can't make out what's being said, though I'm sure there's hints of Latin, Arabic and English. Other, more inhuman sounds make up the aural smorgasbord. I give up. Deciphering the indecipherable is a massive waste of time.

A deck of cards sits unopened in front of me, in the centre of the blanket. I had them specially made on the mainland by a stout Bengali fellow known only as Tat. He owed me a favour and was only too willing to pay it off and see me gone. The man had looked sick and terrified as he handed the pack over. As I had left his modest studio I overheard him whisper.

"*Jahannam chele.*" He spat the epithet out venomously.

I know enough Bengali now to understand the curse. He had called me the Son of Hell.

The deck may be unopened but I know every filthy image inscribed onto every card. The Game can't be played with normal cards, you see. There's no power to be had in those lifeless cardboard rectangles. Even if there was, ordinary playing cards were not designed to hold such power. They would wilt and incinerate in your hands. Cards are just cards, after all. The *Crowley Deck* is more, much more. Invented by the self-styled "Worlds Evilest Man', the *Crowley Deck* contains a power so potent that even the inventor himself lost the nerve to use them. Rumour is that they are made from hemp, blood and the fat of still born infants. Only a mad or evil man would dare fashion such a deck. Only fools and desperate men would play with them.

I guess I'm all of those, bar one—I may be desperate, and mad, and a fool, but I'm not evil.

Not yet.

The ritual passed but I can only recall that night in a haze. There are no specific memories, only impressions so sketchy that the whole thing could have happened to someone else. I remember with clarity the smell of blood, sulphur, vanilla; my grim, desperate pain and my cold, corrupted pleasure. For weeks after, my nightmares swirled into tortured fever dreams.

In the dark of sleep came yellow eyes, the stained and marked teeth of an animal; my frenzied coupling with a woman whose eyes were sunken into the darkness of her sockets: the moans and sighs of the *Fortuna Matris*, with the taste of something long dead on her breath and tongue. The meaty, cloying taste of rot never really left me. It had soaked into my senses, garnishing my every meal with a sour, shitty taste that destroyed my appetite long after the memory had faded.

The other legacy of that night was the loss of my testicles and the little finger on each hand. The rites demanded a sacrifice of flesh and blood, namely my flesh and blood. When I had asked about that, I got a short, snappy answer stating how these were reasonable demands given that for which I asked.

Dealing and holding cards became much more difficult with missing digits. And as for the loss of my testicles, that remains an experience I would rather have forgotten. I soon recovered from my injuries, physically. The security within my own state of mind would never be the same.

All memories of that night dissipated as I returned to the gaming tables with a new fire inside me. The money began to pour in, and the thrill returned with a ferocity I had never imagined possible. My cache rose fast and life began to reshape itself into something new.

I married, and started to think ahead to the future. And in the midst of it, my mentor and my friend vanished. There were no tearful farewells, no last minute drink. He walked out of our hotel and never returned.

Changes began to occur soon after the vanishing. It was imperceptible at first. There were sly sideways glances at the tables and the once-eager whores who had hung around the parlours trying to get a piece of the new *wunderkind*, now shunned me. I didn't really notice. By that time I was married. The days of bedding anyone with blonde hair and silicone filled breasts with the shape and feel of airbags were long behind me.

In Prague, I had a chance encounter with Devon, an old friend of mine from Birmingham. He had seen better days. The solid, well-dressed kid, who had always played a hard-charging forward on the football team, was now a slouched, obese, drab looking non entity — his Stone Island and Maharishi clothing replaced with off-the-rack suits, threadbare and ground to a shine around the elbows and knees. His hair had flattened and lost its colour and his skin had worn to a dull, dirty grey. His eyes had once been luminescent with mirth and steel. Now they looked over-large, hectic and frantic in that dirty grey face, that had once been a lustrous dark brown.

We chatted about the old days; the drinking, the fighting, the heady, adrenaline filled Saturdays marching through Middle England with the BCFC Zulu army, the lunatic Sahota brothers. Those were good days, but Devon remained unenthused as well as uncomfortable.

Something seemed to be playing on his mind. I'd never been stuck for conversation with Devon. He was one of those guys who could chat about anything and never pause. Awkward silences and hidden meanings just weren't his style. As time passed and beer was consumed, I sensed a hidden exchange. He needed to talk about something other than the glory days. I prodded him about it, steering the conversation in a way that would get him to open up. He did, after a time. He seemed surprised, but then he didn't know of my new-found ability to manipulate people and events. He mumbled as he spoke.

He told me that rumours were floating about. People were avoiding me, sensing that something was not quite right, that there was an odd taste in the air when I was near. When I pressed him for more answers, he looked at me tearfully and mumbled a goodbye, leaving a nearly full litre glass of dark pilsner untouched. I never saw him again.

Three days later, he was found floating in the Vlatava River, bound hand and foot and missing his head, great chunks of him gouged out with blunt knives. The word on the street was that he had still been alive when his killer started cutting.

Things began to slide after that encounter. Two major casinos banned me outright. There had been complaints about cheating and other, less savoury practices. A high stakes game of Texas Hold 'Em in New Jersey nearly ended with a bullet in my brain. The invitations to tournaments dried up.

The final straw came in Vegas. Some Texas oil baron had died in the room next door to me. Suicide, or so I heard. His mistress, a bubble-headed bimbo with her brains in her boobs, mumbled about the old coot seeing something coming out of my room while I was out. Whoever this mysterious intruder was, they must have made an impression. The oil man went back to his room, ignoring the bimbo, ran himself a bath, locked the door and quietly slit his wrists.

Why I was punished for that, I'll never know. I didn't really do anything, after all. Things got tense afterwards. Old people in the street began to cross the road to avoid me. Dogs went berserk as I walked past them, howling and cowering behind their masters. Even my wife became distant, drawing away from me when I touched her.

One day, in a less guarded moment, she screamed at me, telling me that touching my skin was like touching a rotted corpse. She apologised, almost in the blink of an eye, but tension remained between us. It was time to get away for a while, to surface from the murk of casinos, high-rollers, suicidal oil barons, seedy Mafioso types and plastic women. An around the world tour with no gambling. That should have blown out the cobwebs.

If anything, the cobwebs became thicker.

They followed me. Everywhere I went, they lurked just out of the corner of my eye.

A grey woman in a rotting lace gown beckoned to me on the tube in London, smiling as she lifted her tattered dress and played with her snatch.

A bulky man, dressed in traditional Moroccan robes, shadowing me in the souks of Tangiers, white teeth gleaming from the darkness of his hood. The teeth had familiar-looking shapes etched onto them but I could never get close enough to see what they were.

A deformed child sat on the steps of a crumbling colonial building in Mumbai, eating the flies that alighted on his skin, looking at me through crusty, white, blind eyes and cackling in Hindi about luck that soon runs dry and Yama and Kali coming for me, destroying me and everyone around me. The child rocked backwards and forwards, his laughter quickly descending into retching sobs as I walked away.

Mumbai: a city to love and loathe in equal measure. I loathed it now. We were attacked on Juhu Beach. The same day I saw the apparition of the child, an hour after watching the spectacular Asian sunset, a fist the size of a boulder smashed into my face. I saw yellow eyes, and heard my wife's pitiful screams, and the high wheezy grunt of her attacker. As unconsciousness swept me away, I smelt something rank and bitter, a pungent odour that I would never forget.

When I came around, the assailants were gone. I had a high pitched whine in my ears. My wife lay eviscerated, her abdomen a hollow, bloody cavity. She had been pregnant with our first child. Her murderer took the foetus and my right thumb.

A day later, my parents died in a house fire, their bodies reduced to charcoal effigies. Soon after, my best friend was found sliced to pieces in his own home, his wife mentally shattered and catatonic.

My brothers disappeared, never to be seen again.

And on and on it went; friends, companions, relatives, all falling to bizarre circumstances.

I discharged myself from the hospital. I couldn't stay any longer. The Grey Woman from London had come for me, falling upon me while I was half asleep. I remember her concrete-hued skin and her eyeless sockets that somehow shone with malice. She came bearing a syringe full of pale green fluid. She whispered in my ear, her voice dry and desiccated like autumn leaves. Her breath reeked of spoilt meat.

"This isn't cheating, you understand. I'm merely stacking the odds in the *House's* favour. We don't lose, you see? We never, ever lose'

A grave fattened worm slid from one of her eye sockets, hitting the floor with a wet splat. Drooling a sick-smelling fluid, she stuck her tongue out at me and wiggled it suggestively. Her hand rubbed her vulva in a frenzy, as if trying to erase a stain from the filthy garment that hung from her wasted frame.

"We're going to have so much fun together," she said, breathless, excited, fading.

She vanished. The syringe hung in the air for a moment before clattering to the floor.

I left India and headed to back Marrakesh, to the solitary sanctuary where this had all begun. There was a man who had the answers. I would get them. By any means necessary.

He greeted me as if he had been expecting me, all smiles and open arms. Something inside cracked, and I gave him a savage kick in the gut. Kersher fell to his knees, gasping, coughing.

I aimed another kick at the little man, my foot connecting solidly with his face. Broken teeth clattered onto the marble floor, flecked with blood. His head whipped back, and he gurgled for a moment before hawking a thick ball of enamel and blood onto the floor. A sobbing laugh escaped his lips. I pulled his head up and stared directly into his wounded eyes.

"Why?"

Why did he give me the knowledge in the first place? Why had everything gone so well, only for it to come crashing down around me? Why was I being isolated, exiled, followed? Why were my friends and family being butchered? I waited for the answer, aware of the blood roaring in my ears. A small, vicious voice in my head jabbered, insisting that I rip that lying tongue out of his mouth and watch him choke on his own blood.

Kersher laughed to himself, red drool dripping from his chin. The same bitter odour that I had smelt back in Mumbai wafted up from his broken mouth, mixed with the coppery scent of blood. That was more than enough for the red mist to descend. My fist crashed into his nose, pulping it even further. I smashed him in the face once more, splitting my knuckles. Blood leaked copiously, staining the white marble floor, slaughterhouse red.

"*Why?*" I bellowed into his ruined face.

His eyes changed. He looked like he was about to lecture an imbecile child. The laughter stopped for a moment. He snorted and spat up more bloody phlegm, onto my shoe, laughing again. It was a tired yet defiant gesture.

"This is what you wanted, and this is what I trade in," he lisped. "And this is what *they* want, my friend."

The laughter stopped and he looked at me with pained regret.

"You were the best of them, almost like a son to me. But, a deal's a deal. I supply the runners, they create the Game. Bets on the outcome are handled by the House."

"Whose house?"

He sniggered.

"*House Asmodeus*. The ultimate gambling franchise, licensed by the darkest of dark ones. I don't know all of the finer details. I'm just an agent, you see. I find the runners, teach them what they need to know and the rest is up to them."

Curiosity was getting the better of me. My anger melted away. I nodded at him to go on.

"This particular Game tests the limits of men. They take bets on how much a man can endure before he loses himself and gives in. Before he takes his own life to escape the horror of what his greed conjures. It's a grave sin, you see. Do yourself in, go straight to Hell; do not pass go, don't collect your two-hundred pounds. You obviously didn't read the script."

I understood now. I was meant to die in India. The deaths of my loved ones had been designed to push me over the edge. For some reason, the *House, Fortuna Devorantum* and *Fortuna Matris* couldn't kill me directly. It had to be by my own hand. They could push, they could incapacitate, but they couldn't kill me directly.

"I'm quite proud of you in a way. No others have lasted this long. Most cracked under all the temptation we threw at them. You're something else. And that makes us nervous. It makes *him* nervous and *he* doesn't like that."

He slumped forward as I let go of him, the realisation hitting with full force. His friendship and his tutelage, was just another form of edge sorting, with me as the tampered deck. He'd seen the desperation in my eyes and reeled me in with promises of easy money, glory and wealth. All for a bet made by forces bigger and darker than any mere criminal or politician.

"There's nothing you can do', he mumbled, "They'll have you sooner or later. No one has ever beaten the House."

I looked down at him in disgust, my rage stoked by his admissions. Shaking my head, I placed my boot over the back of his skull.

"Let them find me."

I drove my leg down, stamping him into the floor. He slid forward. Bone and teeth crunched. I stomped again, harder this time. His body convulsed and contorted. Blood began to seep from under his head. I slammed my foot with all my weight, losing control to my own rage, again and again. He didn't scream as his skull broke like an egg, a slop of grey matter spurting onto the marble. The blood flowed freely now. His body began to thrash, hands clenching and unclenching, his feet beating a dying tattoo on the floor. In my delirious blood-drunkenness, I could hear a chorus of foul angels singing songs of blood and steel, the lyrics telling a tale of blood and sulphur.

A soft, liquid sound of opening bowels signalled the end. I staggered back, watching the last twitches of his life. His chest rattled as his body shut down. He went limp.

The sand takes on a shape: humanoid, rough around the edges like an unfinished sculpture, growing taller by the second. The cards still sit untouched, placed carefully over the symbols of the *Familia de Potestas* drawn on the wet sand beneath the blanket. I wait patiently, still humming songs from childhood.

I don't know how long I stayed in Morocco. It might have been a week, a month, even a year. Time was irrelevant and I had no fear of being discovered. Kersher had no friends. No one would miss him. Maybe I did some other mug a favour. There would be no one to snare lost and desperate men into the Game.

I used the respite to go through the *Speculum Mysteriis*, trying to find ways of beating this thing. It was a long, drawn out and painful process. My Latin may have been non-existent, but thanks to the wonders of Google Translate, I scraped by, gradually unlocking the book's secret, starting with the title: *Speculum Mysteriis, The Mysteries of the Mirror*.

Day after day, I learnt more about House Asmodeus, *Fortuna Devorantum*; the Eater of Luck, and his concubine, *Fortuna Matris*, the Mother of Chance. There was so much more in that book; other worlds, gateways, places where the normal order of things was upside down and inside out, rites of unimaginable power and beings of unimaginable hate.

This was all knowledge that I didn't need at that moment. I found a glimmer of hope, a rite which could be used to turn away the Eater of Luck. It was a dangerous ritual. The power it unleashed could be turned back on the user, even everything around him. If I was to use this suit, the *Familia de Potestas*, I'd have to be somewhere remote, somewhere away from people.

Setting the house on fire, I left Morocco. By the time anyone noticed the blaze, I'd be long gone and the evidence would be ash. The book stayed with me though. There was so much useful information in there. If I survived, I would study it well. I buried it a mile up the beach of my new home and began to settle in, making arrangements for shelter, food and other essentials.

Ang Isla sa Mangtas. I didn't know what it meant. My Visayan is crap, as bad as my pidgin Latin. There was always Google Translate but my iPhone had been bartered for more useful items. Still, there was something about the name which set my teeth on edge when I first heard it. A Thai friend of mine told me about this small island that had been left pretty much alone. He just smiled when I asked him why, tobacco-brown teeth fully on show. The smile didn't reach his haunted eyes.

The friend put me in touch with a fisherman who was willing to take me to the island. There were conditions to this one-way trip, though; he wouldn't set foot on the island and demanded cash up front. It sounded like a great deal to me. The fisherman virtually threw me off the boat and left me and my new home far behind him.

The island was breathtakingly beautiful by day, but the night was rent by ear splitting howls, shrieks and groans. Whatever shared the place with me didn't sound inviting or friendly, or even of this planet. I had a few encounters with some of the denizens in the earlier days. A very strange plant – a towering slick mass that seemed to be a mutant strain of pitcher plant – followed my movements on the rare occasions I ventured into the forest, though I'd never gotten close to it. I get the feeling it isn't love or affection that keeps it on my tail.

And if the plant wasn't enough to unsettle me, there were also strange lights in the night—virulent flashes of colour in the dark of the forest that burnt like a sun, only for a few seconds, but long enough to leave an imprint on my retinas. The ground shook during these freak lightning storms, the sky turning a deep burnished orange, triggering unnameable loathing within me. The storms didn't seem to affect the natives, however. My fellow island-dwellers stayed just inside the perimeter of the forest, leaving me well enough alone, perhaps smelling or sensing something on the air around me that unnerved them. I set up camp on the beach, near a stand of old gnarled trees, and made the preparations for the *Familia de Potestas*.

I waited for my guests to arrive.

I've had some strange dreams in my time on this island. You might say it's a natural effect of the horrors I'd been through, or maybe even the strain of waiting for the end. I wasn't so sure, at first. I'm still not. They feel different. There's a hint of threat behind them, but also a feeling of sadness.

When I close my eyes, I see a city. The skyline is a familiar one but I can't seem to place it. There's a strangeness to it. It's as if the buildings have warped in some subtle fashion the human senses cannot unravel. Thunderclouds, black and heavy, gather in the leaden skies above this place. No lights shine here. It is dead. Maybe the inhabitants are likewise dead and gone, their shadows taking up residence in their absence.

I feel the city calling to me. It's an almost irresistible pull on the soul, a hook pulling me in. I stand and move closer to the edge of the spoiled, murky river that separates me from the imposing citadel. A chill wind ruffles my fringe. I sweep the irritation away and turn. I've been perched on an old car. Its sleek lines and sheer size mark it out as American. The style is classic, the colour blood-red, a white stripe emblazoned down the side.

The car has a presence, a malignance that's almost solid. If I stretch out my hand, I can brush the feel of evil with my fingertips. We have history, this machine and I. Or maybe a future. I can't tell which. The silhouette sitting in the passenger seat gives me pause. Did I have a passenger? I can't remember. The trouble with dreams and nightmares is that there is no sense of time and place. You live in a jumble of images and thoughts. Nothing is linear, nothing makes sense.

All I know and feel is that this is an event waiting to happen, one that depends on me staying alive long enough for this to come to pass. This is important and whatever this car and its passenger represents, I have to be there for this moment.

When I wake from this dream, I feel a pull of urgency. This is why I've stacked the odds in my favour. I've done my own edge sorting. Now I just have to hope that my final gamble pays off.

The shape has become more substantial, more real. I recognise it now. At last after all this waiting, the *Fortuna Devorantum* has arrived.

He's nothing short of magnificent,

Muscular black flesh gleams in the tropical sun. He doesn't sweat but the gloss black of his skin makes him look oiled. He flexes and purrs with self-satisfaction. His shoulders heave as he inhales the warm air. Green eyes bear down on me, contempt and amusement dancing in their fire. A loincloth covers his genitals, a black cape hanging loosely from his immense shoulders. He stretches, the movement luxurious. It makes me think of a cat I used to own many moons ago. Funny how the mind brings up these things on the edge of death.

"You certainly have kept us all on tenterhooks, my friend."

His voice, rich and dark, rumbles up from his chest, seductive yet powerful. There's a grudging note of pride as if I'm his least favourite pupil on the cusp of winning a great prize. "You should be pleased. There hasn't been a runner like you in centuries."

With one fluid motion, he whips the cape off and sits down on the hot sand. I notice the white Ace of Spades motif on the cloak. His emblem and a fitting one. The Ace of Spades is the Death Card, so I've been told.

He raises his flat nose to the wind and sniffs again, his tusks glinting in the sun. His thin, ebony lips twitch into a bestial grin. All I see are teeth. Big, sharp teeth.

"A remarkable place for a last stand, indeed. I take it your boatman didn't translate the name?"

I frown at the odd question. He nods, seeing my confusion.

"The language. This island's name is Visayan for—"

He stops, his smile mocking me. He waves his hand, the gesture dismissive.

"It doesn't matter. You're not long for this world. Translations are meaningless."

He pauses, deliberating over his next observation. Or maybe for effect. You can never tell with a demon. They're harder to read than the Japanese.

"An interesting island though. The fauna is quite unusual, as are its other properties. I can't wait to see what the Americans and Russians do with this place. They should have a lot of fun deciphering its mysteries."

The creature nods sagely to himself. I'm left wondering just what the Americans and Russians have to do with this. If I live, I'll find out for myself. Despite my exile, I'm fond of this island. Interlopers are not needed or required, especially not the Yanks or the Russkies. Bastards to a man, that lot. Mean spirited and unforgiving.

"You're quite a chaotic little bug, aren't you?"

The disdain and contempt in his voice doesn't bother me. The suddenness of the statement does. Is he trying to make a point? Maybe not. It sounds more like a stray thought that has tumbled from his toothy mouth in an unguarded moment.

His jaw, set in a twisted sneer, begins to move from side to side. He's grinding his teeth, presumably out of eagerness or anxiety. My eye catches the etchings on his tusk-like fangs; the ace of spades again.

Fortuna Devorantum, Eater of Luck, leans forward. There's no mistaking the look of joy on that hellish face.

"This Game can be brought to a close at last. Win or lose, House Asmodeus cleans up again. A lot of my friends will be counting their losses. You'll get quite a reception when we arrive."

There's a hint of satisfaction, and a whisper of sadness in his voice. The sport is about to end. Time to find another sucker and roll him. There's no guarantee that the next poor mark will last as long as I have. Quality idiots are hard to find in these stressful times. House Asmodeus will just have to make do with plain, old fashioned idiots instead.

I notice something and look at the creature inquiringly. According to the book there's something missing in this picture.

No Fortuna Matris?

I thought there were two who would come to collect me.

Reading my thoughts, he nods.

"There are other things to attend to. So many lost and desperate souls. We never rest. She sends her regards, however, and she looks forward to rekindling your relationship."

Just him then.

This puts the odds in my favour. One is easier to deal with than two. It's Game on, my friends. His eyes brighten as he spies the cards. Picking them up reverentially, he favours me with a sly look.

"A fresh pack. I could never resist. One quick game before we depart this world? I might even be flexible and let you go, if you win."

I nod, keeping my poker face intact and trying not to smile at his clichéd offer. Why do demons always throw out the old 'last-minute reprieve' offer? Is there some handbook or class for hackneyed monster clichés that these guys attend? Besides, if I win, the Game changes completely. He doesn't seem to be aware of that. The Game hasn't been won often. He's become too complacent, too assured of his own victory. He hasn't taken the variables into account. I have.

This was exactly what I was hoping for. I have spent days fixing the deck. If he plays willingly, the *Familia de Potestas* begins. If I have got the right cards in the right order, I win the Game. Our contract is undone and he would have to leave empty handed. House Asmodeus would never touch me again. There was something else as well, another prize mentioned, but I couldn't translate that segment. Maybe Kersher could have done but he's worm-food now. I'll find out soon enough. All I have to do now is hold my nerve and play. Nothing more, nothing less.

Of course, there is a chance this could all backfire, but I'm willing to take it. The buzz is returning in waves. My skin crawls, tightening up as adrenalin is let loose in my system. My senses sharpen; the waves crashing onto the sand fill my ears; the smells of the sea, of seaweed, our sweat, are almost overwhelming. My blood fizzes, as power builds up in my fingers, toes and groin. I feel unstoppable, euphoric. A manic sense of joy overcomes me and I stifle a giggle. He doesn't notice but just to be sure, I divert his attention.

"Would you like to do the honours?" I point at the unopened Crowley Deck. His overfilled mouth twists into a wider grin. All of his teeth flash at once, an ensemble decorated with the Ace of Spades motif.

The air is alive, the hairs on my arms standing on end despite the blazing sun. Whatever I have set in motion is gaining momentum. It's unstoppable.

The *Fortuna Devorantum* cuts with practiced ease.

Place your bets now. All in.

I keep my face poker-straight and look deep into those eyes. For a brief moment, memories dance in the green haze—my wife, parents, Devon, and so many other beautiful innocents are in the blazing depths, contorted and agonised faces begging for release and relief.

My poker face is still firmly in place. I take one last look around the beach before settling my gaze on the creature. He nods to me, the grin gone. I return the gesture.

"Let's play," I whisper. The waves crash once more, louder than ever. The sound fills my consciousness as I study the hand before me.

Let the Game begin.

A CREATOR UNDONE

THE GODS RETURNED to the Prime Universe in the blink of an eye, war-weary but glad of their triumph. There had been no fanfare, no heralds nor harbingers. They merely stepped back into the realm they had abandoned in haste, yet abandoned for a worthy cause.

The War of Existence had taken a heavy toll on both minds and bodies. Even Gods possessed vessels to carry their essences. Some had broken, fallen by the wayside, a small number even experiencing Soul Death, a phenomenon so rare in the Prime Universe that it was almost unheard of.

It had been a long and brutal conflict. The Enemy had fought the Gods to a standstill and then very nearly to oblivion. Even Shiv, The Eternal Optimist, had moments of dread and self-doubt. The Enemy had used tactics unheard of among Higher Beings. Shiv, Thor, even the Older Gods had been staggered by the sheer cunning and utter ruthlessness of the Enemy.

The Gods fought back in desperation, letting the merciless *Nass Zubaiders*, the *Doomlords* and the highly unpredictable *San Arkanis* loose on the battlefield. The tide turned and the battle was won. The Enemy had fought back to their home, banished, then entombed behind an iron wall of pure thought. The wall was impregnable. No force in the Omniverse could ever hope to break through.

The Gods had little patience now. The interminable fighting and slaughter of various Lower Orders had sapped what goodwill they had left. Their previously forgiving nature was burnt from them.

Shiv understood this. He had hoped his friend Baiame also understood, but he was wrong. To argue with the upper order of Gods had been a difficult undertaking before the War. The Upper Order were not be trifled with. Both younger Gods had done this only once before and counted themselves very fortunate. They had spoken out in favour of humanity, when the Gods and the rest of the Prime Universe had judged the humans unfit and unworthy of continued existence.

From humble beginnings, the Humans had risen to become a paramount force in their Galaxy, a power that expanded with astonishing speed. At first, they had been benevolent, and the Gods looked on the human race with favour and love. However, as rapid as their rise was, so was their fall.

In the blink of a cosmic eye, Mankind went from peaceful benevolence to bloodthirsty belligerence. They became creatures of war and plunder. Whole civilisations were burned from the surface of their planets. Races were betrayed and enslaved. The Galaxy burned from end to end.

The rest of Creation petitioned the Gods for their intervention and intervene they did, although not directly at first. They sent the Lords of Doom, The Black Knights and The Fleshmasters to liberate the worlds forcibly taken by the Human Pestilence. The Race of Man fled before the onslaught, retreating back to their tiny world.

There had been no respite. Earth was bombed, razed, pulverised. Only after the last bit of resistance had been crushed did the Gods stand their forces down and convene, to decide the fate of Mankind. The Abrahamic Ones favoured total annihilation, as did others, from Set to Kali.

The younger god Baiame could not bear the thought of a race being wiped out, even one as evil as the humans. They had made mistakes, but Baiame believed in his golden-hearted way that Mankind could be redeemed. He was a good soul, if a little naïve in the ways of the Omniverse.

Using his eloquence and the force of charm, he persuaded Shiv to be his second. Shiv had his reservations. The Lord of the Dance, Shiv's responsibilities lay in destruction and renewal. He knew no fear, but even he felt a pang of disquiet about this undertaking. The humans had broken the Covenant and now was not the time to be appealing to the Higher Gods. He went along with it nonetheless. Like his friend, he had a weakness for the human race. They were capable of horrifying acts but also of kindness, and their growing intelligence never failed to astound him.

They set out for Mount Meeru, the home of the Ultimate Tribunal. It was here that the weightiest of decisions were made. Within these hallowed walls, entire civilisations were raised or burnt to ashes on the orders of the Convocation—The Thirteen and Nine as they were known informally. Thirteen to hear the evidence, nine to pass judgement. They were the ultimate arbiters of the Omniverse, their pronouncements wise, their judgements balanced. For the Thirteen and Nine, balance was all important. They listened to the young God, admiring his passion and argument. Some of them had even grumbled about the young upstart, at first, only to be swayed by his speech.

He had asked for the humans to be spared, and set conditions to be adhered to. Mankind's previous technology was to be erased, their history wiped, their civilisation to be reset to barbarian levels. He would personally oversee the Humans, guiding them and ensuring that they would never be able to reach the point where they could leave their Solar System.

The Thirteen and Nine agreed. There were conditions. The tribunal made it very clear that failure would rest on Baimie's young shoulders. The punishment for failure would be the severest, the one feared by all Gods—Dissolute Exile. Not even *Mor Animus*—the Soul Death of legend was as frightening. *Mor Animus* was permanent. Once it occurred it was over. Dissolute Exile, however, was eternal and as such, the greatest fear of Gods. The thought of being unable to move, yet being aware of time passing, of speaking yet having no one to speak to, of hearing but having no sound to listen to; this was a punishment that frightened all Gods.

Baiame agreed and began his work. Then the War of Existence broke out. All Gods were required to fight. The young God left the Omniverse with the others, afraid of the war, but also afraid for his charges. Would they cope in a Godless void and thrive, or would they become engines of war once more, hated, feared and despised in their universe? These were questions that would plague the God in the years to come.

Without the Gods, the humans had no guidance, save for some books and moral tales left behind. With no Gods to guide them and help interpret the knowledge, they began to falter and fall back to their old ways; lust, greed and technology for use in war.

The Gods looked down with horror and anguish. For some, the memory of Man's previous fall was but a distant nightmare compared to the war from whence they had returned. For others, the effrontery of Man had to be answered. This petty little race of tyrants had to be stamped on before they caused more mayhem. This time there would be no argument or advocacy. The Gods were not in an especially forgiving mood.

Baiame stood before the Thirteen and Nine Gods knowing his and Man's fate were sealed. Even his friend Shiv had chosen not to defend him. Shiv had left lessons behind for them and they had chosen to ignore them. Man had to die for having the audacity to break the Covenant—never to leave the Sol System.

He had heard the evidence. A small craft had been scooped up by the Flesh-masters on the outer edges of the Solar System. The humans on board were now reconfigured and had been sent back with a Black Knight Craft, the very same craft that had randomly surveyed the Earth over the years. Their punishment would come to them soon enough.

Punishment came to Baimie sooner. For his failure to ensure that Man had learnt their lessons and would not break the Covenant, he would be sentenced to Dissolute Exile. The younger God accepted his fate without argument or discourse. There was no point. If he were to argue his case, he would be struck down where he stood. If he were to run, he would be caught. There was nowhere for him to run to.

Fighting was not an option, not against the combined might of the Gods, Older and Younger. As for exile to another realm, the Gods could not condone that. There was every chance that he could find his way back to the Prime Reality. Dissolution was the best and most effective way of punishing him for his sins.

He was taken to the Grounds of Judgement and there, using sharp edges tempered in the heart of suns, his flesh was stripped away, slowly and agonisingly. His screams rent the air, the tang of his alien blood salting the lips of his tormentors.

His eyes and lips remained where they had fallen. The rest of his body was taken to the Forge of Mithras and disposed of. There would be no way back for him now. His body was gone. In a cruel refinement of the punishment, in order to make it memorable, Brahma ordered Baiame's eyes to be popped like over ripened olives. His mouth and ears, all that remained of him, were deposited in a life casket and jettisoned into the stars.

Shiv watched as the casket jettisoned into deep space, his heart heavy and cold, not just for his friend but for all the Gods. The war had changed them. There would be no more mercy or forgiveness. The universe was about to become a desolate place and this fear of Gods that the Thirteen and Nine created would make the universe darker and colder.

He turned his back on Mount Meeru, the only home he had ever known. It no longer held any attraction for him. The air was poisoned by fear, vengeance and rage, a pollution that, if left unchecked, would corrupt Existence, perhaps beyond repair. Already, he could feel other forces aligning, ready to take advantage of the Gods and their weakened state.

The Omniverse was shifting out of balance and the Gods did not seem to care. The only one that did was now exiled, cast out forever. Feeling the weight of hopelessness, Shiv left the ancient mountain behind. He did not look back. Not once.

Out in the cold reaches of space, a solitary Life Casket spun gracefully through cosmic dust, meteor storms and nebulae. Its course took it further and further from home. Inside the Casket, a God awoke and began to scream.

THE WRITER'S FRIEND

THE PLACE STANK. Harvey Dellar groped blindly for an adjective or metaphor adequate enough to describe the rank scent. He failed. The writer's block was more potent than ever. He couldn't even find a way to describe just how shitty the smell was. He grumbled incoherently, his head drooping as he peered at the ground, searching for the source of the smell.

The warm summer air ripened the fetid odour, giving it substance. Harvey hawked up a glob of phlegm, spitting it out violently onto the ground. He could even taste it.

Harvey's neck began to spasm. He looked back up, arching his neck to drive the stiffness from it. He pulled a battered packet of cigarettes from his pocket and lit one, savouring the blue-grey smoke. The smoke masked the rotten odour that hung over his property like a cataclysmic stink bomb.

This was ridiculous. He had already wasted the best part of an hour searching for phantom cat shit. Mrs Speakmans ancient tabby seemed to have a fondness for crapping in his garden. The haughty feline treated his garden like its own open latrine, wandering in with its tail held high. He had taught it a lesson or two when the opportunity had come. The animal was too old and too slow these days to escape from a well-aimed boot. He smiled maliciously. Maybe the old creature had met its final end. He hadn't seen it for a few days.

He stood over the patch of bare earth, hands on hips, and let the warm sun embrace him, closing his eyes for a moment. It was supposed to be a good summer this year. Knowing the vagaries of the British weather, he really ought to make the most of it. The weather was rarely predictable these days.

He stretched, murmuring with pleasure, his back clicking and creaking. Too many hours had been spent hunched over a keyboard trying to string words together into coherent sentences only for their coherency to fall apart.

Where's the mojo gone, man?

Frustration welled up inside. It was a new and unwelcome feeling for him. The fear that had dogged him from the earliest day of putting pen to paper had come to pass.

Harvey Dellar—up and coming horror writer, winner of Best Newcomer in the Saturn Awards, and the hot tip to take over from the master, Stephen King—had writer's block. No, not just a block. It was a veritable Great Wall of China, imposing, frightening and impossible to scale. *Straits of Cthulhu,* his first novel, had been a tough book to put together, but he had managed to pull together the plot strands, ride it out and turn a mess into a coherent story.

Even Clive Barker liked it, according to an interview with a well-known horror magazine. 'Raw, intense and imaginative', a good quote to have on your next novel, especially by someone as well respected in the genre as Mr Barker.

The roller coaster had started from there. He quit his day job working in a call centre—an experience that he never wanted to repeat—and began writing full time, his mind going into creative overdrive. His next two novels, *Death's Benefactors,* a darkly comic tale of two demonic gangsters, and *Silently Wishing for Death,* had stormed the e-book bestsellers list. The money poured in, invitations to conventions and university speaking gigs flooded his inbox; people wanted to know him. In those quiet moments of clarity, he sat behind his desk, chin resting on clasped hands, and thanked whatever forces governed the universe.

He now cursed those very same powers. The new novel had stalled. The idea was dynamite—a man trekking around the world on a sightseeing tour of the globe's darkest and most haunted places—but it just didn't seem to be hanging together. Three chapters in, and he felt the whole thing slipping away from him. His character, a worldly news presenter named Jay, was evolving into a thoroughly unlikable man, the supporting characters were two dimensional and about a clichéd as you could get, and nearly all the locations he had picked, he'd never visited. He had no idea what the swamps of Louisiana smelled like, or how big Stull Township was.

He couldn't give in. The act of writing was a grind. When a writer was stuck at the coal face, he or she, had to keep chipping away, no matter how difficult it was to coax out the words. It was a matter of professional pride. Dellar hated the thought of being defeated by his own imagination. He had to find a way to whip the little bastard into submission and get it to work double-time again.

Harvey dropped his cigarette, crushing it into the ground with a vicious swipe of his foot.

This is fucking ridiculous. And a colossal waste of my time. Why bother searching for the source of one smell when the whole world stank anyway? Would it really make his situation any better? He shrugged. It wasn't as if he had anything better, and the obsessive compulsive within him wouldn't let this lie.

He continued to scan the ground, his eyes searching for the tell-tale signature of Mrs Speakman's tabby. Something caught his eye in the shade, under the mammoth thorn-filled bush by the fence. He had no idea what the plant was. It had been there when he had moved in.

Hold the fucking phone, ladies and gents. I think we have a winner.

He moved in closer, crouching down to get a better view. The stench became stronger, a cloying rancid fog that emanated from this spot. He hawked another ball of phlegm, grimacing as he spat it out.

The grass was dead, withered and grey, coated with a clear sheen too thick to be dew. The patch was roughly circular, with lines of dead vegetation erupting from it at random angles. An image of tentacles closing on prey briefly flashed through the author's mind. He filed it away for later use. Bare earth dotted the circle, patches where grass had rotted away totally. Harvey, his curiosity aroused, poked a finger tentatively into the mud. He cursed, whipping his hand back as if he had been stung. The ground felt warm and gelid. He wiped his soiled finger on his jeans, trying not to vomit at the sensation. It felt like he imagined it would feel to jab a corpse that had been pulled up from a warm swamp. Harvey shivered, feeling a slight sense of dread.

The patch of earth *felt* wrong. He couldn't say why. There was a quality to its look and feel that tickled the older part of his brain, the part where irrational fears took on a life of their own. He wiped his forehead, his hand trembling. The dread increased a notch as he looked over the oddity. Splinters of white protruded from the ground, all different shapes and sizes. The ground was littered with flecks of the substance.

Can't be—

He stopped himself from finishing the train of thought that had started with the cat and ended with bone. There was only one way to find out and that was to dig. Not an option. He was already on the road to total panic. The thought of what he might find under the earth was close to tipping him over the edge.

Fuck this, I'm out of here. He stood, giving the dead ground one more look.

What the fucks wrong with you, eh? Getting spooked over a patch in the grass.

The self-admonishment brought a half-smile to his lips. The fleeting sense of panic diminished as he walked back to the house. His knees creaked with every step and his legs trembled from crouching for too long. His body was showing definite signs of wear and tear. Harvey still looked good for a man in his early forties; his black hair was still intact, although short and tidy, not wild and youthful anymore. The few wrinkles around his eyes weren't conspicuous unless you were up close, but no one had come close enough to him over the last year or so to notice.

He was too busy to even think about women at the minute, and the wedding band that he still wore out of habit tended to put admirers off. The divorce had been amicable enough, and the ring brought him comfort and helped him to centre his thoughts when he was stuck for a word, a sentence or a story. He fiddled it with it, spinning it at varying speeds depending on how agitated he was.

Harvey stretched and sighed. The day was beautiful, but he had work to do. He took one last, lingering look at the patch on the grass and walked back inside, leaving the door open. .

Trixie watched the scary man-beast carefully. He reeked of fear. She could smell the tang of it exuding from him. Hunger gnawed at her. The *missus*, the old human whose company she kept, hadn't put any food out for her. She hadn't seen her mistress for days. Starving, the old tabby had gone on the hunt, trying and failing to capture anything bigger than an emaciated shrew. Pickings were slim these days. The neighbourhood, once teeming with frogs, mice and other appetising morsels, was now sparsely populated.

The only animals that were left were the loud, smelly long-jaws, barking and slobbering. Trixie knew well enough to keep away from those creatures. It was a lesson hard-learnt, but after losing an eye to a mean and cussed old Shih Tzu named Teddy, she gave them a wide berth.

She watched the two-legs walk back into his box thing, and crept out from her hiding place. Humans had food aplenty in their boxes. Sometimes, they would even leave food out in plain view. She might get caught, but hunger had overridden her keen sense of self-preservation. Keeping low to the ground, she slunk toward the open door. A tantalising aroma of flesh came from its opening, driving her feline senses wild. If she was a barker, she would have been dribbling by now.

Trixie stopped. Her senses rang with a warning. There was danger close by. She couldn't tell where but she could feel the malignancy around her. The smell of food was masked by a scent that she had never encountered before. It was the odour of death. The tabby looked around. There were no long-jaws nearby. She felt uneasy and began to walk around the patch of ground, unaware that she was even doing it.

The earth erupted next to her. Sticky globs of soil showered her. She whirled around, hissing, her ears flat against her tiny skull. A long, red coloured limb, covered in festering yellow sores, was flailing around, as if trying to scent her. She squalled, frozen with fear and adrenaline. The feline had never seen or smelt anything like this before, even when she'd lived with the female human. The smell that came from it was raw and hot. The limb paused. In a flash too quick for her acute senses, the flexible member wrapped around her, and began dragging the cat towards its patch of earth.

Trixie began to scream and yowl as her skin burnt from contact with the stinking fluid that coated the limb. Her fur slid off her and floated to the ground as her flesh dissolved. The cat howled, struggling to escape, her strength failing. With a savage jerk, the appendage pulled itself back into the soft ground. Trixie was sucked under the earth with it, her weak yowls giving way to way to a choking sound as the force of the motion shattered her bones and pulped her organs. The silence returned to the morning air, a few sticky clumps of cat hair and blood being the only evidence of Trixie's fate.

What the fuck was that? Harvey sat up, startled by the screech from the back garden. It sounded like a hurt animal, but the tone of fear and pain was unlike anything Harvey had ever heard before. As a child, he'd witnessed a dog being run over; the thud of the car hitting its midriff and the yelps of pain and fear were still fresh in his memory, after all this time. That was nothing compared to this; there was a crippling fear conveyed by those frenzied sounds.

He walked to the window of his writing room, pulling the blinds to one side. The garden looked normal. The sun still beat down. The sunflowers that he'd planted as a gift for his wife, swayed gently in the breeze. His breath caught in his throat. The dead patch on the grass had grown! It now extended out beyond the shade of the spiny bush. The primal fear returned. His heart hammered in his chest. How could it have grown that quickly? Harvey wiped his face. He had to go and look. Fighting the fear, he pulled his slippers on and trudged downstairs, his unease growing by the second.

The ugly bald patch had grown. It was now over a foot in diameter. It sagged in the middle, giving it the appearance of a shallow crater. The white bonelike shards were gone now, replaced by what seemed to be clumps of hair or fur coated in clear fluid. Harvey frowned and pursed his lips, whistling in disgust at the stink emanating.

I'm not picking that shit up, he thought, looking around for something to scoop the strange fur-ball up with. He stopped for a moment, cocking his head. A strangled cry came from the crater, muffled by the wet ground. The earth at the centre of the depression pulsated for a moment, fluid leaking up through the already soaked soil. The cry stopped. The earth settled. Harvey stared for an eternity, his mind blanked by what he had witnessed. Or at least, he thought he had witnessed.

I'm losing the plot. The stress is getting to me.

Yes, that explanation suited him. Things like this only happened in the books he wrote. Monsters weren't real, demons were just part of the religious propaganda machine, and ancient gods were just fairy stories. The fear receded, not entirely gone, but reduced to a low level hum in the back of his mind. He stood and walked back into the house, a little faster than normal. The sun may have been shining, but at that moment, he wanted the safety net of the house and his writing room.

The sun danced through the slats of the blind, throwing long shadows across the room as evening drew in. Harvey's long fingers ceased their dance across the keyboard, as an alarm broke the silence.

Three hours. Not too shabby, son. Not too shabby.

He rubbed his aching eyes and sat back. The words on the screen blurred for a brief moment before coming back into sharp focus. The writer's block was going. The Great Wall of China was coming down, brick by brick. The words, once so difficult to prise from their hiding places, were now jumping into the light, jostling for attention, begging to be written down. The fear he had felt earlier must have acted like some kind of mental emetic, clearing out the crap in his head to make way for regular movement of thought. It was a disgusting analogy, but then again Harvey was a disgusting person at times.

Beer time. He had earned it. Ok, it was a Thursday night, but it wasn't as if he had a regular job to go to. The days of calling in sick, or stumbling into work encased in a boozy fog were long gone. Not having a wife to nag him about it was also a bonus. In a way.

He still missed her. There had been a few half-hearted stabs at relationships since the divorce, but nothing concrete. Company these days consisted of drink-sodden one night stands, events to be regretted in the morning, especially if they made tabloid news. Which they didn't. Reporters weren't interested in authors in that way. Rock stars and actors were fair game when it came to sexual indiscretions. Writers only made the news when they were the subjects of religious fatwas. Harvey didn't mind. He enjoyed the anonymous celebrity status. Not only could he afford to get shit-faced, he could also do it safe in the knowledge that it just wasn't newsworthy.

He stood and stretched out, the clicks of his joints and spine loud in the silence of the room.

All work and no drink makes Jack a dull boy. He rubbed his grumbling stomach. He would have to feed the beast before even thinking about drinking.

He looked around the room, happy and satisfied with the day's work.

The light in the study changed, colour phasing from orange to a sinister red. Reality shifted for a moment. He became dizzy to the point of nausea. The light seemed harsh, almost alien. The clean lines of his desk and computer took on a bizarre appearance, almost unrecognisable to him, as if he was seeing it for the first time. He felt an aching loneliness, a sickness of the heart that had him reeling. Harvey gripped the back of his chair, closing his eyes and breathing heavily. A babble of voices, harsh and monotonous, filled his head. The language was rough and glottal but he recognised the meaning behind the words. A death sentence was being passed and there was no escape.

He began to count backwards, slow and deliberate, in an effort to retake control. The moment ebbed away, leaving him sick and shaking. He opened his watering eyes. Normality had returned. His breath slobbered in and out. Harvey straightened up, confused. He must be more stressed than he had thought. His body and mind were both depleted. The time for work was over, so he left the room behind, still quivering.

The shadows lengthened and thickened as the sun dipped in the orange sky.

Stigger was a crackhead. He knew this. His family knew it, as did the local police, his probation officer and anyone unfortunate enough to be stuck behind him in the queue at the local shops. He didn't care what people thought of him and his habit. He wore the stigma like a badge of honour, sneering at those who looked down on him. He had the last laugh on them.

Crackhead that he was, he was also an expert burglar. The need for money to feed the gorilla on his back had honed his skills, as had the 'holidays' he had taken at Her Majesty's pleasure. He had learned more about his craft on the inside than he would have thought possible. Lags liked to talk, to show off their skills and impress the youngsters. There was a lot of useful knowledge to be gained inside, if you were prepared to listen, and listen he did.

He had learned the value of patience and observation. Pick a target, stake them out, learn about their habits and routines, sort your escape route out—all of this and more he had committed to memory.

Stigger had been watching the writer fella for weeks now. The man was a creature of habit as well as being stinking rich. He had often wondered why a best-selling author still lived in a semi-detached house in a small Midlands town. Maybe the guy didn't like showing off. Respect to him if that was the case. It didn't really matter anyway. This would be a grand payday. Who cared about why he was still here?

Stigger had waited in the alleyway that ran along the back of the houses, for fifteen minutes. Three o' clock. The writer would be fast asleep by now, as would be most sensible people. It was time to move.

He threw his bag of tools over the fence, wincing a little at the thud it made. The burglar counted down twenty seconds. No lights came on in the street. There was no tell-tale twitch of curtains.

Sweet.

He shinned over the fence, dropping to a crouch in the dark. Years of drug use had reduced him in size from hefty to skeletal, an advantage for someone in his line of work. There was always a fence to climb over. You couldn't do that easily if you were a fat bastard.

The house was dark, it's rear illuminated weakly by the solitary streetlight out on the path. He would have to get the back door open quickly, even though the light was not great. Stigger couldn't take the chance of anyone seeing. The writer was a popular guy around town. He always stood his round in the pubs and did a lot for the community. Getting caught robbing the man would be a good way to get railroaded out of town. He couldn't leave his mum behind. Not now. She was too sick to leave.

Gathering up the little strength he possessed, he dropped onto his front and began to crawl through the dark towards the house. He stopped for a moment to collect his bag, returning it to his back, before resuming his crawl. The place stank to high heaven. Stigger fought the urge to cough, fearing detection. He held his breath for a few moment until the tickling ceased.

Jesus H. Christ. Has he been shitting out here?

The smell grew in intensity. He grimaced as his fingers sank into the ground. The earth was warm. And wet. Stigger frowned in confusion as his hands sank further into the soil.

What the fuck?

He shivered as he felt something lightly brush his fingertips.

Worms? Must be worms. Bollocks to this.

He pulled.

Strong hands gripped his wrists, pulling him forward. His face smashed into the stinking mulch, his nose cracking as it broke. Stigger tried to scream. Sticky, wet mud flooded his mouth, his tongue slick with the taste of rot. The hands, if that was what they were, released his arms and gripped his head. Stigger convulsed. Nails pierced his eyes, pulling them from their sockets. His skin burned as fluid washed over his head. The hands kept pulling at his loosening skin, pulling him further and further into the ground. His mind buckled under the white agony as more fluid erupted from beneath him, a stinking acid that ate into him, dissolving flesh and bone. He could feel things ravaging him, tipped tendrils that broke through his skin, eagerly tearing organs loose and squeezing the juices from him.

A tentacle wrapped gently around his still beating heart. Stigger, blind and mad from the pain, wished for death. The tentacle squeezed, bursting his heart and granting his wish. He became limp. The limbs pulled him deeper into the ground.

His bag sat forlornly on the lawn, a forgotten relic. The earth beside it heaved and bled, grass dying as the chemicals beneath dissolved the roots.

Harvey sat up, regretting the suddenness of the movement instantly. His head pounded monotonously, the repetitive beat of a hangover in D-Major. He groaned and fell back into bed, his skin goose-pimpling with cold. The sheen of sweat had cooled him and the sheets beneath. He felt and smelled awful. He lay there for a few moments, fathoming the reason for his abrupt waking, and the moments before. Fleeting scraps of dreams came to him—impossibly tall creatures with spindly arms and faces hidden in shadow, pointing at him, screaming in accusatory tones.

A purple tinged sky, illuminated by the light of a ringed gas giant, the ground below burning and littered with broken, oozing bodies.

The smell and taste of alien flesh filling his mouth to bursting.

There was something familiar about these random fragments, as if he had lived them. Memories of a former life perhaps. He dismissed the thought. Reincarnation held a fascination for him, but only as a plot point. It was, like all religious theory, a total load of bollocks, only fit to fuel the imagination of backwards Third Worlders and horror writers looking for an angle.

Still, the imagery was striking. Harvey sat up, looking for his notepad. He had kept one on the bedside cabinet ever since Stephen King had revealed that he did the same. Unable to and unwilling to find it, he collapsed back.

Fuck it. If the images were strong enough, he would remember them in the morning. If not, it was no great loss. He had more than enough material to keep him going, even if the writing of it was torturous. His breathing slowed and deepened and his eyes began to close. As he fell asleep, he heard a voice cry out faintly. Sleep took him before he could dwell on it. Within moments, he was snoring.

"For fuck's sake", he muttered. "Really?"

The knock on his front door was insistent, heavy. Harvey stirred his coffee, swallowed two paracetomol dry and walked through to the living room. He felt good this morning, surprising given the amount he'd drunk. The usual fog of fatigue, along with the taste of stale ale, were absent. He hadn't felt this way after a session since his late teens.

Maybe my mojo's come back. He smiled, catching sight of himself in the mirror above the fireplace. He even looked more alive, rested and healthy. The bags under his eyes, the pallor, the defeated set of his face, were no more. He clicked his fingers, pointing at himself and smiling.

"Looking good, kidder." The knocking at the door continued. Whoever it was had heard him. He went to the door, limbering up for confrontation. If it was those two dappy old Jehovah's Witnesses, they would be getting it with both barrels today. His mind felt keen, razor sharp and full of witty comebacks.

He opened the door, mildly disappointed. A man and woman stood before him. The woman, clad in the uniform of the Constabulary, flashed him a winning, even smile. Harvey smiled back in spite of himself. He wasn't fond of the police. Too many encounters with them at football matches of the past had soured him to the boys—and girls—in blue. It was hard to see the good points in someone when their brethren had smashed you over the head with truncheons. Still, she was pleasant enough, an attractive brunette. He idly wondered how he could go about getting her phone number. It had been a month since he had enjoyed a good hard fuck.

The man cleared his throat, ruining the moment. Harvey regarded him with curiosity and a little amusement. He was clearly hungover. The blue eyes, set deep into his long pallid skull, were tinged with red. His greying hair was slicked back, tufts sticking out from the top and sides. His rumpled clothes had clearly seen better days. Harvey felt a twinge of pity for the man. He was clearly going to seed, his soul being relentlessly squeezed by a lifetime in a thankless job. He crushed the feeling of empathy.

Fuck him. He's a copper. Taken aback by the sudden viciousness of the thought, Harvey put his hand out. There was nothing else he could do to hide his discomfort. The man stared at his hand for a moment, as if he was trying to remember what came next, before clasping it in a limp grip.

They shook hands quickly, Harvey resisting the urge to wipe his on his jeans afterwards. The man's hand reminded him of the dead patch in his garden.

"Are you Harvey Dellar?"

Harvey nodded, forcing away a smile. The poor guy sounded rougher than he looked. His voice had the nasally twang of too many cigarettes and far too much alcohol.

"Sorry to disturb you. I'm Detective Constable Toseland, this is WPC Mann." Harvey winced as he caught a whiff of stale alcohol from the Detective Constable. He must have really overdone it last night.

"Pleasure to meet you both. How can I help?" He flashed another smile at the WPC, pleased when she responded. Toseland cleared his throat noisily.

"Just a few questions. Nothing major. We're just following up a couple of missing persons reports." Harvey frowned at this. Missing people *were* major, especially in a town like this. The one murder they had had a few years back had rocked the place to its core.

"Who's missing?"

"Your neighbour, Mrs Speakman", Mann piped up. "Her step son hasn't heard from her in over a week. She doesn't appear to be home. We've checked." Harvey thought for a moment. He hadn't seen her for a while either. Mrs Speakman's house was directly behind his. She often popped her head over the fence to say hello. Why hadn't he noticed this?

He knew the reason why. He had been too preoccupied with his own writing to notice. Feeling shame, he asked about the others.

"Young lad by the name of Tim Maitland. His mum hasn't seen him for three days."

Toseland handed him a photo of a young boy. Harvey studied it. The boy had a cheeky grin on a face framed by an untidy but fashionable haircut. He was clad in a Liverpool FC shirt, holding his thumbs up at the photographer. Harvey shook his head.

"I know him. He lives with his mum and aunt just up the road."

Harvey knew the women through his ex-wife and he had chatted to them in the pub a few times, but they weren't close friends, more acquaintances. Timmy's dad, from what he knew, was a lazy shit who had become a bit too fond of battering the boy's mother about. The thug had left them a couple of years ago. Soon after that, Denise Maitland's sister had moved in with him.

"Last time I saw him was last Saturday morning outside Tesco with his mum. Just to say hello. I was off to Birmingham for the Comic Con." Harvey smiled at the memory. It had been a good day, a panel appearance with some other British horror heavyweights, capped off by meeting two Doctor Who actors, and Avon from *Blakes 7*.

Toseland looked crestfallen. He was probably under a lot of pressure from his superiors. Mann, on the other hand, seemed thrilled to be talking to a writer, a successful one too. Harvey calculated the odds of getting her phone number to be extremely high.

"Ok, well thank you for your time. If you see anything, please give a call."

Toseland handed him a card, Harvey feeling a mild twinge of disappointment when he noted the number on it. It was the DC's number.

They said their goodbyes, WPC Mann giving him more than a cursory look over and a flirty smile. There were possibilities there. He could sense it. He could almost read her mind.

Harvey closed the front door and made his way back to the living room. His coffee was cold. He left the cup where it was. He stood for a while, debating his next course of action. Part of him wanted to go and check the strange markings in the garden. Every time he thought of it, the image disappeared, as if his mind were pushing it away. Anyway, the urge to write was upon him. He could feel the fire in his fingertips. His imagination awoke, roaring.

Fuck it. This was too good an opportunity to pass by. He could sort the garden out another time. Humming an old UB40 tune, he bolted upstairs, eager to begin.

The day passed and the evening drew in. The sun sank, leaving behind streaks of orange cloud and a lingering heat. Harvey sat, hunched over his keyboard, the writer's block gone, the pent up story now breaking down the huge wall in his imagination that had seemed invincible before.

His back was sore, his eyes hurt, but the sheer joy of creating numbed these pains. He had written for most of the day, only stopping for a piss, a beer and a cigarette. One of the perks of being divorced was that he could smoke in the house without receiving a barrage of abuse. That had been a definite no-no in their married days. If he'd wanted to smoke back then he had had to go outside, day or night, rain, sleet snow; it didn't matter. Now he didn't have to set foot in the back garden unless he wanted to. He stubbed the cigarette out and took a long swig of his drink, grimacing. The lager was flat and warm. It was gin and tonic time. After this chapter.

He fell into the work, thoughts of booze now swept away as the story came together, piece by piece.

It was dark outside. The street was quiet, apart from the occasional person walking to the pub, walking the dog, or just walking. People chatted, argued, made love, jeered at the telly, drank and generally lived out their normal, everyday lives. It was a normal night in a normal town.

In Harvey's back garden, there was an unnatural gloom and a tension in the air. He would have felt it himself had he gone for a smoke outside. The air was heavy with a sense of foreboding and menace.

At around eight o'clock, the widening patch of polluted earth cracked open. A clear fluid flooded out of the cracks, pumping up from somewhere deep below. It soon filled the crater with a stinking miniature pond. Pockets of gas exploded on the surface, releasing more decay.

A man walking his dog past the fence noted the smell and wondered if the drains were blocked around here. Certainly smelled like it. As he walked on, the smell was quickly forgotten. Time was getting on and *Match of the Day* would be on soon. Let the owner of the house sort his own drain problems out.

The earth heaved and roiled as it began to give birth. A pair of mud covered arms slowly grew out of the puddle, hands gripping the dry edges of the bare patch. The arms flexed, pulling at the earth. A dripping form pulled itself from the mud-pool and onto the grass.

Friend rolled onto its back, breathing in rasping gulps of air. Ribs and other bones protruded from its half-made chest. The creature grimaced as it struggled against the constraints of half-life. More substance was required to keep cohesion. The raw material it had been lucky enough to gather so far was at odds with itself, unstable. It needed stability.

Friend held its hands up, inspecting. The hands were skinless, raw and dirt-covered, twisted coils of muscle and tendon exposed to the air. The dirt scratched at its exposed nerve endings, driving the creature wild with anger. It had to get clean before the fury took hold. The thing slowed its breathing and closed its eyes. Clear liquid seeped from the cells of its skinless body, becoming a torrent and a balm, washing the mud away and soothing its dangerously raw flesh.

Friend stood. Slime and mud sloughed from its tall, thin form. It felt its face, its touch deft and light. Its face felt oversized and exaggerated. It was hardly surprised. The creature had relied on its own memory of how it used to look in order to put itself back together. Reconstruction was not an exact science, or so it had been told.

The nubs of its teeth felt large, sharp and overexposed. It had no lips. It staggered, trying to reorient itself. This world's air was rich and heavy, its gravity stronger than the creature was used to. It would take some time to adjust. It had to buy itself that time. The creature was exposed and vulnerable. The forces that had almost destroyed it would come searching, sooner or later. It needed refuge.

The creature looked at the house and sniffed. The mind that had drawn it to this location burned as bright as a star. It could sense the frustration and longing in the dark, twisted consciousness. This mind had drawn it, as it had tumbled through the *Schism*, an anchor point in which to enter this world. There were so many twisted minds to choose from on this planet, but this particular one held a fascination for the creature. The mind's owner was like Friend itself, in many ways—both were bitterly disappointed with their fellow species, both were striving to make their lives better, both were sacrificing much to gain their objectives.

It had made mental contact subtly at first. A forceful, direct contact would have destroyed the other's consciousness instantly. Even the lightest of touches had disrupted the human's train of thought.

He could be left to scribe no longer.

Friend was not strong enough to fix the damage. The animals had been too small, their minds too primitive to nourish Friend's own consciousness. *Magicks* required raw power. The older humanoid and the youngling had boosted it, giving it much-needed strength. The ravaged one, however, was the key. His physical form was revolting, but the decay and corruption in his soul was energising. Friend had reached out to this human, stroking his nervous system back into place so that he could scribe better.

Friend was pleased. This human had enabled it to escape and hide. It had even given it a name, after a fashion. The creature had found this word in the human's mind, liking the sound and the imagery associated with it. It was time to make acquaintance with this human, this *Haaarvey*. Friend gingerly made its way to the house, eager to meet the scribe. There was much to discuss.

Harvey was deep into the book. He was outlining a part with a new character, a young policewoman, Maisie Donovan, and her older, cynical, alcoholic friend, DC Mcdonald.

He crinkled his nose against an itch.

The words unfurled thick and fast, paragraphs taking shape before his eyes, powering the plot to new and unexpected levels.

He sniffed.

This is going to be the best thing I've ever written, he thought. Discordant synth music filled his ears, a haunting lamentation that spoke of frozen landscapes and shape-shifting monsters. He readjusted his earphones and continued to type.

He rubbed his nose, pulling with his thumb and finger, sniffing out of habit.

His hand stalled mid-pull. He sniffed slower, his back becoming rigid. A familiar smell painted a miasma across the back of his throat. It was the same as that ball of slimy fur he had found on the grass earlier. He shook his head and paid it no mind. Some of it had got onto his jeans earlier. Nothing that a hot wash couldn't sort out. Besides, he was getting tired. His eyes burned furiously.

An insistent droning suddenly filled his ears, obliterating the music. He shrieked, yanking the earphones out. The sound echoed around his head.

"What the fuck—"

"*Waaaa-zeee-fooooook.*"

Harvey froze. His heart smashed against his chest. He stiffened. *That was not real.* He gulped.

"*Izzzzzel reeeeel. Mmmm, aye zzzzzzreeeeel.*"

The voice had a buzzing, clicking tone to it, the sound of an insect trying to form human words. The tone was cold and bleak, no inflection to be heard.

What the fuck is in my house?

The smell was overwhelming and thick, permeating every corner of the room. Harvey began to tremble. A cold sweat washed over him, brought by the malignant presence now sharing his space.

"*Aaaalarm not needed. No harm. I mean you no harm.*"

Harvey frowned despite his fear. The voice was becoming more coherent by the second. The buzzing in his ears also faded.

"*Magicks take time to work in this realm, it would seem. Apologies of mine, you must accept. No harm to you, do I intend?*"

His confusion grew.

Has Yoda invaded my house? That'd explain the stink. Fragrance eau Dagobah. He laughed, a brittle splintered sound.

"Is my syntax more understandable now? I hope so. It would be so much more favourable to our friendship, if communication was clear and understood by both parties."

Harvey laughed again, harder and louder this time. The situation had gone from terrifying to incongruous. Yoda had turned into a bureaucrat.

"I am not Yoda, whoever that may be. Nor am I a bureaucrat. It was that kind that sentenced me to death. I have no love for cowardly pen-pushers. In this, we are alike."

Harvey swallowed, trying to dislodge the lump in his throat.

"Who are you? How do you know me?"

"Formal introductions work better if we converse face to face. If we are to become friends, that is."

The chair, unbidden, spun around.

Harvey looked up and pissed himself at the sight of the dripping, malformed creature that stood before him. Its eyes fixed on his. The dark orbs glittered with intelligence, malice and hunger. The creature's face was almost skull like, the teeth too sharp to belong to any man. Its features were lop-sided, its head oversized and bulging. Bright, bleached bone showed up through open wounds, reminding Harvey of the bare patch of grass. Harvey's mind jabbered at him, trying to convince him that this was not real.

The creature dipped its head close. Harvey gagged at the stench. It stroked his cheek tenderly, leaving a snail's trail of stinking slime.

It whispered. *"Friend. Your mind guided me here. You must give me succour and shelter from my enemies. In return, I will help you."*

Even in the grip of terror, Harvey couldn't help being curious. How could this half-finished creature help him? And what it did it mean by guiding it? The creature began to cough, a hacking sound that gave way to a bubbling, gurgling laughter.

"Such impatience. Such curiosity. I was correct in my assessment. We truly are kindred spirits. All inquiries will be answered shortly. First, I must present to you a token."

The creature put its hand to an exposed piece of green bone at its temple, slicing through the growth with a razor talon. Its fingers gripped the squirting extension and it tugged. A fragment of wet bone *splutted* onto the floor.

Harvey whimpered and bit his lip, bottling the scream that longed to explode within him. The creature forced two fingers into the hole and wrenched hard, pulling free a piece of itself and holding it in front of Harvey's eye. He curled his nostrils against the stink wafting from the lump of dripping matter.

"*The Token*", the creature said breathlessly.

What was he meant to do with it? Eat it? The creature shook its head energetically as if it was offended by the thought. Harvey's curiosity grew. If this thing meant to harm him, it could have done so by now. It was strong, despite the decrepit state of its body. The randomly sized talons on its spindly fingers could slice through his skin with ease. He relaxed slightly. The creature put its hand out, the green mass on its palm quivering and contorting. Insectile legs sprouted haphazardly from all over the token's surface, a gristly sound. The many legged blob stood on its owner's palm, legs shaking. It began to sway side-to-side as if it was searching for something.

"What...what is it?" Harvey asked, at last finding his voice. The creature made a strange sweeping gesture with its head.

"*The Token*", the creature repeated, its voice solemn. "*With this, we join. I will have refuge, you will have stories to tell and magicks to work. Nothing will ever be beyond your reach again. This I swear to you.*"

Harvey considered this for a moment.

Never stuck for inspiration again.

It seemed too good an opportunity to pass up. Harvey nodded. "I accept. What do I do?"

"*Nothing at all. The Token knows what it must do.*" The creature sighed, its breath smelling of rank, abandoned tombs. "*Please relax.*"

Harvey exhaled.

The little blob leapt onto his face, landing just under his nose. The writer fought the urge to sneeze as he felt two gossamer thin appendages explore the opening of his nostrils. The creature held its hands up in an imploring gesture.

"*Relax, Haaarveeee.*"

The thing erupted with a delighted *sqee* and scurried up his nose. Panicked, Harvey shouted and squeezed his nose, trying to squash the little bastard.

Too late. He could feel the mass of the tiny abomination squirming into his sinuses, blocking his airway.

Desperate for breath, Harvey opened his mouth.

"Get it out of me," he cried in panic. The creature shook its head again.

"The Token does its work. We will be joined."

Harvey fell to the floor and began banging his head, trying to dislodge the intruder from the micro-caverns of his skull. Pain flared as the creature nibbled, biting hard through the soft tissue as it burrowed deeper.

Harvey sobbed. Bone crunched. Pain speared him as the creature bit through into his cranial cavity, where the lack of nerve endings made the intrusion unfelt and unknown, save for the sounds filtering through his inner ear.

Blood and tissue leaked from Harvey's nose and he began to convulse. The thing wiggled deeper into his brain tissue, causing him to fit. Harvey trembled and rolled onto his front, beer leaking from his mouth along with strings of mucousy vomit.

The world darkened. His face crashed to the floor.

Harvey wiped the steam from the bathroom mirror, and inspected his face, looking for blemishes. His skin, still pink from showering, radiated perfection. He smiled, his teeth whiter and more even than they had ever been. The wrinkles around his eyes were now gone and the paunch he had been developing from too many liquid lunches was gone too. He was a new man.

The creature, now known to him as Friend, had explained everything when he had come to. Friend had pulled him to his feet and apologised. The creature hadn't come to hurt him, only to save him from a life of mediocrity and failed dreams—the future he faced if his writer's block returned. They were now joined. The thing in his head was a part of Friend. It shared its and Harvey's consciousness, as well as some of Friend's abilities.

As the creature healed and grew stronger, so did Harvey. There would be such sights to behold and many *magicks* to learn and put to use. Friend was going to make Harvey rich and powerful. Nothing would ever be beyond the writer's reach ever again. In return, all Harvey had to do was keep Friend safe and feed him when necessary.

With what?

An image flashed up in their shared mind. The rational part of him, the old Harvey recoiled at the sight. The new man embraced the vision in all its blood-soaked glory. There was still an element of caution however.

What if people suspect?

No one will suspect. My magicks will keep you in shadows. No one will remember your face unless we will it. Besides, one cannot write of murder if one never experiences the sheer delights of taking life. It is a privilege few ever experience. You will enjoy it. I sense that much.

Harvey smiled. Friend was going to show him a new way of living, one he had only ever imagined and lived on paper. He dried himself and walked past his study. He had considered getting back to work, but that could wait.

Friend was hungry, and as a good host, Harvey had an obligation to make sure that his guest was fed. He'd pick something up on the way back from the pub for them both.

What do you fancy, Friend? Blonde or brunette?

An eager thought came back.

Let us be extravagant on our first night together. That policewoman, Mann, was it? I can show you where she lives. I can also weave a little attraction magick. She will be eager and suppliant.

Harvey laughed and clapped his hands. Friend mirrored the gesture. The writer put on his coat, eager for his new life to begin.

ONE NIGHT IN MUMBAI

TEARS FROZE on his face. He scrunched the stiff muscles around his eyes and cheekbones. A thin rime of ice cracked, sliding from his cooling flesh, only to be replaced by more icy tears. It was an exercise in futility. He knew this. The knowledge did not stop him from repeating the exercise.

The wind bit through his winter coat like a knife, seeking exposed areas from where it could leech his warmth and cast it off into the deep dark blue of night. The camp was close. He could sense it, or rather he could sense the warmth of human life. In the dark, howling throat of the Antarctic storm, the heat of human bodies shone like beacons to his borrowed eyes.

The wind cut underneath him, trying to grip his legs and throw him off balance. It was not the natural phenomenon he was used to. Animal rage permeated the black night, pricking his senses. It was a familiar feeling. His collective consciousness knew the taste of this anger. It had haunted him for countless millennia, from the glory days of ancient Greece, to the plazas of Chandigarh. It was alive, a hunting animal sent by the creatures out there in the dark spaces, those that Man had not had the time or the inclination to explore, until recently.

Mercer shook his head in despair. Mankind had ventured into unknown territory without learning a simple truth—the Cosmos was hostile, impersonal. Blind entreaties to deities and arrogance were no armour against the creatures that waited on the other side of the Schisms, nor could they be judged by human standards. There were things out there that had no moral compass as Man understood it. To avoid their scrutiny, one had to tread carefully and use a deft touch, not blunder into the unknown, lights blazing. His despair turned to disgust. Would they ever learn?

Mercer shook his legs, still powerful after a journey that would have killed a normal human. He muttered something in a language older than civilisation. The wind shrieked and uncurled away from him, slinking back into the night, wounded, running to its masters for aid and comfort. The man laughed and resumed walking, pushing his way through the snow. In the distance, he could just make out a blur of blue light. He was nearly there. One last, great push for safety. He put his head down against the wind, still muttering in a glottal language of snarls and whistles.

He reached the edge of the camp, the cold, azure glare of exterior lamps a welcome sight after the void of the Antarctic night and the bilious green light of *Arkonius*. The injured man allowed himself a brief respite, smiling with gratitude at the final end to a long journey. It didn't last. Pain, white-hot and gnawing, exploded within. He swayed, unprepared for the assault on his ragged senses. He breathed in suddenly, wincing as something inside came loose from its moorings, increasing the agony. A low moan became a gurgle as blood begin to pour from his mouth. The scarlet ribbon became a flood, flowing too quickly to freeze. He sank to his knees and bent forward, mouth wide open as his life poured from within his wracked and tortured frame. The red puddle iced over as it hit pristine snow.

The torrent slowed, allowing him to straighten. The numbness of shock was fast approaching. He had to get moving. If he didn't, he and *they*, would perish. Nerves screamed as he struggled to his feet.

The *Bisala Enzadi* had hit him harder than he thought. The creature, taller than a man, with huge fists and hook-like blades on its fingertips, had cornered him during his escape from the city. It was too large for him to fight directly, even with years of combat skill gifted to him by the Lazlo Gestalt. Ducking and feinting, he had kept the *Enzadi* at bay, an incredible feat. *Bisala Enzadis* were masters of the ancient *Bunduki* martial art, Steel Hands.

With its build and strength, the creature should have torn him open. Only luck and a well prepared knife attack had saved him from death. The dying *Enzadi* had still managed to deal a crippling blow in its death throes. The sneaky bastard had waited until he was almost on top of it before smashing a clawed hand into his side, crushing the left half of his rib cage.

This hurts so much. Never felt pain like this before.

A voice chimed in, from deep within him. Lazlo. Or at least one of the many components of Lazlo. He struggled to recognise which one it was.

You have. Or have you forgotten the Conquistador and his spiked club, already? It only seems like yesterday to me.

He recognised the language – Nahuatl, language of the Aztec. The voice could only have been Ichtacha. An image came to him, unbidden— a raven-haired, fiery young woman, olive-skinned and innocent looking. The filthy Spanish dog had tried to take her, thinking that her small frame meant helplessness. In an eerie foreshadowing of his fight with the *Enzadi*, Ichtacha had beaten the Spaniard, stabbed him, only to be bludgeoned by the dying man. Life was indeed circular.

Of course. He smiled. How could I forget?

Reminisce another time. We're dying. You have to get inside now. While you still have the chance.

He nodded grimly, seeing the sense in her words. If he died here, Lazlo would perish too. That could not happen. The planet and the Omniverse – the very tapestry of existence – depended on Lazlo and the knowledge the creature possessed. If it died out here, so would the Omniverse.

With a gargantuan effort, he staggered to his feet and ploughed through the deepening snow to the main camp entrance, pushing his way through the door, into the warmth. Light speared his sensitive eyes and he cried out, collapsing to the floor. Bit by bit, measure by measure, Mercer felt his body shutting down as organs crumbled, swimming in a soup of blood and cells. The Gestalt began to stir, readying itself for a familiar journey. Captain Danning was close by. It could feel the man's presence. He was their only hope. Without him, the next hour would be filled with dread and agony as the host body, Mercer, broke down. The Gestalt would leave an eternal existence drowning in a sea of clotting blood, shit and decay before the darkness of *Mor Animus*, Soul Death, claimed it.

Mercer's essence began to fade. He could feel himself being drawn into the creature that lived at his very centre. His life was over. He was resigned to this. He would live anew, disembodied, but alive, as part of Lazlo's mind. But would Lazlo live long enough? He waited as Mercer's body began to shut down.

His eyes snapped open and he gulped hard. His senses came flooding back to him. He lay in a bed, not the most comfortable of resting places, but a bed nonetheless. The numbing cold of Antarctica seeped from his muscles and bones, chased into the ether by the soupy heat of a Mumbai night. Captain Danning – The Captain, as he was known to one and all – lay for a moment more. There was no hurry to get up. He relished the heat, letting it permeate his body. Sweat lathered him, a consequence of life in this strange and intriguing land. He closed his eyes. The cacophony of Mumbai by night invigorated him. It was an assault unlike any other on Earth, a stimulation of the senses that extinguished lethargy, even in the stifling heat.

He'd left the window shutters open, an old habit ingrained into him by previous visits to this land. He had hoped the stale air of his room would be cycled out into the night, but it hadn't. There was no breeze—just the odour of his own sweat, sharp yet sweet, mingled with the rich scent of spice, bleach and ancient earth.

The Captain sat up, shaking off the last dregs of sleep. His senses sharpened. Lazlo was waking too. He enjoyed the sensation. When the Gestalt awoke, it was like opening your eyes to a new world. Every angle, every contour of the world, was starker. Smells, sounds, thoughts: all were enhanced tenfold. His energy levels increased dramatically. His reasoning skills were honed. Having Lazlo residing with him was like finding the Fountain of Youth. The creature squirmed within, sending a wave of happiness through his system.

Opening his eyes, he stood and sauntered over to the dust-smeared mirror in the corner of the small room. His appearance never ceased to amaze him. It wasn't vanity. It was sheer marvel. At an age where flesh began to sag and muscles began to slacken, he was an anomaly. His body held firm, every part still in the places that had been ordained for them, not an ounce of fat to be seen. Another pleasing side effect of the *conjoining*.

He winked at himself. The part of him that was still Captain Paul Danning had a vanity that Lazlo felt a little uncomfortable with, but never tried to quash. That would be against the rules. The Gestalt didn't evict the host's personality, nor did it try to change the personality in any way. That wasn't the purpose of the meld. It never had been. It was about the joining of minds into a cohesive unit, a pure, symbiotic relationship. The human elements received the wisdom and knowledge of a life measured in millennia by becoming a part of the Lazlo Gestalt, and the Lazlo Gestalt gained a sanctuary that was mobile and easy to defend, as well as the chance to experience more life.

The Captain had been blissfully unaware of this existence. Until that fateful night in the snow and ice, he had been a mere soldier — formerly of the British Army, then inducted into the secretive world of Unit Cabal. He had seen more sights than he cared to, sights which threatened his sanity. His presence in the frozen continent had been a Unit Cabal mission. The task had seemed simple enough; safeguard his old friend Will Mercer whilst the reticent archaeologist poked through some ruins that had been found out in Droning-Maud Land. After the jungles of the Congo and the Belize Incident, the mission had been a welcome break, as well as a chance to catch up with a dear friend.

Never been more wrong, have I?

He returned from Antarctica with a wider understanding of the universe than before. He now understood just what faced his delicate species out there in the Void. He also had a near limitless supply of knowledge to choose from. And yet, Lazlo's curiosity about this world amazed him.

A Gestalt could live a million millennia and never get bored, the creature had once explained. There was always something for him to do, especially in a reality and a place such as this. Earth kept him busy and intrigued. Just being with people was a gift in itself. When Lazlo had first arrived in this plane of existence, so different to his own, he had looked upon Earth as a pleasant, if rough, little planet. Time and the knowledge he gained from others told him otherwise. Earth was more than just a blue orb hanging on the tapestry of this strange black universe.

Earth was a Shatter-point, a junction in the folds of reality. Its presence was vital, not just for the survival of the universe, but for all realms and realities. The third child of an insignificant star held the Omniverse together. It was the fulcrum around which Life itself revolved. Malignant forces could hold all of Creation hostage if they ever gained control of this place.

The Gestalt had all sworn this would never happen, not while they remained alive. They had all signed up to the Covenant long ago, when the nations of the Earth were united as one single mass of land. This place was to be protected at all costs, even if it meant the everlasting dark of *Mor Animus*. The price was hefty but it would be paid in full.

And paid it was. Where there had been many Gestalts, now there were few, not enough to fully uphold the Covenant. War, disease and ever increasing incursions from other places had decimated their ranks, scattering the survivors to the four winds. Lazlo was one of the last.

The Captain felt a twinge of loneliness and sadness. He knew who the strong pangs were for. As much as it had admired and respected its fellow outcastes, there were only two losses that had broken the creature's heart, if it possessed one—Maya Rosemont and Servilius – Lover and Friend. The Captain turned his thoughts inwards to try and comfort Lazlo. The other minds joined in, wrapping him in warmth and security.

Thirsty, the old soldier poured himself a glass of water and walked over to the window. Outside, the city heaved, from the maze of alleyways and slums, to the glittering towers of the financial heart of India. The people went about their business, oblivious to the things happening out of the corner of their collective eyes. The human capacity for self-deception was exceptional, definitely unique in all of the Realms. If a man didn't want to see something, he could easily convince himself he hadn't seen anything.

The human slivers within the Gestalt murmured their amusement— Danning, Cornelius, Anatolia, Ichtacha, Chan Khong and others, whose names were now lost in the mist of time, forgotten even by themselves. Lazlo's skin rippled with delight. It had found humour a baffling concept at first. There had been no laughter in the realm of its birth, only an austere existence guided by principles of logic and emotionless harmony. This new emotionally chaotic experience had frightened all of the exiles. They had been unprepared for the rawness of life here. Time and assimilation led to appreciation and the eventual embrace of these feelings. Laughter was no longer alien to it.

Assimilation had also given the human elements space and a new perspective from which to judge their former species. They had come to see humanity, rich in diversity, faults and quirks, as a cause for celebration, not despair. Even Danning, cynical and abrasive towards his fellow men, now had a greater respect for them. Time and knowledge softened his attitude. He sipped his water, stretching his enhanced senses outward to touch the world beyond.

The tumultuous sea of humanity shouted back at him. So many conflicting emotions—joy, love, despair, hate. His nerves jumped from the contact. A younger, untrained Gestalt would have collapsed under the strain, but Lazlo had been around far too long to let simple emotions drown him. Shock spasmed through the Captain's system. The sudden jolt caused the glass in Danning's hand to catapult out of the window and smash in the deserted back street below. His nerves writhed at the agonising telepathic contact. He had not expected that, those acidic pools of hate amongst the bustle of humanity.

Ten grim consciousness's – black with hate and evil intent – sang joyless songs of a malevolent ideal. The intensity was almost inhuman. He sucked in his breath sharply. Beads of sweat sprang from his high forehead, trickling down his proud nose.

Something was wrong. The violence of those minds was like a beacon of burning fat and blood, a foul smelling, blazing intensity. The Captain reined in his senses, pulling the tendrils of thought back to a safe distance, expanding the range once again. There was death on the air tonight. He had to stop it.

The Captain sucked air into his lungs. As he exhaled, he opened his mind fully and ejected it out into the night, letting his thoughts expand and settle over the city. His nerves sang again, something nearby pulling him in. It was as if the city had been pocked with several voids, black spots sucking the life and joy out of the surroundings. Brutal hunger radiated from these dead zones. There was a psychic odour around the voids, a whiff of tombs and old blood.

The Gestalt's enemies had found him, moving their puppets into play. The monsters' signature presences had been camouflaged by the dark thought of men who come to Mumbai only to slaughter.

The Captain pulled his thoughts back. He felt fouled by the contact, as if he had bathed in rotten shit. He was confused by this sudden turn in events. Ten men were about to commit atrocities for nothing more concrete than an idea, a falsehood fed to them by devious, unscrupulous old men. It was an evil both the Captain and the Gestalt despised—men who claimed to be wed to an idea, sending other people's children to kill and die. Evil was not a concept confined to the Earth. The Omniverse was full of bloodthirsty races and tyrants – *Naas Zubaiders, Flesh Masters, Doomlords.* Yet to Lazlo, who had seen these and more, the nature of their evil did not shock. These races were born that way. They had no other concept to balance against. Human evil was all the more shocking because of their innate capacity for good. People were not born monsters. They were twisted that way by others who should have known better. He had to stop them. He knew this. But...

There was more to consider here. The voids of hunger, tainted with a nuclear malevolence, were obviously non-human. The signatures were too diffuse, muffled by the murderers and the throng of Mumbaikers, making them difficult to identify with any form of clarity. The Captain bit his lip, thinking furiously. There could be any type of Morbius Entity out there - *Bisala Enzadi, Knights Weird, Dread Priests,* maybe even a *Pnakot.* He winced in pain as he bit a little too hard.

Pnakotus!

Could it be? The odour around the presences had a slight tang of *Pnakot* blood – bitter and almondy. The sense of hunger matched the feelings he had had the last time he met Archon Morbius' Royal Guard.

Ten killers and a possible squad of *Pnakotus* loose in a city like Mumbai. Gestalts rarely believed in coincidences. The study of logic during their youngling phase, coupled with study of the Omniverse, destroyed any belief in such phenomena. The Omniverse was a cold, organised place. There was always a plan. Nothing ever happened by chance, only by meticulous engineering. Something had gone to immense lengths to pull this together—ten terrorists to distract the population, giving the *Pnakotus* freedom of movement around the city. The police would be drawn towards the city centre, leaving this area at the tender mercies of anyone ruthless enough to take advantage.

The Captain began to run through options, unaware of the ribbon of blood trickling down his chin. In his reverie, he had bitten too hard.

What to do first?

The men were a threat, but they were merely human. Dangerous, yes. Intelligent? Maybe. The minds he had touched did seem to be a trifle dim, accustomed only to obedience, not individual thought. The *Pnakotus* were not only dangerous and intelligent, they lacked pity and morality; true depraved predators.

Not even Hell with its pantheon of depraved and disturbed *Praetors*, *Plutarchs* and lower demons had the imagination and mental diseases of the *Pnakotus*. Lucifer was a mere snake oil sale man, a gauche con artist. His pantheon of demons were egotistical prima donna. The forces of Hell were a triviality when set against Morbius Pnakot, the High Arkon of the Wastes and his Entities.

That creature knew no boundaries, no moral centre, and his hatred for humankind, a hate he shared with the denizens of *Pnakotorum Arkonius*, blinded him to all reason. The Gestalt, conjoined with Mercer, had barely managed to blast the *Arkon* back into deep hibernation. It had taken all of Lazlo's strength and magicks. As Morbius tumbled back into deep sleep, his dreams and thoughts leaked out into the world, a poisonous cloud of dark thought that soiled the minds and bodies of the unprepared. There was no known cure for infection, only immolation. The screams of his Unit Cabal squad—Thrower, Danzig, Randhawa, Egerton, Toseland—still haunted his dreams. In his mind's eyes, he saw corrupted bodies that shivered and convulsed as fire flaked the flesh from their bones.

The creatures' mission would be simple—revenge on the interloper who had dared to imprison their leader, destroying much of their city and a large number of their kind. The creatures wouldn't rest until they cracked open his bones and used his marrow as lubricant for their masturbatory self-pleasure. And that would only be the beginning of his torment. If they managed to take him back to Morbius and awaken him, the ancient being Lazlo would learn a new definition of suffering.

Corpus Mori—Flesh Death—was an unpleasant and painful process for all of the souls in the Lazlo Gestalt, but *Mor Animus* was something far worse, something feared by all beings who lived in the Higher Reaches. The pain was beyond the comprehension of normal lower order creatures; the knowledge and experience lost to a Soul Death was incomparable. Dominus Servilius had once told him that even the Gods themselves feared the final oblivion of *Mor Animus*.

The memory of his friend brought up a deep sense of loss and pain.

As well as fearing it, the Ethereal Ones were also well versed in the art of inflicting the Soul Death. The day he had used that skill to put Servilius down was one that would haunt the Gestalt for centuries to come. The memory came unbidden from a vault deep inside his mind. He could still smell the blood, high and ripe on the hot wind, the clashing of swords as Roman centurions fought desperately, hand-to-hand with the Barbarians from the North.

He tried to push the memory away. The old pain was a distraction he could ill afford. It was no use. The memory was too strong, too insistent. Something had unhinged Servilius. Whether he had snapped on the day or whether this had been happening over the course of time was irrelevant. What mattered was that a Gestalt had lost control of his minds; all of them. The Captain remembered the look in the older man's eyes and shivered. There had been ferocity, a cold vicious rage that he had never seen in another human. The Dominus that had been Lazlo's friend and mentor since the Exile, had gone, erased from existence. The creature that then stood before him radiated contempt and hatred for all forms life, even Lazlo. He had raved disjointedly, broken sentences pouring from his cracked lips.

"They have all gone, Lazlo. We are the Gods now. Thirteen and Nine no more, merely a void. We have to fill the gaps in Order, you see? *Do you see?* The Gods have abandoned us!" Servilius had lapsed into incoherent mumbling, pacing backwards and forwards. At times, he clawed at the air, as if trying to grasp invisible tormentors. Lazlo had begun the Last Rite, hoping that Servilius would be too distracted to notice.

"I'm sorry, my friend." Lazlo had turned his face to the sky, screaming his despair as the energies of the Rite poured from him, a deep maroon cloud that oozed from pores and orifices. The release was too much for him; he was too young and inexperienced to be able to contain the ritual. His mind ignited in a blaze of red light. Veins bulged beneath the surface of his host skin, splitting and shedding precious fluid. Before he passed out, he watched Servilius fall to his knees, skin and muscle liquefying. Darkness took him. He accepted gratefully, not wishing to see the final end.

When he awoke, Servilius was gone. Nothing remained save red-flecked armour, sandals and scattered pools of blood on the dusty earth. It was a sad legacy for one as great as the Dominus.

Danning wiped a lone tear from his cheek and pulled himself together. Ancient wounds still ached. Perhaps they always would. He'd had a few millennia to learn the truth of this.

Maybe a Gestalt does live for too long.

A distant sound of machine gun fire and screams assailed his keen senses, bringing him back to the here and now. The attack had begun.

A few streets away there stood a row of deserted, fire-gutted houses. The locals avoided these places, kept away by fear and, for some, guilt. The owners were long dead, their lives torn from them by knives, kerosene and burning tyres. The few survivors had left Nariwalla Colony, unable to bear staying in the place. The memories of neighbours turning against them, baying for their blood, had soured them against the place. The rank injustice of seeing the very people who had murdered their kin walking the streets with impunity, in some cases even holding government posts, shattered their faith in a system that was supposed to protect all.

The houses now stood as mute testimony to a time when the animal lurking in the human heart had been unleashed with devastating consequences. The buildings only stood now because a local Pandit who had tried to save the murdered, had allegedly cursed the Colony. Furious at the mob, he had decreed that if any of the shells of plaster and brick were touched, then the whole of Mumbai would be engulfed by flame and blood. With a final touch to show his seriousness, the Pandit had committed suicide in one of the houses, pouring kerosene over himself and lighting it as he sat in the still smouldering ruins of the wrecked building. The mob, unnerved and frightened, fled and never returned. Residents avoided this part of the colony when they could. The lane, closed off at one end by the wreck of a house, was as quiet as the grave.

The silence suited *Navi Rakhasha*. She needed time to meditate, to gather its energies and clear its mind. The prey would be more of a challenge than the pathetic fleshy, two-legged creatures it normally killed. She may have been bred for slaughter, but the powerfully-built being didn't like leaving anything to chance.

Rakhasha sat cross-legged on a floor still stained with old blood. She sensed the grimy echoes of pain and misery, a constant litany of agony inaudible to lower species. The being's mottled grey-green skin rippled with delight. The agony of the innocent was delicious.

Tubes of flesh writhed on her head, the eyes at the tip of each tentacle closed, as the creature pulled itself deeper into a cleansing trance. An eye-bearing tendril on each side of her neck darted around, keeping watch for any signs of danger or disturbance. It was virtually impossible to take a *Navi Rakhasha* by surprise. The thing would have smiled with pleasure had biology allowed it to. *Rakhasha* possessed no lips. Her face was a cavernous maw that opened and closed, like a fleshy, glistening flower. Rows of saliva-drenched, hooked teeth gleamed with a phosphorescence of their own. A black scabrous tongue unfurled, moistening the multitude of eyeballs with clear, stinking fluid.

The creature gasped and moaned in orgasmic delight as new sensations assailed it. She opened her eyes and sniffed. Her mouth watered at the stench of cordite, blood and shit. Saliva dripped onto the dusty floor where it writhed. The delicious feeling of death battered her, making concentration difficult. There were other killers out there. The murderers were only human, not its kind or any other. It was just Man showing his inhumanity, killing in the name of a god that that had left the Realms long ago, even before *Rakhasha*'s time. No matter. Humans were like insects. Food and sport; nothing more, nothing less. Once *Morbius* revived, Man would be shown his true purpose at the end of a meat hook or in a death camp.

Concentrating hard, the creature pushed away the pleasurable sensations of death and slowed its breathing, clenching its fists. Talons of sharpened bone dug into the fleshy parts of her palms. She made no sound. She couldn't feel pain, lacking the nerves for such a sensation. Thin runnels of black, stinking fluid dribbled from its injured hand onto the dust floor, disappearing into the ground.

Navi Rakhasha paid it no mind. She could afford to lose a little blood. There would be chance enough for replenishment once the Gestalt was captured. The creature ventured deeper into its trance, awaiting the perfect moment to attack.

Sunil Bandari loped excitedly up the stone steps to the top floor of the guest house, all arms, legs and birds-nest hair. His usual reticence was gone, dissolved in the face of the news he carried. Captain Sahib needed to hear what the boy had to say. On the way back from the train station, the boy and his father had been waylaid by Munshi Quadeer Baba, an aging *kabob* vendor who had been pitched up outside the small station since the time of Partition.

There were men in the city, he reported grimly. Well-armed, organised, murderous men. Mumbai was under siege and all were in danger—Hindu, Sikh, Parsi, Nazreenee, even Musselman. These *goonda* bastards didn't care.

Sunil's father listened carefully, uttering a shocked "Hai Ram', as the old man continued his story. A friend of a friend of the station master had even stated that the killers were from over the border, from the so-called 'Land of the Pure'.

"Would that really be so surprising?" The old man spoke in rapid fire Marathi, becoming more and more agitated as he spoke of the neighbours. His older brother had been killed in action in '65. He had no love for Pakistan, even though he shared their religion. He was Indian. That was all there was to it.

There had already been murders in the district. Maybe sympathisers, collaborators looking to start a wave of communal violence. Two policeman had been found dead in the *maidan* further down the road. The *maidan*, a small piece of walled scrub-land, dotted with a few forlorn looking *peepul* trees, was optimistically called a park by the boys who played cricket there and the clandestine lovers looking for space away from the eyes of overbearing parents and gossipy relatives.

The area was full of lathi-waving policeman, ancient British-era revolvers strapped to their waists. They fought the crowd away from the crime scene, not wanting potential evidence to be lost.

Munshi had carried on with his tale. Screams had been heard in the park, cries of anguish and horror that had torn at his old heart. They were the cries of men who had seen *Iblis* himself.

Some burly Sikh taxi drivers had run into the park, only to emerge shaking and crying. One of the drivers vomited into the gutter. The policemen had been torn to pieces, they had said. Skin, chunks of flesh and blood now littered the dead grass. The driver who had vomited claimed he had seen someone running away from the bodies and disappear into an alleyway leading to the back of Nariwalla Colony.

There was something else, something that only the Munshi had noticed. He may have been an old man but his attention span put a youngster like Sunil to shame. He had seen a creature flying low through the night sky, not long after the screams had died down to a whimper.

At first, the old man had paid it no mind, thinking it was a hawk or some other type of bird. Then he had slowly become aware of being scrutinised. Something was watching him. Telling his prayer beads with his right hand and muttering the Kalma, he had looked up.

The creature had paused directly over him, its ragged, membranous wings flapping slowly as it observed the chaotic scenes below. It had crossed its powerful looking arms in a gesture of satisfaction, as if it was enjoying the show. A single drop of blood fell from the sky, landing on the pavement in front of the little old man.

He knew then that the police would never catch the killer. The creature shook. It was laughing! Yellow, glowing eyes locked onto Munshi's. In the fire of that gaze, Munshi Quadeer Baba saw Hell. The creature pointed down at him, a ragged, dark angel passing judgement on an old soul, before flying off in the direction of the old Nariwalla Colony. The old man sighed, muttered something about omens and the End of Days. There was a rattle of gunfire from farther up the road, emphasising the old man's fear.

Lal had thanked the old man and pulled Sunil away, fear in his eyes.

"Sunil. Listen to me. You have to go back and tell Captain *Sahib* about this. Tell him to stay in the house. These bastards are looking for *ferangee* to kill!"

Sunil, his heart pounding, nodded. His father had not looked this fearful in a long time. Not since the day his mother had died, mown down in the street by a car. The killer had never been found.

"Ok, *Vadila.* But what about you?"

"I'm going into the city. There will be casualties." Lal straightened up, a little pride in his face. It had been a long time since he had used his medical training. He had given up being a doctor soon after his wife's death. The Guest House had been hers. Keeping it open was a way of keeping Kavita Bandhari's memory alive. He looked at his son, his pride and love for the boy almost overwhelming. He looked so earnest, so serious. Much like himself. Kavita often used to tease the pair about how little they smiled. Lal touched his boy's cheek, tears suddenly stinging his eyes. He turned quickly, hoping the boy didn't notice.

"Go on. I'll be home soon."

The Bandharis parted ways, Lal stopping and turning for a brief moment. He smiled and made a shooing gesture.

Sunil turned and sprinted all the way back to Mrs Bandhari's Best Guest House, taking the long way around. He didn't fancy bumping into the men with the machine guns, and Munshi's story about the man-bat had unnerved him. It was better to stick to lit roads than chance the dark passageways of the Colony.

Reaching the top floors he stopped for a moment, his breath rasping in and out from his lungs. His side ached with a stitch that felt as if he was being pulled inside out. The manic dash back to the Guest House had pushed him to his limits. He leant against the wall, the cool plaster feeling wonderful through his thin cotton shirt.

A door opened and a head popped out. The man looked as impeccable as always, not a silvery hair out of place, his face clean shaven and strong featured. Only his eyes betrayed anything out of the ordinary. There was an ancient wisdom beyond those eyes. Sunil straightened and tried to speak between huge gulps of air. The older man held up his hand in a placating gesture.

"Easy, son, easy. Get your breath back first."

Sunil nodded, sucking air in desperately. Rivulets of sweat poured from the haphazard stack of black hair perched atop his head.

"A glass of water is needed, I think. Come in, Sunil."

Sunil nodded, following the Captain into his room, relieved at not having to talk just yet. The room was neat and tidy. A bag sat packed and ready on the bed. Was he leaving? Had he already heard about the gun-waving bastards on the streets? The Captain poured two glasses of water, handing one to the boy before sitting in the old wattle chair by the window. Sunil accepted the glass gratefully and sat on the bed. His breathing returned to normal.

He felt a pang of sadness. He didn't want Captain *Sahib* to leave. The man was a model guest. There weren't many paying customers who looked after their rooms as conscientiously as the white *sahib* did. The normal clientele; backpackers mostly, with a smattering of migrant workers, pilgrims, aspirant Bollywood actors and petty criminals, treated the guesthouse as just that—a guest house. Some were better than others, but none of them kept their rooms as tidy as the Captain.

Sunil had also developed a fondness for the old *Gora*. He was like a pale uncle, always ready to dispense advice, share stories of his army days, or merely to listen to worries and woes of a boy on the cusp of becoming a man. The Captain also showed a respect and reverence for India not readily shared by other foreigners the boy had met. His knowledge of customs and religions astounded the boy, and his command of Hindi, Marathi, and Punjabi was superb. He was a true son of the soil, more so than the cohorts of the Shiv Sena. The soft-looking English gentleman was an enigma to the boy, kind, but frightening in an indefinable way. Sunil wondered what lay beneath the genial surface. The Captain set his glass down.

"What's happening out there, son? I thought I heard gunfire?"

Sunil, happy for the chance to practice his English, told him everything. His words, pronounced correctly and with perfect inflection, tumbled out of him in an excited torrent. The older man listened, his brow becoming heavier by the second.

Sunil stopped. The Captain looked at the bag then back to Sunil and smiled. There was worry in those eyes despite the grin. Was he thinking of running for it? Would he even be safe? If there were gunmen out there, would they target the older *Ferangee*?

"Where's Lal?"

"He's gone into the city, Sahib. To help with casualties. He did not say where."

"Ok."

He paused, a look of contemplation on his face.

"Are any of the guests still here?"

Sunil shook his head. They had all checked out, with the exception of The Captain and an old Rajastani labourer called Moola Ram. Ram had gone out earlier, but had not returned. Only Sunil, the Captain and a few gecko lizards remained.

The Captain nodded

"Ok. That's good. First things first. I want you to go back to the station and wait for your father. It's out in the open, but at least you'll have people around you. Understand?"

Sunil shook his head defiantly. "Why, Sahib? Why do I have to go? What about the guesthouse? What about you?"

The Captain laughed softly.

"I'll be fine. Now, take this."

He produced a manila envelope and pressed it into the boy's hand. "Give that to your father and thank him for everything. Thank you for everything." The old man mussed the boy's thick black hair and gently pushed him out the door. "Now go. Quickly. We haven't got much time."

Confused and a little frightened, Sunil left. He trudged back down the stair, disconsolate. He would never see the Guest House again. He was certain of that. Something in the Captain's eyes told him. Destruction was coming here too. Maybe this was the *Natraj*, the last terrible dance of Shiva that would usher in the end of time and space. He stepped out of the main door then down the path, stopping to take one last look at his childhood home. His mother's dream; Mrs Bandharis Best Guest House.

The old place had seen better days. The exterior walls were chipped, the paint from the window frames was peeling away and the house had a curious list to it, as if it was about to topple over. It wouldn't matter much if it did. They had no neighbours. The Guest House sat at the end of the lane by itself. His grandfather had brought this place soon after the upheaval of Partition. It had belonged to a Muslim family who had fled in the opposite direction. Somehow this had seemed fitting. It had become a home for a refugee in his own homeland, a homeland torn apart by the whims of greedy, short-sighted men. Eventually, under the watchful eye of his mother, it had become a hostel for the weary, a refuge of a different sort.

Not anymore, Sunil thought glumly. That thought made him angry. His father had tried his best, but his heart and spirit were no longer in it. Sunil knew that he had only carried on in Kavita's name and also to provide him with some safety and stability. Losing a parent was hard. Losing familiar surroundings would be a wrench too far.

His defiance burned inside.

He would not leave. This was his house. He had the right to be there. A Bandhari needed to be there. He knew this without knowing why. Whatever was transpiring depended on him being there. This was his *dharma*.

He turned and headed back to the house. There were plenty of places for him to hide away from the older man and to keep himself out of any danger, until the time was right to show himself.

A pair of glowing eyes watched the boy make his way back to the house. There was a flap of leathery wings and a shadow took flight.

Navi Rakhasha was ready. The Battle Meditation was complete. The *Scion*, Munshi Baba's man-bat, had returned from its recon flight. The Gestalt was at the guesthouse and the *Pnakotus* were in position.

The human pawns were playing their part to perfection. The poor deluded fools really believed they were doing the work of their God. If they knew the truth, they would have killed themselves there and then. Their handler was a true devotee of Morbius, clothed in the skin of a wanted man. Humans were so easy to manipulate. Promises of paradise, heavily-thighed virgins and rivers of wine were more than enough to incite murders. *Rakhasha* huffed with disdain. Such a stupid species. When the time came to cleanse this vermin from the universe and claim the beautiful Earth from them, *Rakhasha* and her sisterhood would be there, ready and willing to chew on the bones of the fetid, insipid human scum.

Navi Rakhasha drew herself to her full height in one lithe movement and stretched. Her skin pulsated as black blood began to flow, nourishing muscle and bones. The tendrils on the creatures head writhed like a nest of snakes, sluggish after a meal. The *Scion* croaked, its head jerking, arms waving in agitation. *Rakhasha* grunted and made a dismissive gesture. She didn't care for trivialities. If there was a young human at the scene, all the better. The younger ones were so much more tender and tastier, especially when the meat was seasoned by the chemicals of fear. The Scion bowed its head, unfolding its wings and taking into the air. *Rakhasha* took one last deep breath, savouring the ghosts of past and present.

The Captain stood at the window of his room. He hadn't left the guest house. That wasn't the plan. Something had stopped him. The voices of the Gestalt, those fine souls who had shared his consciousness as he had shared their bodies, had been unanimous. There would be no running. Even if he ran, Pnakot and his *Knights Weird* would catch up with him. There was no place to hide on Earth. The only safe refuge would be another Realm and that was a near impossibility. Most of the tears between realities had been closed for millennia. The Gestalt would fight to its last breath, if needed. One Last Stand. Maybe the time was right. A long life had made him weary.

If, by some chance, they survived, they would lend assistance to the authorities. There had been several explosions in the city. Whatever was going on was big, bigger than he and the residents had first thought. He felt surprise and shock emanate from the financial quarter. This attack had caught everyone out.

Lazlo had no choice but to concede. He was a democratic Gestalt. He had witnessed the birth of Democracy in Greece, had even helped shape it in his own modest way. It would have been hypocritical of him to go against the wishes of the majority.

The Mumbai night wasn't as frenetic as usual. The sounds of life had taken on a strange, muffled quality. It was as if the air around Mrs Bandari's Best Guest House had become thick and soup-like. Danning sniffed. There was a slight scent of something off in the air. It brought to mind ozone, rot and blood — the stink of *Pnakotorum Arkonus*.

He smiled grimly. At least it was warm this time around. The small voice of Mercer chirped its agreement. He watched the skyline and the street, stretching his senses to their outer limits, steeling himself against the panic and death of the siege of Mumbai. On the fringes of consciousness, there was a blank, a howling void with a centre of hate. The smile turned to a frown. He hadn't ever felt anything like this before. Not even Lucifer's mind had felt like this. This was something new and as such, something dangerous.

Considering his options, he froze. In the dark of the yard, something detached itself and walked into the light that shone through the open lobby doors. His breath caught in his throat as another shape revealed itself. The creatures stood, illuminated, the light dancing on the slick sheen of mucus that dripped from them. They were identical in every way, with corpse-grey skin, their arms bent at odd angles from the elbows, the feet seeming to have been cut off and then reattached backwards.

Pnakotus!

A thrill of horror and recognition came from the Gestalt. There was no mistaking the rabid, simian features, the lopsided symmetry of their bodies. The creatures looked up at him, screeching like rabid monkeys in a zoo for the damned.

Recognise me, do you? Danning thought, amused. *Here's me thinking you were thick.*

As one, the creatures howled again, and charged into the guesthouse. They were surprisingly agile given the strange angles of their legs and feet. Danning came away from the window, relieved. *Pnakots* were pack creatures, relying on weight of numbers to defeat their prey. Two would be easy to beat and they were not in Antarctica. This was India, familiar territory for the Captain and the Gestalt. He grinned.

Easier than I thought.

A voice replied. It had a bubbling quality to it, the many voices of past lives coming together to give counsel. This was the first time it had happened to the Danning Host. It was the true voice of Lazlo; a multitude of minds working in total agreement.

Caution, my friend. You have forgotten to ask one simple question. There are only two Pnakotus. Why?

The Captain paused, realising the oversight he had made. Why only two indeed? Why was there not a swarm of them? Where these two that confident of taking the Gestalt themselves? No. *Pnakotus* were pack animals, but without the guidance of Morbius or his second in command, Scorpius, they were devoid of any form of intelligence.

The answer dawned on him. There had to be something else guiding these two monkeys. Lazlo hummed in confirmation.

A light, deft touch is required, Captain. Charging into battle is never a safe option.

Agreed.

He made his way to the door. From outside, he could hear furtive footsteps that stopped at his room. He gripped the door handle and braced himself.

One, two, three…..

Navi Rakhasha and the *Scion* stood in the yard outside the guest house. She could almost see the bright flare of the prey and the more diffuse signature of her *Pnakotus*. She tried to focus, but the excitement and rage distracted her. It had been too long since *Rakhasha* had faced an enemy worthy of her time.

She looked up. There was a crashing sound from the top window. *Rakhasha* seethed. The *Pnakotus* had given away their presence. It took all of her self-control to stop from going up there and destroying every living thing in the room. The creatures still had a job to do. After the prey was subdued, the Pnakots would be punished; as slowly and painfully as possible. *Rakhasha* was very familiar with *Pnakot* physiology. She would make them scream until their throats burst, for nearly ruining everything. Killing the policemen had been reckless enough. Giving away their position to the enemy was unforgivable.

The *Scion* croaked. Its work here was done. It had found the Gestalt and thoroughly surveyed the area for any danger to *Rakhasha*'s plan. All it wanted to do now was leave this burning hot, dusty country, and return to Antarctica, away from the noise, dust and filth of humankind.

Rakhasha cast her many eyes at the *Scion*. There was no need for the creature to stay. The task it had set out to do was now complete. The *Scion* was a scavenger and a coward, of no use to *Rakhasha*.

The creatures stood for a moment, regarding each other. Tension soaked the air. *Rakhasha's* contempt for the bat creature was obvious. From the moment she had been summoned here, the many eyed being had made no secret of its feelings for the *Scion*. The winged monster's pride in its royal lineage had been dented by this interloper. It flapped its wings in a disdainful manner, fervently hoping that the commoner could not interpret the gesture. The *Scion* was a long way from home, bereft of the support provided by other high-born Morbius Entities. It swallowed its pride.

Rakhasha savoured the *Scion's* discomfort. She had no time for these high-born types. They were the same in the Realms; little creatures born to lives of privilege and ease. They had no idea of the cruel reality of the Omniverse. Existence was greased by the blood and the fat of the vanquished. Everything else was mere window dressing. One day, it would teach this pathetic winged upstart the truth of this.

The *Scion* bowed its head in mock respect and took to the sky, relieved to be away from the filthy commoner. *Rakhasha* watched it for a brief moment.

A shockwave from above convulsed through its mental link with the *Pnakotus*. *Rakhasha* roared in agony and surprise as the pain drove the creature to its knees. She clutched her mighty head, tendrils writhing frantically as white-hot light blinded it. The scent of charred *Pnakotus* flesh singed her nostrils. The creature leant forward, vomiting thick, blood-tinged gruel. The *Pnakotus* had failed! She felt their life essence being torn from their bodies and cast into the Void. Staggering to her feet, *Rakhasha* severed the mental link to her dead soldiers. She had to attack now before the prey fled. She dug the bony spurs on the back of her arm into the brick and began to shimmy up the wall. Rage burst forth. The *Gestalt* was about to learn the lessons of blood and pain.

The Captain pulled the door open, preparing to unleash a wave of power at the *Pnakotus*. Instead, he saw a thin, teenaged Indian boy, trembling in the hallway. He grabbed Sunil's arm and pulled him into the room, slamming the door shut behind him.

"What the fuck are you doing here? I told you to get out of here and go to your father!" Even Lazlo was angry. This boy's presence put them all in danger. "You're going to get the both of us killed."

Sunil's bottom lip trembled and his almond-shaped eyes filled with tears. The Gestalt felt an immediate surge of regret for his outburst, sending soothing waves out to the Captain. The boy was only sixteen and Lazlo was....he couldn't quite remember anymore. It must be in the thousands, at least. Feeling ashamed, he muttered an apology and mussed the boy's hair again.

"Captain *Sahib*, this is my home. My grandfather came to this old *haveli* with nothing but the shirt on his back. His home, his family, all gone in the Partition."

The Captain bowed his head. Guilt gnawed at his collective mind. Lazlo had been somewhere deep in the Amazon at the time, searching for more of his kind, unable to help a land he loved dearly from tearing itself apart. The stories he had heard from survivors years after, made his blood boil. Such terror, such hardship, such inhumanity. Lazlo could have stopped it. He knew it. Yet he never had the chance. He looked at the boy. There was a steely hardness around the eyes, a firm set to the jaw. Sunil was not going anywhere.

"The Sikhs say that you should face all things in high spirits, even death. That's what I intend to do, Captain *Sahib*. This is my home. It was my mother's dream. I cannot leave."

The Captain laughed softly. "Your mind's made up, then. Ok, you stay. But the moment, things go bad, you run. Run and keep going."

Sunil nodded. A shadow of fear fell upon his dark features.

"Captain *Sahib*. There are things out there. I hid from them in the old store room. Once I felt safe, I came to you."

The boy seemed to be taking it in his stride. He was scared, but he didn't act too fazed by the presence of the *Pnakotus*. He had talked about them as if they were normal people. Interesting. The Captain clapped his hands together.

"Right! Listen carefully, young man. These things will attack as soon as they get in here. *Pnakotus* aren't great thinkers. They tend to go straight for their prey. In this case, me. The moment they come through those doors, you get out of the way and get out of here. Understood?"

The boy nodded, then looked around the room as if he were searching for something. His eyes lit up.

"Sunil, what have you seen?"

"A weapon', he said grinning from ear to ear. He walked across the room. "I'll show..."

The door exploded inward as two shapes crashed into the room, dust billowing behind them. There was a cry as they smashed into the Captain. He flew across the space and onto the bed. The creatures unfurled themselves, chittering. Sunil backed away into a corner of the room, obeying the white sahib's instructions to keep well away. The pale, slimy things circled around the bed, looking at each other, barking.

Danning straightened and squared his shoulders.

Right, you bastard. Time to show you how Millwall do this.

He roared at the monster, beckoning it with a gesture he had not used since the Nineteen-Eighties.

"LET"S GO THEN, WANKER!"

The thing closest to the door leapt onto the bed and straddled him, pinning him to the thin mattress. The old man grabbed its legs and tried to pull them apart, but they wouldn't budge.

It's stronger than before. It's stronger than before! The *Pnakotus* sensed his distress and began to cackle and howl. To Sunil, terrified in the corner, it sounded like the laughter of Hell itself. Danning strained against the creature astride him.

It looked down at him, its misshapen face somehow simian and canine at the same time. The dark pits of its eyes glowed with triumph, drool hanging from its wide mouth. The creature turned its head to one side, regarding him the way a butterfly collector studies a rare specimen. The *Pnakotus* purred with delight, then lashed out with a taloned hand.

The Captain screamed as elongated fingers tore through his shirt into the soft meat beneath. Skin and muscle parted, blood quickly bubbling through the rents in the Captain's stomach. He choked as red spittle spilled from his lips. The creature stepped back for a moment, licking juices from its fingers. It rolled its eyes in ecstasy.

The Captain looked down at himself, groggy and in shock. A slick grey coil of intestine spilled out from his ruined shirt. The *Pnakotus* chirped in delight and dove forward, gripping the organ with a firm hand. It looked into The Captain's eyes, a sick smile on its lips, then yanked. The Captain bucked and thrashed as the creature undid him, pulling his gut loose. Blood misted the air between them.

He coughed out a sticky plug of clotted blood. A creeping sense of vertigo now took him, shock and blood loss combining to sap his strength. He wouldn't last long. *Corpus Mori* was approaching. Soul Death would soon follow. The Gestalt began to jabber, panic stricken as it realised the creature's intention. It was going to eviscerate the Captain, pulling the protective shield of organs from the man's dying body. The Gestalt Nest would be exposed, easy picking for these foul scavengers and whatever force had sent it.

The Captain, almost overwhelmed by the surge of emotion, tried to push his killer from him but the effort was too much. His arms fell limply to the side, his body jerking as the *Pnakotus* continued to empty him. There was nothing more he could do.

Sunil closed his hand around the lamp and picked it up carefully. He was teetering on the edge of shock as he watched the dirty grey monster tear into his friend. The Captain paled, his life blood spurting and soaking into the mattress. The other *Pnakotus* stood with his back to the boy, watching the slaughter in rapt fascination. It hadn't made a move to join its companion yet. It was content being a voyeur to the slaughter. Every now and again, a soft cooing sound came from it, as if it were spurring its companion on. Sunil's nerve snapped and a raging anger boiled up from within him.

Without thinking, he screamed at the top of his lungs and charged the *Pnakotus,* stabbing the lamp into the thing's slick body. The thin glass bulb shattered with a popping sound. The *Pnakotus* shrieked as electricity surged through it. Smoke seeped from its eyes and ears as it cooked from the inside out. It convulsed, its teeth shredding its lips to ruin, its bony hands clasping the air frantically in front of it. It screamed once more before flames boiled from its mouth. Its eyeballs steamed in their sockets, liquefying to seep down its face in thick, gelatinous tears. The creature sighed, a plume of foul smelling smoke erupting from its ruined mouth, before crashing face first to the floor.

The other creature stared in abject horror, its attack now forgotten. Its spawn sister crumpled to the floor and curled up like a salted snail. Within moments, the dead creature began to melt, its skin splitting. Stinking black fluid poured from the open cuts onto a floor already stained with blood. Sunil turned his head, his eyes stinging from the acrid steam. He coughed, holding his arm across his nose to block the thick smell.

One down. One to go.

The Captain was close to blacking out. Dark spots erupted across his vision, coalescing together to form a thick weave of dark. The end was near. He knew it. A normal man would have been dead minutes ago. It was only the enhanced power of Lazlo that kept him alive now. Barely.

The *Pnakotus* had ceased its attack, its shock and grief at the death of its spawn sister turning to rage against the young human male. The Captain knew what it was going to do. Before it could leap off, he used the last of energy to grab it by the throat. The creature sqwaked, surprised. It grabbed the Captain's wrist, trying desperately to break his grip.

You're not going anywhere, son.

The voice of Lazlo spoke up. The Gestalt sounded strong, despite the close proximity of death. *Do not let go. We only have one chance at this.*

Danning frowned. *Chance at what? An explanation would be great around about now.*

No time. Let's just call it a.....party trick? Is that correct, my friends?

Other voices in the Collective Mind murmured their agreement.

Danning. I need you to let go. Let go and trust us. All of us.

Let go? I thought you told me to—

Not of the creature. Let go of YOU. Trust me.

The Captain scowled. This was no time to be cryptic. But then, what options did he have? He couldn't let Lazlo die.

Ok. Do what you have to do. But if this goes wrong—

I know. It's my fault.

The Captain smiled. Lazlo was trying to be funny. At least he had experienced that. It almost made his death worthwhile. He closed his eyes and let go.

The *Pnakotus* began to wail and claw at its face, its talons leaving furrows in its cheek, bloody marks across its forehead. Sunil watched, confused and more than a little frightened. A warm glow suffused the Captain, a golden radiance that came from within his violated body. He let go of the *Pnakotus*, his body beginning to slump into the bed.

Squealing, the creature leapt up and came crashing down onto the sticky floor, smashing its head repeatedly against the stained floorboards.

Sunil jumped back as it reached for him. He was horrified, yet fascinated.

The *Pnakotus's* eyes had rolled back, exposing the whites. Veins bulged from the skin and burst, spraying thick, black ichor into the air. With one final screech, it tore its own face off and threw the dripping mask at the injured man on the bed. A cold, blue blaze of light encased it, before glowing white hot. The creature vanished, leaving behind a last trace of a wail and the smell of roasted meat.

Outside, the *Navi Rakhasha* climbed for the roof.

"Sunil." The voice sounded very weak and very old. "Sunil, come here." The boy shook off his malaise and rushed to the blood soaked bed. The red streaked crater in the man's abdomen pulsed with dwindling life. Sunil choked back a sob.

"There's...no time for that... Mourn me later. There's something I need you to do..."

Sunil nodded, the tears rolling freely despite Danning's admonition. The Captain weakly beckoned Sunil closer. "Listen to me very carefully.

There's another one on the roof. It's not like anything else I've...I've ever met."

"How do you know?" Sunil said, his voice full of tears. His friend, the crazy old white sahib, opened his eyes and smiled.

"I just do. It's a gift. One that I think you're worthy of. For the moment, just listen to me, ok?" Sunil nodded, not really knowing what else to say. The Captain smiled and let his head fall back on the bed, his breathing shallower with every passing second.

Rakhasha waited. The prey weakened. The vital essence, once so bright, came more and more diffuse. She had to get the knowledge needed from the Gestalt before he expired. Without it, Archon Morbius would be trapped in deep sleep forever, unable to take his rightful place at the highest pinnacle of Creation. This world was the key. Once it had been cleansed of Humanity, the work could begin.

Mankind was a grave worm, anyway, unfit to participate in the affairs of the Omniverse at large. They had tried once before and that had been an utter failure. It would be much better to clean this filthy stable, before the infestation had a chance to spread again.

Rakhasha tensed, jumped —

—and came crashing through the flimsy ceiling into the room below. A cloud of plaster obscured its many eyes for a moment. As the dust cleared, it looked around. Lying next to its huge feet was a curled up form, smoke rising from it. The creature salivated as the smell of roasted flesh hit its nostrils. First the prey, *then* food.

Soundlessly, *Rakhasha* raised her left foot and brought it down on the baked skull. Bone crunched as the head cracked open, *Rakhasha* grinding skull and brain into a thick green paste.

Someone laughed, then coughed. The giant swivelled its head to the bed, which was soaked in human blood. Slick crimson pooled around the figure, filling every niche and valley between his body and the bedding. The man's eyes fluttered open. He smiled.

"Been waiting for you. As ugly as expected." He laughed weakly.

Rakhasha moved closer, her mouth opening and closing faster in excitement. A voice came from deep within the chasm of teeth and tongue. It was soft and feminine, a faint lilt to it, almost Caribbean sounding.

"Morbius. You have the key. Tell me how to awaken him and I will end your suffering."

The Captain coughed again before lapsing into silence. The *Rakhasha* gripped his chin and yanked the man's head towards him. His eyes glazed over with pain, the light of life so desperately weak now.

"Did you hear me, Lazolo?"

The man nodded.

"I did….and it's Lazlo, actually. Or it was Lazlo."

Rakhasha was confused. Why was he not afraid? Was he insane, tainted by eons living with the filthy humans? She gripped the man's jaw tighter. "Death or Truth? Which is it to be?"

Danning merely chuckled, then sighed, a sound so weary the creature nearly stepped back from the agony of it. He closed his eyes. "Neither." Danning whispered. "Now fuck off!"

Rakhasha's roar drowned in the blast, as the Guest House became a ball of flame.

Sunil Lazlo-Bandari stopped and turned. The fireball that had once been his home could be seen over the rooftops. From all around him came gasps and cries and the sounds of people running, shouting for the police and ambulance service.

Nodding, Sunil walked away, heading for the train station. He winced and rubbed the small of his back.

It's ok, said a voice deep in his mind.

The Gestalt will take some time to settle in. It will require rest. You won't hear from all of us for a while, just me.

Sunil recognised The Captain Sahib's soothing baritone.

That's right. I'm your guide to being a part of the Lazlo Gestalt. I envy you, in many ways. So much to see, so much you will learn. It's a rebirth in ways you'd never imagine. Oh, that was a nice touch with the propane gas bottles by the way. Very inspired.

Sunil had been surprised that the gas bottles had been full. It was unlike his father to keep so many full propane cylinders on the property. He had been afraid that one day the house would be blown off the face of the planet. As it turned out, his fear had become reality, but how? Had he been guided in some way to make sure there had been a large enough supply to guarantee the house's destruction? Or was it merely a happy accident?

It didn't matter to Sunil so much now. Lazlo was safe, as was Mr Danning. Sacrificing his body had been the only way to get out of this, but the Captain showed no signs of distress. That old body had served him well, but it was only a house, not a home. He was enjoying the freedom of not being tied to it anymore. They all did. They were now in a young body, about to take his first steps into the larger world. It was akin to being reborn.

Sunil smiled at that thought and reached into his pocket, his hand curling around the envelope the Captain had given him for his father. Now that he knew what it contained, it eased his guilt about not being able to save the guest house. His father would be a very rich man soon.

In the distance, he could see a glow from another fire. It looked like it was coming from The Oberoi Hotel. The incident was carrying on, unimpeded. Despite wanting to, he knew that he couldn't get involved just yet. The Gestalt needed time to knit itself to his body and soul. If he were to go into danger now, he and his new-found friends would be vulnerable. He sighed, cursing the murderers now loose in the city.

There'll be another time, son. If there's one thing we Gestalts have a surplus of, it's time. Sunil nodded his understanding. One day, he would go to the source, the cowards behind these cowards. He would find the man responsible and rip his still-beating heart from his chest.

For now, finding Lal would suffice. There was an eternity for everything else.

The boy smiled and walked away from the remains of his home, into the Mumbai night.

WHATEVER HAPPENED
TO PETE THE NEAT?

CRACKS.

Funny, I never took much notice of them before. Well, you don't, do you? There's too many of them. If you were to try and count every single crack you came across in the course of a day, your mind would — well, it would crack wouldn't it?

Not to say that I take a keen interest in cracks. Only the big ones. The ones that people make a point of ignoring because they don't want to see what's waiting to come through. They don't want to take a peek through the gaps, to witness just what lies parallel to our experience, our own existence. I don't really blame most folk for that. I wish for the days when I walked around in blissful ignorance, happy and content with our little world and my place in it. Those were good days.

I live in small-town heaven. Day to day, unremarkable — you could even say boring. On the surface, at least. Small-town Britain is better at hiding its secrets than the big city. They like to drag their sordid little secrets kicking and screaming out onto the front page or the morning news with a sick pride — look at us! We're fucking horrible and we know it. Here, out in the wilds of the countryside, we're a bit more considered, a bit more 'sussed', as the Cockneys would say. We have our secrets, our oddities, even our strange off-the-wall occurrences. It's just that we like to keep it in house or under the table. No dissections by talking heads and those useless social commentator types, not for us.

The secret stuff is often discussed in hushed sessions around corner tables in the pubs. Heads are kept down, voices are barely raised above a whisper, banter ceases when someone outside of the circle approaches. We like to hoard our information, keep it held close, and dole it out piece by precious piece. Being loud and lairy is just gossiping isn't it? Leave that shit to the tabloids.

Even a place like this has tales that defy explanation, extra undercurrents to certain stories that, again, are discussed in whispers. Like Mad Mike's disappearance. Everyone knows that he did a runner. Owed money to some serious people from Leicester, so I've been told. What they don't tell you is that he must have been in a hurry. A friend of mine who is a copper tells me Mike must have been travelling very light. He hadn't packed much. He hadn't packed anything. All his clothes were still in wardrobes and drawers. His passport was found in a box on top of his fridge. He even left his wallet and keys behind. Unusual, yes. Especially when you consider the house was still locked up, even the windows. Our friend tells me there was something weird about the whole thing. The house smelt funny. Like rotten eggs, shit and vanilla. They even found blood. Mike's blood, as it goes. You could tell my mate was a bit freaked out. His face crinkled up as if he were about to cry.

A few weeks later, I found out why. Apparently, he had been left in the house, alone, waiting for the forensic team to arrive. He was checking around the place when he heard this sound. It was like a moan or a cry of pain coming from the living room. He makes his way downstairs and there, lying on the floor, is a man with little skin left. My friend said this guy had been flayed alive. The skinned man looked up at him, cried out and then just vanished in a cloud of smoke.

My copper friend left the force soon after that. Can't really blame him.

There's been other strange stuff going on. Pets going missing, people going missing, strange noises being heard in the fields at night. Murph, one of the lads who lives down that end, told me he smokes inside the house after dark. Refuses to step out in his back garden. His missus gives him earache for it, but he puts up with her. He won't go into detail though. Whenever I press him, he just tells me to leave it and gets the drinks in.

Oh, and did I tell you we've got two writers from here? They've both buggered off to the big city now; local boys done well. Horror writers, funnily enough. They've come from the right place. There's something not right around here. Terry, the old bar manager, used to say that the Devil had a hold on this place. Even claims to have seen him once, in this very pub. He never comes out with that when he's sober, mind. Only when he's had a few.

I'm sure everyone around here has their own strange story to tell.

I do. It's one of the local legends. Pete the Neat and his disappearance. He was a good kid, earning good money in the building game, going back up to Newcastle to see his mum every other weekend, always good for his round—an all-round top boy. One night out of the blue, he just vanishes—leaves the pub, a little tipsy but not smashed out of his tree like some of the other youngsters you see around here.

And that's that. Never to be seen again.

Six months now, not a trace. His mum, bless her, well she's beside herself. I don't blame her. If that was one of my kids, I'd probably be six foot under with the worry and stress. That makes it so much harder for me to keep the secret and carry the burden.

People still speculate though. That will never stop.

In the round table session, on a Thursday or Friday night, people still ask that question—whatever happened to Pete the Neat? I normally try and squeeze my way out at this point. Thank God for the smoking ban. The topic is raised and I'm straight out of the back door, cigarettes in hand. I don't want to be around when the boys start speculating. I really don't think I'd be able to keep my mouth shut any longer, so I make myself scarce. If I was to tell them what I saw that night, they'd lock me up in a rubber room straight off, no questions asked. Even I question myself on the odd (very odd) occasion when I look back and try to analyse what happened. It all seems too surreal for me to make sense of it. I'm the only man on the planet who knows what happened to Pete the Neat and I can't say.

Promises were made as well as threats. I know his mum's suffering and the cops—not that I care about those wankers—are going mental trying to figure this one out, but I've got me and my own to think about. After what I saw that night, the thought of going through the same or watching one of my family going through it, is more than enough to buy my eternal silence. Maybe writing it out of my system will help relieve the guilt, spread the burden. Maybe it won't. Worth a try, I suppose.

Anyway, here's what happened.

It was a normal Saturday night. Nothing untoward or unseemly, just the usual—girls dressed up in their finest, the lads trying their best. People flitting in and out of the decent selection of pubs and eateries in search of food, drink, company and so much more. I don't really go in for that type of night out anymore—too sedate for that these days. Early forties life and an early forties body does that to you. You slow down, your capacity for a good drink diminished as the years creep up behind you and cosh you around the head the next morning. Happens to the best of us. The mind is willing, the body not so. Life takes a great delight in reminding you of this when your head is down the toilet, and fifty pounds worth of booze is pumping from your gut.

As the sun dipped low in the summer sky, I wound my way through the revellers, smoking a cigarette, casting appreciative glances at the women, exchanging banter and handshakes with some of the men, three pints and a double gin and tonic percolating nicely through my blood. The scent of perfume, aftershave and fast food permeated the air— the odour of a Saturday night in full flow.

I knew my destination. It was pre-programmed, a route hardwired into the neurons from years of routine and repetition. The 'Pack,' as it's affectionately known, loomed large, an old defiant building, warm and inviting despite its reputation with some of the locals. As I've said, strange things happen around here, some of them revolving around the Pack. But those are tales for another time, too numerous and some of them too bizarre for me to even hint at. I have enough trouble trying to tell this particular story.

I walked into the cool, inviting bar, casting my gaze around, giving a brief nod to those familiar faces in various states of inebriation. They responded, some quiet and considered, others loud, but all friendly. Except one. Pete the Neat sat at the very end of the bar, back up against the wall behind him. He looked as immaculate as ever, designer clothes wrinkle free, clean shaven and not a hair out of place. A half empty pint glass sat next to his right hand, the drink flat and lifeless as if it had sat there all day. That in itself was unusual. Pete was quite the drinker, not normally a man to leave a beer untouched for too long.

I waved at him. He didn't seem to notice. He just stared into a space far beyond me, his eyes wide and frightened. His face was pallid, the colour of sour milk. Dark circles of flesh stood out from under his eyes. A light sheen of sweat greased his forehead. He sat rigidly, as if rigor mortis had set in, not noticing the swirl of activity and life around him. I swallowed the sense of unease that had materialised from nowhere. I don't scare so easily. The feeling was unwelcome as well as unusual.

I stepped up to the bar, ordering my drink and trying to ease back into my Saturday night. The unease remained. I could feel something else in the room with us, something dark and malignant, a magnet drawing joy and life to itself. Looking around, I saw nothing—just a pub full of people enjoying some much needed time off from the world. Terry, the mournful looking bar manager, took my order, slightly cocking an eyebrow at me. Maybe he could see my discomfort. If he did, he didn't let on. He just added a double whiskey on the house to my drinks order, muttering something about me needing it, before taking my money. I downed the free drink, shivering as it burned its glorious path to my stomach, and ordered another. Pete didn't move. He sat in the corner, frozen and unnoticed by the throng.

Closing time. The room spun lazily around me. The double whiskey had not been the brightest of ideas. There was a bill to be paid in full when morning came. For now, I ignored it. Tomorrow could be dealt with after a good sleep. I stood, slow and careful, counting to ten. The room didn't stop spinning. It never did. The counting was just a habit left over from my youth. As I said my goodbyes, a shape shambled past me, head down. It was Pete, leaving without a farewell to anyone, not even to Dan the Man, his best friend and drinking partner. No one even noticed. Why didn't they? He wasn't a small man—his height made him conspicuous. It was as if he had ceased to exist, a ghost journeying through the living one last time before crossing the threshold into another realm. A faint haze trailed in his wake, the colours twisting and roiling like a transparent tornado. He scuttled out of the door.

I'm not sure how long I stood there, gaping at the sight I had witnessed, blaming the whiskey for the illusion. Without thinking, I said my goodbyes and stepped out into the night.

To this day, I still can't figure out what it was that made me follow him. The feelings were mixed, ambiguous. Was I curious? Was it through a subconscious need to help him? Or was there something else pushing me, wanting me to witness the demise of another? I'll never know. To be honest, I'm not even sure I want to find out. Answers can lead to more unpleasant things than just further questions.

The main street was quiet. The revellers had either staggered home or moved on for new pastures in pursuit of more alcohol. I looked around frantically for any sign of Pete, but there was none. I knew where he lived and the route he would take home. It was the same as mine, across the park. That was where I would go. It was on my way home anyway. Nothing lost there.

I sobered up. That's never happened to me before or since. The gallons of alcohol, the crazy carousel effect of a world seen through the eyes of inebriation, evaporated, leaving me dry and a little frightened. I tasted ruin and defeat in the cool, summer night air. It grew in strength as I shuffled down the small side street and into the dimly lit park. I hesitated. Beyond the warm sodium of the streetlamps, the park opened expansively, more like a field, really, with a few goalposts, a basketball hoop and a skate ramp that had seen better days and much bad behaviour. It loomed, dark and threatening. I'd walked this way more times than I could count. It should have held no fear for me.

Swallowing, trying to dislodge the greasy lump in my throat, I walked, looking around nervously. The path veered off to the left into the dark, the squat, ugly shape of the Recreation Centre obscuring the main body of the field from view. I stopped again. There was a whimper in the night, short and quiet, but enough to stop me in my tracks. The rational part of my mind told me it was just kids, or even a drunken couple taking advantage of the night and the isolation. The deeper, more instinctive part told me otherwise. There was fear in that sound, a deep and terrible dread.

Fighting the urge to run, I carried on. I had to see, had to help. I rounded the corner. The one forlorn streetlight was out. The night held sway, its inky stain blotting out all underneath the broken lamp. In the distance, I could see more orange streetlight; safety and my home, within reach, yet so far away. I heard the sound again, coming from the black depths of the field to my right. I turned, peering into the dark. There were shapes down there, how many, I couldn't be certain. It could have been one. It could have been a hundred. Common sense told me to leave it, go home and place an anonymous call to the Boys in Blue. I turned to walk away.

"Help me."

I froze, listening hard. Was I hearing things? Was my tired and drunk mind trying to fool me?

"Please, someone help me."

The pain and terror in the voice was unmistakable, as was the voice itself. It was Pete's. Without thinking, I dove into the night, moving quickly but carefully down the gentle slope.

"Pete," I cried out. "Pete!"

A soft sobbing came from nearby. I homed in on the sound, reaching the darkened little piece of tarmac where a sturdy basketball hoop was fixed into the ground. I looked around.

"Where are you, Pete?"

"Up here," he managed say, before lapsing into sobbing. In the pitch black, I could just about make out a shape lashed to the clunky backboard of the hoop. It reminded me of a crucifix. Pete's arms were stretched out to the side. He snuffled softly.

"It's ok, mate. I'll get help and get you down."

A voice spoke. "You'll do no such thing. He is up there for a very good reason. If you interfere, you join him." The voice seemed to come from everywhere and nowhere, a chorus, a low rumble in agreement with itself. A soft red light began to glow all around me. I shivered. There was something in that light, a tone that made me uneasy. Gradually, the light increased. On its outer edges, I saw silhouettes of all sizes and shapes—tall, small, thin, and stocky. A large shape dislodged itself from the main body, stepping into the red twilight. I squinted, unable to make out who or what it was.

"So sorry. Please allow me to illuminate you."

The light changed from soft red to a harsh white glare. I cried out and clapped my hands over my face at the sudden change. The figure laughed, more amused than malicious.

"Humans. So fragile. I've turned it down. You can look now. I slowly opened my burning eyes, looking down at the floor as they adjusted. The light was a little softer, but still quite harsh, rather like a powerful torch.

I looked up.

My bladder let go. I dimly registered piss gushing down my leg, shock smashing all rational thought from my mind at the sight of the creature before me.

The thing was bone white and humanoid. It exuded a regal air, the stance and posture oozing arrogance. The creature had no face. Its head was fleshless, the bone yellow and mouldering. A single eye socket adorned the centre of its face, gazing blankly at me. Something glistened in that gap. It could have been an eye. It could have been anything. The skull was misshapen, the jaw hidden by a long slope of bone, the remnants of two tusks, the ends splintered and broken, hanging from the shelf.

The creature was also very naked. My terror increased at seeing the long, stiff member that jutted from its pelvis, bone white. It tapered to a sharp point, bringing to mind an elephant's tusk. Blood greased the phallus. The creature made a self-conscious noise in its throat, wiping itself down with a bony palm. It looked at me, somehow contriving to appear coy, before licking its hand clean, carefully watching me, gauging my reaction. There was nothing I could do but stare. It had no features, but I could tell it was amused. The shaking of its shoulders and the grating sound emanating from it left nothing to the imagination.

"So sorry. One does get carried away when one has fun. Now what can we do for you?" It gestured into the darkness beyond our little pool of light. The things out there fidgeted. A long, sore-covered arm extended from the dark towards me. I could do nothing. The fleshless one slapped at the arm.

"Leave him. He has no part in this." It pointed up to the hoop. "Unlike this one who dared to break a pact with us."

My gaze followed the direction of his arm. My teeth ground together as I took in the sight. It was indeed Pete, naked, lashed to the metal frame, and skinless from the neck down. Open-mouthed in horror, the bile churning at the back of my throat, my eyes pored over every detail, every injury.His leg muscles had been flensed from the bone. I could see nicks and scrapes from the knife or whatever they had used on him, marking his femur. Large chunks of muscle had been torn away, the wounds ragged with teeth marks. Only his face and head remained intact. His eyelids fluttered alarmingly. For a moment, they opened. His gaze was distant and filled with agony and regret. Incredibly, he smiled.

"Sometimes a deal isn't worth the hassle."

He laughed softly before lapsing back into half-consciousness. I turned my head, trying to look intimidating, well aware that this was futile in piss soaked jeans. The elephant-headed monster giggled.

"You like?" It was mocking me.

"Why? Why torture the kid like that?"

A chorus of wailing laughter came from the gallery in the dark.

"He made us a deal, you see. We supplied the items in question for a modest fee. It was a small ask. He let us down."

I frowned, my anger growing at the patronising tone in this half-formed monstrosity's voice.

"How?"

"He wouldn't kill the person we asked him to. We're not allowed, you see. There are certain rules that have to be adhered to, and certain types we are not allowed to molest in any way."

A grudging sense of admiration for the half dead boy reared in my mind. He was willing to go through this so as not to kill. That was a type of bravery unseen in this day and age.

"Who was it?"

The creature shook his head.

"I'm not at liberty to reveal such. Suffice it to say, when the child in question reaches adulthood, it will not only be protected, it will also be a threat. That's why we need it removed. Count Raum was very clear on this, wasn't he, little Petey?"

Pete did not respond.

My anger increased, perilously close to rage. This thing had tortured my friend because he wouldn't kill a child? I clenched my fists. The thing wagged a finger at me.

"Ah-ah. Not a good idea. Strike me and you become involved. My advice? Walk away. You can't save your friend now. Just walk away and forget about us. Unless of course you want to do a deal? Count Raum can be summoned very easily, you know."

I looked down at the ground, the acidic stench of my own piss stinging my nostrils. The thing was right. Pete was too far gone. He was almost dead.

Alive, I could at least get some form of revenge on this strutting, preening monster. I looked up at Pete, murmuring my sorrow and apology. The things in the darkness all snickered. I glared out at them, a challenge in my look, before turning my attention back to the main mouthpiece. I nodded.

"Ok. You win. I'll walk away. No deals though. You make me sick."

I hawked up a wad of phlegm and spat at the creature's feet.

"You…spat at me!" There was disbelief and anger in its voice. "You cheeky fucking runt. You dare to defile me?" It tensed, as if ready to spring. Somehow, I knew it couldn't touch me. I wagged my finger back at it, smiling.

"Ah-ah. I wouldn't do that if I were you."

The creature held itself back, frustration boiling from it.

I turned and walked away as quickly as I could. Not once did I look back. To do so would forfeit my soul. This much I know.

I dreamt of Pete for the next few nights. I could see him in the dark, shivering, bleeding, a red and black mist wrapped around him like a swirling and angry shroud. As I watched him, deep furrows opened across his torso, the skin parting then expanding outwards, wounds prised open by invisible hands. Blood streamed from him like rain. He whimpered again as the skin was lovingly pulled from the muscle, peeled away strip by strip. The flesh beneath glistened in the unnatural red light. Veins pulsed frantically before opening up to disgorge precious fluid into the night. He began to convulse as his skin folded back from sticky musculature, filleting from his back, along with his scalp, even his face.

He whispered.

"Forgive me. Please. Forgive me."

To whom this was addressed I would never know. It could have been the child he was tasked to kill, the creatures who had taken his life—maybe the agonised apology was to me for being dragged into this lunacy. I would wake up in the dead of the night, a fist jammed in my mouth to prevent a scream from bursting forth. As I rushed back into wakefulness, I could hear that smug voice, a voice I was growing to despise by the day.

"Sayonara, my friend. I hope we meet under more convivial circumstances."

That was enough to dispel my fear. One day, I was going to make that elephant-headed fucker suffer. Until I could figure out how, it would be back to life as normal.

I never walked through the park again, by the way. Too much of a risk.

So there you have it. That's what happened to Pete the Neat. Do you see now why I could never tell this tale out loud? I don't want my intentions revealed. One careless word in the wrong ear and it could have the worst consequences for me. I'm going to get revenge for Pete, and to make sure that kid, whoever he or she is, grows up safely. I need the advantage of surprise. So for now, my lips remain sealed. If you're reading this, then I've succeeded. If I've come away alive, I may even tell you how it ends. For now, we'll leave it at this.

INTERLUDE MINOR: DARROW

DARROW GRIMACED as he finished the last bite of a tasteless meal. The energy was welcome, regardless of the fact that everything tasted of cardboard.

Join Unit Cabal, they said. See the world as you've never seen it before. Experience the worst catering outside of British football grounds. He put the fork down, discreetly belched and leaned back in his chair, wishing for a cigarette. All Unit Cabal installations had a strict no-smoking policy. He would have to go through two checkpoints, a weapons check and a blood test, just to get off the grounds. It wasn't worth the hassle. He had always promised himself he would find the health and safety genius behind that protocol and eviscerate the little weasel slowly.

He checked his watch. There was still an hour to go before he had to return. An hour to kill with nothing to do. Maybe a smoke break would be worth it.

Fuck it. Plenty of time yet.

He stood and left the near-deserted canteen area. The installation was quiet. Most officers were out in the field these days. The needs of the hour demanded it. There were more incursions into their world every day. It was as if the human race had started to attract more attention. Hardly surprising, given the amount of shit they had flung into outer space—radio signals, probes, even that stupid *Star One* mission. What an expensive failure that was. Three years and no word back from the three astronauts. They must have died by now.

Darrow took a slow walk down the featureless corridor, lost in his own thoughts. He had been attached to *Unit Cabal* for a year now and still had been given no hint of a bigger mission. Just interrogation duty— illegal immigrants, Al Queda operatives, strange cult members—the same scum he had dealt with during his years in the Met. Only the location had changed, apart from the pay. The money was better; the work certainly wasn't. He had decided to give it another year. If nothing changed, then he would hand his papers in and he would return to normal life. Fuck the National Security Act, fuck *Unit Cabal.* Fuck them all. All talk and no action. Nothing interesting ever happened around here.

Cameron smiled. The last few stories had been most entertaining. Null had a way with words, that much was evident. He had found himself lost in the tales the strange man wove, thrilling to the twists and the turns. The last one had been excellent. He craved more.

"Then you will have more."

Cameron closed his eyes again, briefly wondering why Null's voice sounded deeper than before. Maybe it was his story telling. Yes that was it. It was Null's narration voice—soothing, calm, ethereal.

"Concentrate, Cameron. The next tale is about to be unveiled to you. A most interesting recount. I picked this one up in the Midlands, I believe. It's a cautionary tale. Please enjoy."

Cameron sat back and listened with rapt attention.

L.L.T.C (LUCIFER LOVES THE CLASH)

WRITING THIS could get me killed. Or worse.

What could be worse than death, I hear you ask? Believe me, there are worse things. Much, much worse. That's not some hoary old cliché pulled from the patented 'Late Night Horror Bag of Cliché'. These are serious matters.

I definitely don't want the God Squad getting their grubby mitts on this manuscript either, or any other religious fuck-tards for that matter. You've only got to surf the net to see how they deal with people who have sinned in even a minor way. My infractions would be more than enough to inspire downright medieval retribution from those arseholes.

I'll play this one safe. This stack of scribblings is going into a strongbox, only to be released after my death. I call it 'Afterlife Insurance'—insurance against holy rollers turning up on my doorstep armed with knives, guns and millennia old books. For a start, I have no desire to be 'saved' as they would put it. And what has Heaven got that could possibly attract me? Harps, clouds and Sarah-fucking Palin? Do me a favour, and get the fuck out of my face with that shit! It's a con, and all you sheep out there have fallen for it. You've even paid out your life savings to sick old pastors and smiled whilst they shafted your kids. Mugs!

This is my shot at the big leagues—all my desires fulfilled on Earth and a cushy after-death number that involves minimal harp action and no dumb-arsed preachers. What am I on about? Well you'll know once you've finished reading this.

If you are reading this, then I'm long gone, taking my place at the Right Hand of the Prince in Necropolis. Either that, or I'll be languishing in Liverpool surrounded by the bastard sons of American Tele-Evangelism. A fate worse than death indeed.

It all revolves around one night, a night that still seems like a surrealist dream or a bad acid trip. Did it really happen or was it all just a fugue, a by-product of an exhausted, half drunken brain? I mean, paranormal activity only happens in shit films in this day and age, doesn't it? And it's not as if I live in some small American town straight out of a King novel, or a dysfunctional, inbred little Lovecraftian burg. I live in a small market town, nestled deep in the not so wild but still rolling green fields of Northamptonshire. Nothing really unusual happens around these parts.

It's a nice enough place, even if it's imbued with that nosiness that I'm sure is universal in small towns—everyone knows what everyone is doing and who they're doing it with; whose kids are drinking and making nuisances of themselves around the skate-park; whose front door has been smashed in by the police on the hunt for drugs…

We know who's knocking who off, who's got a drink problem, who's good friends with the slot machines. We even know the good stuff—births, marriages, lottery wins. Every week, or maybe even every day if you like a drink, we all gather in our favourite hostelries, and shoot the shit about these and other things, putting the world and the neighbours to rights, putting events into their little boxes to be labelled up and shipped out as opinion.

It's a steady and stable place, this old town of mine. The countryside is pretty stunning—if you mentally block out the dual carriageway. The kids are ok—when they're not out to impress each other or being a pain in the arse for the sake of it. The people are not bad—as long as you know who is who and treat them according to social convention.

It's just another market town in Middle England I suppose, liveable, pleasant even, but not spectacular. So why did the Devil himself come here, to our small town on a balmy summer's evening? That's the million pound question. There are no easy answers. I'm not even sure that there's an answer, full stop. But visit us he did.

Make no mistake about it, it couldn't have been anyone or anything else. Even if there wasn't an accompanying flash of light, sulphur-smelling smoke, a cackling coterie of demons or Hitler with a large pineapple shoved up his rectum. It was just him, armed with offers, temptations, a strange tic in his left eye and, believe it or not, quite unexpected good taste in music. The Dark Prince was having some downtime on a job. He had come to shoot the breeze, have a pint and listen to some decent tunes. And it wasn't heavy metal.

Yep. You read that right. Satan doesn't like heavy metal, black metal, in fact any kind of metal. It'd be fair to say that he loathes it. If word of this got out and it was believed, the whole Black Metal scene would implode overnight. Now, I don't see that as a bad thing. Awful fucking dirge music. Maybe I should publish this just to help rid the world of shite like Mayhem, Blasphemy and Deicide. The planet would be a bit quieter, if not more peaceful, anyway. I'll hold onto that thought for the moment.

Back to the story. So we're in my small market town, on a balmy summer's eve and in a small boozer called the Woolpack, or the 'Pack,' if you're a local. I'm in there, still on my first Guinness and plotting the night's course of drunken mayhem. I'm also figuring out what to put on the jukebox to replace the shitty Euro Trance Techno bollocks that's pumping out of the speakers.

Sparky is late yet again. Not unusual for him. The little fucker'd be late for his own funeral, and mine too, probably. He's my best mate, wingman and general trouble-buddy. We're the dynamic duo—Sparky and George; always ready for a drink or two, always with an eye for the ladies—unless of course the eyes are so alcohol soaked that we can't focus on our drinks let alone women.

Since I'm still relatively sober, I try and make long and meaningful eye contact with Tina and her gaggle of friends over at the far end of the bar. She's obtainable, as are a few of her friends, so I'm hoping for a result tonight. And it's at this point that things take a sharp left into the Twilight Zone.

Here's what happened.

I stand at the bar, shifting my glance from the mirror behind the optics to the girls at the other end of the bar. That habit of furtively checking myself out in the mirror was, and still is, a really annoying habit, but what can you do, eh? It's a lifelong habit; some people pick their noses and flick the remains at other people, I continually check myself in any reflective surface I pass. My eyes still looked ok, a tiny bit glazed but still very much focused. I'm only on pint number three. The bloodshot eyes, the slack doughy face and the perpetually wet, slightly open mouth will come later as surely as night follows day.

Terry, the morose man-mountain of a barman was off down the other end of the bar with the girls and Mad Mike, the scariest man in town. Every town has a Mad Mike equivalent; the guy that you treat with respect and a measure of caution. The guy who'll give you time of day regardless of your race, politics or even your face, but will go to *Defcon Four* for reasons only known to himself. I give him a wave. He doesn't wave back. He finishes his drink, puts down the glass, takes a good look around the bar with an odd look of regret on his face and makes for the back door, his shoulders slumped in defeat.

There's something about his bearing that's a bit off centre. He's not his normal self. I dismiss any concern as Terry lumbers over, a seventeen-stone mass of tattoos, ponytail and a bit of a funny damp odour. Ordering my drink, I smile at him. He doesn't smile back, he just maintains that sour-faced weary look that reminds me of Droopy, the dour cartoon dog.

Life and soul of the party today, aren't ya?

It's best to leave that thought unspoken. He's in a mood about something, and number one rule of the House is don't piss off the Bar Steward if he's having a bad day.

Terry sets the pint of Guinness and blackcurrant down on the sticky bar. Things must be bad. He hasn't even wiped it down. He mumbles the price, I give him the money and head back to my favourite spot, a little alcove by the door, and settle in, waiting for my dearest but slightly aggravating best friend to make his grand entrance. From my vantage point, I'll be able to sling a beer mat with some accuracy towards the back of his head. Saves on having to get up and tap him on the shoulder.

The shitty Eurotrash has given way to some chancer from one of those 'talent shows' on the telly. That's fucking *it*, I decide. Time to give the pub a music master-class; The Jam, The Stone Roses, a few cheeky New Order tunes, The Clash, maybe even that Spear of Destiny tune that was big when I was a kid and, for some reason, has been an 'earworm' for the last few days. I know how to pick an achingly cool, yet not too 'out there' selection of music. It's one of my many talents. At least *I* think so anyway. Let Sparky sort The Smiths out when he gets here. If no one else likes it, then I can just shift the blame onto him. It's a tried and tested tactic and the poor sod still hasn't worked it out.

The music choices made, I sit back down and settle down to some serious people watching. I say people, but the pub's still a bit sparse tonight, especially for a gorgeous summer evening. People are still making their way home from work or getting ready to come out. The only reason I'm here is for an early finish. I don't mind. Bit of peace and quiet for a change. The girls have all gone off to the back part of the bar and congregated around the pool table. I can hear the raucous laughter from here. It's a good omen.

A couple of older gents sit in the corner amiably chatting about the wife, kids, times gone by and times to come. An image of Mad Mike swims into my consciousness. That's unexpected. There's still something bothering me about the way he left. He had the demeanour of a man about to face an execution. The look in his eyes was something that I'd never expect to see from a total psycho; fear. He seemed to be scared shitless.

A sudden chill tickles the nape of my neck. It lasts for no more than a second, but it takes me by surprise. There's a faint smell of something rotten. Probably the glass washer behind the bar. It always stinks like a sewer in the summer. Terry just shrugs and says "It's getting fixed," when it's mentioned. He must be using the world's slowest plumber. The thing's been like that for months.

The smell and the chill are gone as suddenly as they appeared. I'm a bit puzzled. I have a mental shrug, take another sip and close my eyes for a moment, letting the sweet sounds of Oasis sooth me.

Something drifts into my consciousness. It's a sound unlike anything I've heard before. It's far off, as if it's in the distance, but at the same time it seems to be coming from all around me. Drowsiness overtakes me, making my limbs feel leaden and my eyelids glue together. I can't open them. The sound is like a million hornets flying in over the top of a vast, unknowable hill. There's an undercurrent to the sound, like moans or tortured screams. The veins in my temples begin to throb as my nervous heart ramps up the blood pressure.

In the projector screen behind the lids of my closed eyes, I see a place bathed in a harsh orange-red glare that hurts the optic nerves. Great tower blocks jut upwards from broken, sewage-filled streets.

Shapes hurl themselves from the top of these structures, hitting the ground and opening like ripe fruit. A leathery-winged thing, like a man, but the size of a Boeing, buzzes past my vision so close that I see through the ragged holes in the fine membrane of its wings. The unnatural moaning is coming from the streets. There's a never ending column of people, men and women, some bearing gaping wounds, their internal workings spilling out to join the mass of stinking shit and pulverised suicides on the street. Others have no skin at all, their denuded faces twisted in screams of torment.

There are shapes moving around the column of tortured flesh, poking, prodding, and biting the unfortunates. I can't make out their features—the faces are like tallow being melted under hellish heat—but I can feel their intent. They want to maim, hurt and destroy. There's no kindness in this place, only malice, death, blood and shit.

This twisted city sits on the shores of a vast red lake. Boats of all descriptions plough their way through the thick red fluid, their bows covered in clots of maroon. An old steamboat like something out of Huckleberry Finn holds my attention. There's a skinned man lashed to a pole by barbed wire and nails. His mouth is wide, a horrid wailing sound erupts from him, an infernal horn alerting others to the vessel's passage. I try to make out the writing on its side, but dark clumps of matter obliterate most of the lettering. It's called The Lady F—

I hear my name called out from the sickening wall of sound, indistinct at first, but steadily getting louder. Oily drops of sweat run down my forehead. The smell from that lake is nauseating. I want out! My nerves are near shredded by this city, this landscape, the brutal torture.

With a jolt, I return to the present. Perfume, beer; I hear cars, Tina, Liam Gallagher.

"Welcome back, George. I apologise for the impromptu trip. The Summoning has a weird effect on space-time, especially if someone with your abilities is a bit too close to the Vanishing Point." A hot clammy hand touches mine and I almost scream.

My eyes fly open. My heart's going like a jackhammer, my head and my stomach roil with the scent of old blood, meat and sour milk. I look down at the hand, sweat dripping into my eyes. The fingers are long and thin. The nails are perfectly manicured, except the thumbnail that looks raggedy from years of being chewed. It's a perfect piano-playing hand, I think to myself and giggle, my sanity warping for a moment before snapping back into its normal everyday shape. I look up.

The owner of the hand looks me straight in the eye and for a second, I see that hideous red-orange glow. It subsides at once into a normal looking pair of hazel eyes, set into a long and pleasant face. The man has a bit of a pallor that contrasts with his mop of black hair and his beetle-black eyebrows. He's got a faint grin on his face, amused by some private joke. Maybe I had a funny turn and that's his source of amusement?

I pull my hand away and grab my drink, gulping it down. In the blink of an eye it's gone, but there's a full pint sitting next to it which I'm sure I never bought. My confusion shows on my face. The man snorts, his version of a choked-back laugh. One eyebrow raises and he points at the drink.

"I thought you might like another." His voice is very distinct. It's deep and a bit rough, as if he's smoked a whole box of cigars whilst wearing a gas mask. The accent's hard to place as well. It could be local, it could be foreign. It changes. The hairs on the back of my neck rise. This man scares me. There's a presence to him, a feeling that I can't put into words. It's a feeling of wrongness. He doesn't belong here, not in this pub, not in this town, not even in this reality. I look at his face again. It looks normal enough, a bit too thin and long, as if he's been squeezed in a vice. Everything is in its normal place, yet it feels artificial, as if his face is just a mask, worn for the occasion.

He's even dressed dapperly—expensive looking shirt and suit combo, no tie. Physically, he looks like a strong wind could bowl him down the street. He's absolutely no threat and yet here I am, neck hair standing to attention and my bowels feeling almost liquid. My stomach gurgles as I move. The man points a long, bony finger at my abdomen and the feeling subsides almost immediately. No sickness, no feeling like the world is about drop out of my arse onto an unsuspecting public. Nothing at all.

He just smiles again and points at the jukebox; 'Live Forever' goes out with a screech like an old record having the needle suddenly and violently pulled across it.

What the fuck?

The place goes silent for a minute before crunching guitar chords and a solid stomping drumbeat fill the air. I recognise it instantly: 'White Riot' by the Clash.

"Sorry, my friend. Terribly sorry. As much as I love Oasis, I'm in a Clash sort of place tonight'.

Two things cross my mind in that moment. Number one is a pretty obvious question; how the fuck did he just do that? Number two is a little less obvious and more surreal—did I put 'Never Take me Alive' by Spear of Destiny on after the Oasis track? My brain seems to be working on several different totally unrelated tracks at the moment. Random disconnected thoughts roll through my mind. Part of me wants to leave now, sprint home and hide. Yet another part, stirring in the dark, recognises this man, is intrigued by him and wants to know more.

He smiles as if he can feel the turmoil. The expression on his face makes me think of a shark lunging in for the kill. His eyes are as glassy and as dark as black marble. His eyebrows crease in concentration. The air shimmers for a moment. There's a slight popping sound, and from out of nowhere, a tall glass appears. It's filled with clear liquid and ice. Condensation drips from the glass onto the table. He takes the slice of lime from the glass and swallows it whole before taking a leisurely sip.

The thin man smacks his lips, and puts the glass down.

"Bacchus always did know how to mix a good G and T."

Bacchus. I'm sure I've heard that name before. It sounds maddeningly familiar. I try not to think on it too much. My head hurts and my heart feels as if it's about to burst from my chest. The urge to get away from this geek is maddening. But I can't move. Whether it's from terror or from some other unknowable urge, I just can't summon up the energy to get up and walk out. The best I can do is to curse Sparky for being late. If I get out of this alive and sane, I'm going to kill the little bastard for it. I summon up enough energy to speak.

"Problem?" I manage to croak out. He shakes his head.

"No problem at all. I'm just wondering why a man with talents such as yours is wasting away in flea pits like this when you could be doing so much more? You think that yourself on a regular basis, don't you?'

"I'm sorry?"

He laughs. I don't. How can he know just how dissatisfied I've been feeling? I don't even talk to my friends about that and this guy seems to know within five minutes of meeting me. He seems to know about the wasted opportunities, the lack of luck, the feeling of not being in control of my life, the resentment against life itself. The man nods, his face sombre all of a sudden. I'm not liking this. I feel transparent under that gaze. It's as if he's peeled everything back, all the defences and walls I've carefully constructed over the years. I'm feeling vulnerable. He looks at a spot somewhere above my head.

"I've helped a lot of people in your position. Some have responded to the challenge admirably. Others have, unfortunately, fallen at the last hurdle and repented, cheating me out of what is, and always has been mine. You'd be surprised how many I've seen over the long years, all wanting power and glory but not being lucky enough to get them."

He leans forward. I can smell something strange on his breath. It's not alcohol. The smell takes me back to chemistry lessons at school. It's a rotten smell, a combination of eggs and rock. I realise with a start that it's not just his breath. The smell's coming off him, stronger and stronger by the second.

"You are a man in need of a new direction, yes? A man who needs a new cause to live for, a new reason to get up in the mornings, rather than having to face the unending mundanity of life. You need power and purpose. All this I can give you, and so much more besides."

The tone of his voice is confidential, as if he's about to impart the greatest secret of life to me.

"But not today. I'm on a schedule, you see. Busy, busy, busy. This is just a pit stop and a chance to enjoy a beer, some music, maybe even drum up some new revenue for the Pit. I've had a hankering for the Clash for some time. I do love their music. Can you imagine how distraught I was when Joe Strummer went elsewhere? A good, principled man, a great musician. Incorruptible. Anyway, I don't get much of a chance to listen to them at home. Fashion and opinion has dictated that I like heavy metal, so they're the only musicians that come to the Pit."

The Pit? Must be a new music venue around here then. Haven't heard anything about it though. Tommy boy would have told me by now. He was in the industry you see. If working at HMV counts as being in the music industry, that is. Our Tommy's a bit of an odd one.

Maybe that's what this exceedingly creepy bloke means by helping. Could he be offering me a job?

"Personally I can't stand Heavy Metal these days, but with all these suicides supposedly caused by it, why look a gift horse in the mouth? And the publicity that one gets from the God Squad is priceless." He laughs. "Those idiots never will learn, will they? Even when they arrive at the Pit, they're still as obnoxious and as self-righteous as they were in life. We shunt them off to Liverpool these days. The other Cities in Hell won't have them and I certainly don't want the likes of Pat Robertson running around Necropolis. The man bores and irritates me.'

Liverpool? Cities in Hell? I am really confused now. And as frightened as I was before. Something's dawning, a subtle realisation of just how much trouble I'm actually. In that damp, firing bundle of nerves and meat in my head, a connection's being made between the Pit, sulphur, heavy metal and that lunatic vision I had earlier.

The man's smiling again but it's wider this time. Much wider. It's taking up most of his face. Tiny, needle sharp teeth fill his mouth. A long ulcerated tongue with a hole at the end shoots from his mouth and into his drink. A few drops fly from the glass and onto the stained table. There's an obscene sucking sound and within seconds the drink is gone. Tiny drops of blood squeeze from his pores like sweat and begin to ooze down his face.

I can't move. The terror crashes down on me like a block of lead. The creature shakes with mirth. The diseased looking tongue grows even longer, and gently licks the blood of his face. His skin has turned red and corrugated, a landscape of large pores and patches like rough eczema.

"I'm sorry about that. I had to drop back to my natural form for a moment. Keeping up appearances is exceptionally hard work. Anyway it's time for me to go to work."

Two horns sprout up from the blood-matted hair. Amazingly, Tina walks pasts, tips me a wink and heads to the toilet. Can she not see the oozing, bloody mess sitting across from me? The thing shakes his head.

"No one can see me. The only reason you can see me as I am is because of your latent abilities and your hunger for more than this Earth can give you. It gives you an edge over most and it called out to me. If you had just been a normal workaday, mortgage, kids, then die kind of guy, I wouldn't have bothered checking you out. I'd have just collected Mike and been back in Necropolis by now. Times running short and I'd better get moving. Nice to meet you, George. Have a think, eh?" His face sagged a little around the mouth as if the gravity in the room had tripled. "The offer still stands, until the day you die. I'd love to work with you."

At least I know now why Mad Mike was looking so glum. I wonder briefly where he'll end up—Necropolis or Liverpool? Personally, I'd take Necropolis. I've been to Liverpool.

He hasn't left yet. I wonder why. Time's obviously a factor, but he's going out of his way to convince me to sign up.

"Join me. You'll get to learn the story behind these fairy tales your kind has been told. There are very few people in the world who understand these days. Just think what that would be like. Knowledge that not even the Pope has. It's a great deal. The life of a king, the afterlife of a scholar and a prince. You may even rise to my Court one day. There is a vacancy, in fact. One of my favourites has retired to concentrate on his gaming business. I could do with some new blood."

I'm really hoping that he didn't mean the 'new blood' comment in a Dracula type of way.

Despite the major head-fuck that seems to have descended on me and totally ruined my night, I'm intrigued. Modern Life is Rubbish. Blur were definitely on the money with that one. I'm just as trapped on the cosmic hamster wheel of life as everyone else, running in a circle eternally with no hope of getting off. Whatever Hell's got to offer might be worth the risk. It's got to better than Heaven. I mean what's God got? Cliff-fucking-Richard? No thanks.

"I must go now. Things to do. But think about my offer. You'd be a valuable addition to the team."

The creature stands up and points to the jukebox, then to my wallet. The guitar intro to 'Going Underground' kicks in, closely followed by

Paul Weller singing about his life being in a rut. Appropriate choice. This thing really does have the measure of me.

"A favourite of yours, I believe. Mine, too. Anyway, I must go. Have a think. If you decide to go for it, I've left a card in your wallet. He's a rep for me in this area." The creature's face begins to melt and run together like a melting red candle.

"See you again, very soon, George." There is a flash, a sound like a wrenching scream of agony and with that, The Devil disappears, leaving me in shock and the pub stinking of blood, sulphur and the aftermath of White Riots from days gone by.

And that's that. He'd left in the blink of an eye, leaving me with a head full of questions and fears, a bank balance of two-thousand pounds and a calling card for someone called Reverend Bliss.

Sparky arrives soon after and we drink as if a new Prohibition was about to be called. And life goes on much the same as it did before; work, drink, football, music; the occasional woman. Nothing's changed much. That two-thousand pounds just doesn't get spent, no matter what I do. That in itself is great, especially as the fine fellows at the bank don't really seem to be asking any questions. Even so, I can't seem to make the break from work. I cling to that job as if it were a life raft in a sea of uncertain times. Oh, and Mad Mike? Gone. Completely disappeared. There's been talk about drug dealers or Mike pissing off the wrong person. I know differently but I daren't tell anyone. Some things are too much for the ordinary man to understand.

I wake, go to work, go out, around and around the Hamster Wheel with no end to the tedium in sight. Bliss's card stays in my wallet. I never got around to throwing it away. It's like a part of me keeps hold of it, just in case, until the mundanity of life gets too much and I finally give in.

At some point, I realise that I just can't do it anymore. The thought of another day on the Wheel is too much. There's too much of life that's passing me by while I sit in an office. The words of a man—a creature—offer me more. The frustration's been building into a head of steam. It's time.

Reverend Bliss' card is sat next to my keyboard. I'm excited, nervous and maybe a little scared, but sometimes you have to take a risk if you want to leave the hamster wheel behind. It's time to make that call, take that leap of faith.

I tell you one thing though. I'm not going to Liverpool. No fucking way on this Earth. Or even Hell. That's a definite.

I wonder if there's a Birmingham in Hell?

DUE TO A LACK OF INTEREST, THE APOCALYPSE WILL NOT BE TELEVISED.

APOCALYPSE. A word that carried weight and portent.

It was a word that brought to mind hideous, blood-soaked images—creatures of tattered wing and horn-tipped claw rendering the bodies of sinners to scraps of skin and meat; angels with flaming swords preparing to fight the good fight; whores of ancient long dead cultures and a star named Wormwood. Even the so-called pagans had their names for the cataclysm – *Ragnarok, Kali Yuga, Frashkereti.* Names did not matter, only the end result—utter annihilation, abominations of desolation, *Kalkis, Madhis* and other heralds of the End of Days; madness and death coalescing into the End of Everything.

When the end came, it should have been an arresting spectacle, an effects-laden extravaganza holding the rapt attention of believers and non-believers alike. It didn't work out that way. The end, or rather the beginning of the end, was largely ignored, buried under a cornucopia of shit news: budget cuts, racist policemen and vapid, soulless celebrities. Besides, there had been so many false alarms before. Why should this day be any different?

J.D's day started with little fuss or incident. Every day did. Another day on the hamster wheel, reporting 'stories of local interest.' He had long ceased caring. Ambition and drive had been burned from him. Such games were for the young and ruthless these days, like that posing wanker, Quigley.

He awoke, showered, dressed, stubbed his toe on the strangely canting dresser that occupied one end of his bedroom like a wonky, wooden Jabba the Hut, and made his way downstairs. This was mundanity at its best—a game he was tired of playing but did not have the energy or inclination to get out of. His world dull and routine, but at least it was safe. There was a steady pay check at the end of the month and he got to have his face on television. Granted, he never got the great news jobs—the court cases, political scandals and the like—but he still managed to get out into the world and encounter interesting, quirky people. And the old grannies from The Women's Institute, with their bake-offs and whist drives, could always be relied upon to feed him. They loved him.

The work was dull and safe. He had the odd pang from time to time, the longing for something meaty, like a murder or even a football riot. But it was not to be. He didn't have the gossamer thin good looks and sharp designer sensibility that Quigley had. That boy was destined for bigger things. J.D would remain provincial.

He leaned against the kitchen work-top waiting for the kettle to boil. The day beyond the window looked strange—bright but with a lethargic cast to it. The few clouds in the morning sky were thin and wispy.

Lurid science fiction tales of Hadron Colliders and tears in the fabric of reality stirred in his mind. The Collider Mark Three launch had been big news earlier in the week. The naysayers had been lively on the internet, swapping theories and anecdotes about the catastrophe awaiting them all. A smile came to J.D's lips. Internet nuts were amusing, if nothing else. He stirred his coffee, absent mindedly gazing into nothingness.

His phone buzzed, startling him. Coffee slopped from the cup, splashing the work top. Putting down the cup, he picked up the phone, groaning as the name flashed on the screen.

Mad Murray. The bastard. The Jock other Jocks were afraid of.

Waiting for a few seconds, he composed himself. He hated speaking to his commissioning editor at the best of times. The man was abrasive, abusive and blunt, all qualities that were enhanced ten-fold by the strong Glaswegian accent and the raspy, cigarette-roughened voice. Murray had been his boss for ten long years, treating the reporter as his favourite whipping dog. If there was a shit, demeaning job to be had, the editor always made sure it headed straight to J.D. If he was having a bad day and needed someone to take it out on, there was always J.D.

The abuse had worn the reporter down, his confidence sapped. If J.D. were to be as brutally honest, it was Murray who had sapped his ambition from him. But he put up with it. Where else could he go? In the world of media, Murray's word carried weight. He could make sure J.D. never worked in television again.

So this was how his morning would start—stuck on the phone with a chain smoking socialist that nonetheless harboured the heart of an elitist snob. The media scene was infested with people like this— people who wore political views like a shirt and changed them often to suit their own agendas and those of their wine bar cronies. J.D. loathed the little slick-haired bastard, but he gave him the work, and they didn't have to spend too much time in each other's company. J.D. wasn't trendy enough for Murray's wine spritzers and identity politics brigade. That suited J.D just fine. Semi embarrassing memories of the time he had nearly chinned some reporter from the Guardian reminded J.D. that he was not part of their set and never would be.

He breathed in deeply and pressed the answer button. A gruff Scottish voice barked into his ear. He winced

"Speak to me, fanny *boz*."

"What can I do for you, boss?"

"Don't come into the office. I need you to head out towards Leicester way. Got a story for you. Some crazy farmer. Horse shit and yokels. Right up your street." J.D. looked up at the ceiling in despair. What would it be? Prize bulls? New born foals? He was seized with a savage urge to tell his boss where to stick the job. The urge passed swiftly, to his relief.

"Ok, shoot."

"Mullen's Farm, out Kibworth way. Old Farmer Giles has been seeing weird shite in the sky, strange noises; all that jazz."

J.D. frowned. How was this news? And why hadn't the police been called in? If it was just kids messing about, which it more than likely was, wasn't it just a public nuisance thing?

"Why hasn't he gone to the Old Bill?"

There was a crunching sound from the other end of the line. Murray was grinding his teeth. A bad sign.

"Because they'll cart him off to the loony bin or just laugh their balls off at him? I don't fuckin' know. Just get your useless arse out there, see what the old bastard wants, make a half way decent story and get back here. Mac and Earl'll meet you there."

J.D. brightened slightly at this. Mac and Earl were good lads. He had worked with them before. He grabbed a pen and notepad, carefully noting the address details, double checking. The last time he had not checked, he ended up at a mosque instead of a Sikh *Gurdwara*. That had been embarrassing, earning him the screaming down of the century from his boss as well as the contempt of the local Sikhs. The head priest, the *Giani*, had spoken to Murray, requesting that the reporter never be sent again. If he couldn't tell the difference between a mosque and a temple, he couldn't be very bright.

Murray signed off with his usual venom-filled diatribe against J.D., his parents and his whole family, and slammed the call to a close. The reporter took a moment, breathing deeply. The encounters with his boss always left him like this—tear filled, helpless and hopeless. Again, he briefly considered throwing in the towel, before discarding the idea. The bills had to be paid, after all. No one else would do it for him.

He finished his coffee, scooped up his car keys and left, taking a last, lingering look at the small, boxy house before pulling away.

The drive to Mullen's Farm was uneventful yet pleasant. He roared down winding country roads, appreciating the vista before him - rolling green hills, small wooded areas, and solitary farmhouses nestled in amongst small woods—lonely outposts of civilization in the wild. The sun sat high in the azure sky, no longer sullen but shining with a clear, crystalline luminescence. The light enriched the land below, making it seem fuller and lusher.

J.D. was in a good mood. The encounter with his boss was now a distant, unpleasant memory, the windows cranked down, the stereo blaring out Oasis. He sang lustily, trailing off at intervals while he looked around for landmarks and listened to instructions from the flat-voiced sat nav, following the winding roads deeper into the Northamptonshire countryside. It was a good day to be alive.

Mullen's Farm.

J.D. swore loudly and viciously as he passed the sign. He mashed his foot down on the brakes, not bothering to check for traffic behind.

There was no point. He hadn't passed a single car for at least a half an hour. The roads were deserted.

The car screeched to a halt.

Fucks sake!

Quickly, aware he was blocking the country road, he performed a spare, efficient three point turn and drove back slowly until he reached the entrance. It was little wonder he had missed it. The entrance to the farm sat concealed from the road by giant trees and bushes of a type the reporter didn't recognize. Botany had never been his strong suit. Plants and trees held no fascination for him at all. His earlier good humour vanished, replaced by a sullen moodiness that increased as he drew closer to his destination.

Swearing incoherently to himself, he swung the Audi into the concealed entrance-way and paused.

He turned the music off, an inexplicable dread seizing him.

I don't want to go up there.

The driveway up to the farm was dark, with trees interlocking to form a dense canopy. Sunlight filtered through the gaps. Verdant light made the way alien and threatening. He wound the window up, the gesture partially soothing the otherwise crippling fear. The urge to throw the car into reverse and scream away from there was almost overwhelming. Sweat sprang up on his top lip, the car's air conditioning chilling the liquid. A skeletal finger lightly traced its way up the reporter's neck into the sweat-dampened hair on the back of his head.

What the fuck's this all about? This isn't right at all.

Something seemed off-kilter. His own sudden plunge in mood concerned him. J.D. was a natural optimist, a fairly happy-go-lucky guy. Sudden mood swings were not his style. That wasn't to say he was permanently and irritatingly happy all the time, even he had his moments. But when the moment came, it was for good reason and never this intense. He pushed the feelings down. If he ignored them, maybe they would dissipate. That was how it normally worked.

He gripped the steering wheel and coaxed the car forward at a snail's pace. Any faster and the urge to speed would overtake him. It was an unknown road with unknown quirks. Proceeding too quickly could lead to an accident or even worse.

No, he decided. *Slowly and steadily. That's the ticket.*

Five minutes stretched seemingly into five hours. The back of his shirt dampened and his heart thudded against his ribcage. Eventually the canopy opened up and diminished, the full metallic glare of the sun a welcome relief. The woods parted to reveal a ramshackle farmstead. There was an unkempt garden that looked more like a scrapyard, full of rusting farm equipment and old, broken garden furniture. Weeds and long grass cocooned the dead hulks, vines wrapping around the machinery like tentacles. The farm house squatted amidst the chaos and decay, forlorn and crumbling. The building canted alarmingly to one side, as if the vines that encased it were pulling the house into the ground. Dusty, darkened windows stared out into the world, sad and mournful. It was a place that had seen better days.

J.D. pulled the car over to one side, switched off the engine and sat for a few moments, taking in the scene. He felt sadness at the neglect. There was an air of lost hopes and shattered dreams about the place. He imagined the back-breaking routine, the struggle to keep life going against the odds stacked against them—banks, foreign competition, a government that sequestered itself away from the people it ruled, uncaring and unforgiving, and a land that grew ever more unwilling to give up its fruits for the benefit of its owner. His own life concerns seemed trivial by comparison. There was always someone worse off. That was a fact of life that kept J.D. going in his darkest moments.

He stepped out of the vehicle, the heat sticky and cloying after the cool, air conditioned confines of the car, pausing a moment to slip on some very expensive sunglasses. Image was key in the game, according to the meticulously dressed Quigley, even for a low level local reporter like J.D. He had to look the part, no matter how expensive the accessories and how ridiculous they made him feel. The glasses did little to diminish the intense glare of the sun, its light harsh and piercing like a floodlight turned up to maximum. J.D. rubbed his forehead, massaging away the beginnings of a headache. It was going to be a long day. He looked around. A shiver ran up his spine. The eeriness was palpable.

There was no sound, just a void of noiselessness. It was the same unearthly silence you got before a storm, a void where sound had been sucked away to leave a steel-tasting vacuum. Cow shit and hay, the familiar perfume of the countryside, slung his nostrils. It was neither unpleasant nor unwelcome. The reporter had lived near villages and farms for most of his life. The odour had formed part of the backdrop of many summers. He trudged towards the house, still looking around as if he expected to see someone behind him.

"J.D!"

The voice, deep and rich, came from the side of the farmhouse. He smiled in recognition as a stocky Asian man strode out to meet him, hand outstretched. The sunlight bounced off the man's balding pate. His shirt clung to his stocky frame, patches of sweat growing at the armpits. The men exchanged greetings and handshakes.

"What's the deal, Mac?"

A nervous grin creased Mac's round face. His brown eyes darted back and forth. He licked his lips, scowling.

"No idea, mate. We've set up around the back. Come and have a look."

J.D, concerned at the man's anxious air, glared at him.

"Why all the cloak and dagger shit? And where's the farmer?"

Gesturing with his thumb, Mac giggled. It sounded nervy and brittle, making J.D. feel more uncomfortable.

"Round the back with us. Earl's with him, just setting up the sound. Seems alright enough, but he could do with a bath. The guy stinks, man."

J.D blew out his cheeks in exasperation and anger.

"Mac! Why the fuck are we out here in the arse-end of nowhere? Is this another one of Murray's stupid little digs?"

Mac's manner became serious. A glint of fear sparkled in his eyes.

"It's better if you come and take a look, mate. We might have the story of the century here."

His voice changed abruptly, tremulous, confused and scared. Abruptly, he turned, beckoning the reporter to follow. J.D wiped the sweat from his forehead, took another look and followed. The dread sat in the pit of his stomach, percolating away.

"Ok. So, what am I looking at here?"

They stood, four men staring up at the brilliant sky. Mac and Earl had set their equipment up as efficiently as always. They didn't skimp when it came to their craft. The men were professionals, both very good at what they did. Earl stood as if he were on an army parade ground, his boom mike held across his chest. Despite the heat of the day, he was clad in an old army surplus parka jacket, the huge garment hanging from his bony shoulders. His t-shirt drew periodic sour glances from the farmer, who evidently didn't approve of the message or the wearer. Earl had that effect on people. His long hair, spiked up at crazy angles, and his voluminous collection of old punk t-shirts never failed to raise a sneer from people like the farmer and the trendies, like Quigley. Earl didn't care and neither did J.D. Earl was one of the best sound guys in the business. If he wanted to wear a t-shirt that proclaimed 'Fuck Art, Let's Dance', then fair play to him. There were too many sensitive types in the world. It would do them good to have their sensibilities shaken from time to time.

Mullen spoke up. He was a solid looking man, the archetypal farmer in every way—blunt features weathered by a lifetime in a back-breaking occupation, wellington boots caked with dried mud. He wore a body warmer. A battered and stained fedora perched on top of his head, wisps of grey hair erupting from the bottom at random angles. His bottom lip stuck out as he spoke. His words trembled slightly. J.D. tried to maintain eye contact, a show of respect for being on his land. He noted the red-rimmed eyes, soft green irises in a sea of broken blood vessels. The bottle obviously had a grip on him. The unshaven cheeks, red nose and tremulous quality to his voice gave it away. And, the fog of stale whiskey fumes emanating from him when he spoke. Mullen was, like his farm, in bad shape.

"Well, that's why I called you here."

J.D. did a double take at the man's accent, far removed as it was from any stereotypical portrayal of the rustic farmer type. He spoke in a flat, neutral manner, a slight East Midlands twang, but not strong. "I noticed it last night. About elevenish. The dogs, well they were going mad you see. I came out to have a look. Next thing you know, there's a flash of light and the dogs have gone." J.D. raised an eyebrow.

"Gone? How do you mean?"

The farmer reached into a pocket, pulling out some foul smelling strips of leathery material. "I mean, like this. These were their collars." He offered them to the reporter. J.D. was taken aback. Mullen's eyes filled with tears. "They're all I've got. Me wife passed on last year, the boys are all over the place. The dogs were all I had." The pain in the farmer's voice stabbed at J.D's heart. He understood the neglect and decay Mullen chose to live in. The man was isolated, alone and adrift from other people, stuck in a house that he no longer had the inclination to maintain, and a business that no longer worked for him. He gingerly took the collars from Mullen's thick, calloused fingers and inspected them, grimacing at the odour. It smelt of burning hair, fat and something more pleasing to the nose. Mint. He coughed, dislodging a ball of phlegm and swallowing. Spitting it out on a stranger's property would be bad form. He had made that mistake once before.

The collars were coated in a thin layer of white grease, streaked red. Puzzled, he handed the strips of leather back to the distressed farmer and pointed up at the sky with one hand. He wiped the other on his jeans, trying to remove the slick grease.

"You think this has something to do with your dogs?" Mullen shook his head.

"No. Not that. There's something else up there. On the other side, you understand. I've been hearing it all night. Like a moaning sound. Then screeching. At about two this morning, it started babbling. All these strange words like nothing I've heard before. I've been around Poles, Pakistanis and all them. It wasn't any of those. I had to have a tot to try and block it out. Ended up finishing the bottle. That worked for a time." J.D. nodded his understanding. That explained the redness of the man's eyes anyway.

"Seems to be quiet now though."

Mullen nodded, the gesture fatigued.

"Stopped when I was passed out. There's hasn't been a peep so far. Just those weird things poking around. Can you see 'em?

J.D. stepped forward, trying to get a closer look at the thing, a chill creeping up his spine. His dread increased a notch.

Above them, the azure of the sky was torn by a crack. It was difficult to accurately measure how large the hole was. The more the reporter concentrated on it, the more it seemed to shift and blur as if it knew that the men below were observing and measuring it. It seemed to flatten, then expand and then flatten again, growing wider with every expansion. Thin filaments of *stuff* poked through the hole, questing and searching the space around it before disappearing back.

It's tasting the air. The thought startled him. It wasn't alive whatever *it* was. Strange, certainly. Unexpected? Most definitely. But not alive. This was one for the scientists. He would make his report, get Murray to air it, and leave it with people far more qualified and clever than he. Reporting from the Twilight Zone wasn't in his remit, at all.

As he watched, the crack opened up, wider this time.

Silence. It was total, suffocating.

Even the birds had stopped singing.

The hairs on J.D's neck raised in stiff salute as the atmosphere became heavy with expectation.

He heard the men shuffling nervously behind him. His annoyance grew as tried to mask his own fear. It was time to take control of this situation. Wasn't that what Quigley would do?

He turned, an angry look on his face.

"What the fuck's the matter with—"

A low groaning stopped him dead. It boomed from the sky, echoing around them. Mac's eyes widened, Mullen became pale. Earl raised a quizzical eyebrow but that was the extent of his response. He wasn't an emotional sort. He was too stoned anyway.

The groaning sound continued for a moment before tailing off into an ear splitting keening. J.D. clapped his hands to his ears as the pitch became too intense to bear. It was no use. The sound seeped through his hands as if they were not there. Pain spiked behind his eyes. He screamed, sinking to his knees. The pitch became higher, rattling the filling in his molars. He felt a warm gush as the blood vessels in his nose let go. The world canted sideways, then became dark. He keeled over.

"Wake up, man, wake up."

He groaned, pushing away the insistent hands that kept shoving and shaking him.

"No school today, mum. It's a holiday." He mumbled incoherently as hands dragged him up to a sitting position.

"J.D, shape up, man."

Annoyed, the reporter lashed out groggily. A hand smashed his cheek, whipping his head to the side. Clarity returned to him, the slap stinging his face. He looked around. Sickening pain lanced his head, reaching a crescendo before subsiding into a low level buzz. His vision clearing, he noticed a peculiar tint to the daylight. The world looked greener than before.

Have I had a stroke or something?

He moved his legs and arms and looked up. Mac crouched in front of him, his face pale, almost beige. His lips and chin were coated with crimson, trails of blood leading from his nose. They all had nosebleeds, it seemed. Mac's eyes were large, agitated and lined with red.

"Thank fuck you're awake. Look man, we've gotta get the fuck out of here. That thing's got even bigger." His voice was panicky, the words tumbling out in a rush.

Irritated and groggy, J.D. pushed him away and struggled to his feet. His senses cleared and returned, but the green tint to the daylight remained. Mac spun him around, pointing back to the strange portal.

"Look at that. You can't tell me that's normal."

J.D. looked up.

What the ever-living fuck is going on here? His mouth dropped open at the sight above them.

The crack had increased in size and become rounder, yet jagged. A rotten, emerald light spilled from the hole in the sky. He felt relieved. He wasn't having a stroke. The relief evaporated. There were sounds coming from the hole, slithering squelching sounds. He gulped, turning to the others. Earl had his boom mike raised, headphones on, his face blank as he recorded. Mac looked terrified, as did the farmer. J.D. stepped up to him, his face within kissing distance. He jerked a thumb toward the hole.

"That noise! Is that what you heard last night?" Mullen merely nodded, his face ashen, his lips moving in a soundless incantation. The man was very close to losing his mind. The squelching became a fraction louder. The reporter considered his options. This was beyond the scope of any of them. Maybe it was better to let the authorities take care of it. Or maybe it was the biggest chance ever gifted to a struggling, disrespected, low-level reporter. The idea appealed. This could be the event that would propel him past his smug rival and his horrid boss.

He looked over at Mac. "Have you called it in?"

Mac shook his head.

"Why not?"

The darker skinned man snorted in disbelief, gesturing at the green tear. "Have you fucking seen what's going on? What's the point of calling it in to Murray? I called the police." Mac really must have been terrified. He had no love for the boys in blue.

"What did they say?"

The camera man shrugged. "That they were aware of the situation and that the army was on their way. People can see the light as far away as Leicester, Kettering, even Brum. When I told them about the other stuff, the guy on the phone said, and I quote, "what stuff?""

J.D. turned this over in his mind. They were at the epicentre of this, able to see clearly what others at a distance could not. The footage shot would be pure gold. A news item with him at the helm would be award-winning. Live contact with an unnatural phenomenon. It had to be alien, of course. What else could it be? J.D. reporting live, making first contact with people from the stars. His excitement stirred, a long-forgotten feeling. He hadn't felt like this for a long time. It was almost unwelcome and uncomfortable. His big chance, the big break he had been waiting for. They had to strike now before someone else, maybe even that floppy haired idiot Quigs, got in on the act.

He looked at Mac and smiled. "Get behind that camera."

"Why?"

"Why do you think? We're about to become famous. You, me, Earl, Mr Mullen here." He slapped the farmer on the back heartily. "We're about meet an alien."

Mac knew there was no point in arguing. He could see the glint in J.D's eyes. It had been a long time since he had seen that. The reporter had lost his sparkle over the years, the fresh-faced enthusiasm souring and curdling into a morass of bitterness and under achievement. This could be his big break. Mac didn't have the heart to steal this moment from him, despite his own terror at the surreal situation. This was Northamptonshire, after all. Why would aliens form a portal here? Of all the places in the world, this was the least likely. He thought about it no further, taking his position behind the camera.

J.D, mike in hand, stood directly in front of him. Earl stood to one side, holding the boom mike out of shot.

"Have you got the portal thingy in shot?"

Mac gave him a thumbs up.

"Ok. Let's do this."

Mac began rolling.

"I'm here at Mullen's Farm, at the edge of Northamptonshire where a strange and frightening event is taking place. A weather phenomena has appeared in the sky above this gorgeous piece of countryside that will leave experts baffled and religious people fearful. Joining me now is Mr Mullen, the owner of the farm. Mr Mullen, when did you first become aware that something was amiss?"

Mullen didn't speak. His lips kept up their soundless litany. His eyes were huge and hectic. Beads of sweat coursed down the old man's face.

J.D. sighed.

Amateurs. He poked the old man out of shot.

"Mr. Mullen, when did you-"

"Hail, Mary, full of grace...."

J.D. hissed in annoyance. "Mr. Mullen, please. I'm trying to do an interview here. You're going to be all over the news, maybe worldwide. Come on. Work with me on this."

Mullen screamed, a high whooping sound of terror from the depths of his soul. Earl dropped the mike. Mac stepped away from the camera.

"Fuck's sake, what?"

Mac said nothing, his eyes transfixed on the spot above J.D's head. The reporter turned, dropping his mike. He felt a warm gush as his bladder let go.

Tentacles hung from the crevasse above, lazily unfurling and stretching until they reached the ground a few feet away. The salmon pink tendrils shone wetly, a clear fluid dripping from them. Mullen's dog collars flashed through the reporter's mind. The ear splitting groan from earlier shook the sky. Despite his terror, only one thought went through his mind.

"Keep filming, Mac."

"What? Are you out of your fucking mind?"

"You heard. We need a record of this. Earl, pick that fucking mike up. I'm going to call Murray and tell him to clear the decks."

"Are you mad?"

J.D. shook his head. This had to be recorded and broadcast for posterity. He pulled his phone from his pocket, hitting speed dial, all the while watching the tentacles warily. They didn't seem to be doing much, just stretching, liquidly and luxuriously, massaging each other as if they had just awakened.

Come on, come on, dickhead. Answer.

"What, prick?"

J.D laughed. The Scotsman was as gracious as ever. The boot would be on the other foot soon.

We'll see who the prick is when I fire your arse back to the fucking Gorbals, sweaty!

"Murray, its J.D. Clear the schedule and get ready for the biggest thing to happen since Jesus." He was aware he was babbling. He took some deep breaths, trying to slow down. It would do him no favours to sound like an out of breath, excitable school child.

"You mean that funny looking light out your way? Not interested."

J.D frowned. The editor must have heard the rumours.

"Yeah, that one, now listen."

"Forget it, son. Weird weather and mass hysteria. M.O.D.'s already put the word out. Besides, today is Budget Day. Even if I wanted to, I can't clear the schedules. You know how *she* gets if we fuck about with announcements."

J.D. bellowed incredulously into the phone.

"*What?*"

"Don't take that tone with me, son, or you'll be on the Nat King Cole in seconds. It's not news-worthy enough. Record it, send it back, the boys'll put it on Look East tonight."

J.D. trembled in anger and fear. The hole had widened. Whatever owned those tentacles would be falling out soon, stepping onto the soil of a new world. This had to be recorded and reported. Why couldn't the Jock bastard get his deep fried brain around that?

"Murray, listen to me. Listen close, right? There are fucking tentacles dangling from a green hole in the sky—a hole that's getting wider by the minute. It's a fucking portal to somewhere else and it ain't Kansas. Oh and get this! There are weird sounds coming from that portal, weird shit that I've never heard before. Mr Mullen's dogs were vaporized in the middle of the night. And you're telling me that the Budget's more interesting than this?"

"Aye. That's about the size of it."

Black shapes began to gather around the edges of the hole. He squinted, trying to get a clearer view. From this distance, they looked like stickmen. Winged stick men. The shapes struck a primal chord of fear on his soul. He swallowed, suddenly inspired to try a new tactic with his obstinate boss.

"Murray, listen. You're a God Fearing Man, right?"

"Aye."

"Well this is some Revelation shit happening right here above me. Potential apocalypse. Please, you have to let me air this." Pleading filtered through his tone. He was starting to sound like a child again, a child begging for one last chocolate, toy or any other treat.

Murray sighed and gave a rattling cough, a decades-long love song to smoking.

"One last time: the Government are on it. In the Government, we trust. Besides which, the Apocalypse has been predicted more times over the last thirty years than I've had hot dinners. No one cares anymore. Get over it. Film what you need to, head back to the office and we'll run it tonight. In the meantime, you'll have to excuse me. Busy day. Budget and all that. Sayonara, prick."

There was a click as Murray hung up. J.D. suppressed the urge to launch the phone at the frightening shape above. He looked down. Maybe there was another way to get the editor's attention. He clenched his jaw together, the decision made.

"Mac, you still filming?"

"Yeah."

"Good. Keep rolling. Anything happens to me, get out of here. Understood?"

A hand gripped his shoulder.

"What are you planning, J.D?"

He noted with surprise that it was Earl. The quietest man in the Kingdom had spoken up.

"Just watch. I'm going to try something. I mean, these things haven't tried to harm us, have they?" Earl's grey eyes bore into him.

"They vaporized Mullen's dogs, J.D."

"Vaporized, my arse. It was probably a teleporter, you know, like the one out of *Blakes 7*."

J.D. was clutching at straws. He knew this, but he had to go through with his plan. Years of frustration, lost chances and missed opportunity boiled over. He was going and that was final. Shaking free of Earl's grip, he advanced.

This is probably the most genius idea I've ever had. Or it might be the most colossally stupidest idea I've ever had. There had been plenty over the years, that was true. But this was a true leap into the unknown. The pay-off could be tremendous. If he didn't try, he would never know, nor be known. Time to take a gamble and trust in karma, destiny, or whatever the fuck it was that had eluded him and ignored him for most of his life.

He exhaled sharply. He was committed now. For better or for worse, he had to see what would happen. Maybe nothing would. Maybe this other-wordly visitor would be friendly. Just because it looked different didn't necessarily mean it was harmful. He swallowed, his heart hammering in his chest. As he drew closer, he noticed the smell coming from the tendrils. It was unlike the smell of rot and fat that had emanated from the broken dog collars. The smell was green and pleasant, rather like wild mint. He smiled. At the very least, the visitor would smell good while it tore him apart. He pushed the thought away. Now was not the time to be spooking himself.

He reached the tentacles and paused, studying them. They didn't respond to his presence, continuing to massage each other.

So far, so good. They don't want to eat me then. Not yet.

The reporter stood, admiring the ripple of muscle beneath the taut, slick skin. The limbs were thick and strong. They could snap him in two or crush him to a pulp without any effort at all. He stepped a little closer.

A thinner tentacle unfurled from the mass, and reared above him. It seemed to sniff the air around it before lowering in front of him. J.D's heart jack-hammered in his chest. The tentacle didn't seem threatening. He cleared his throat.

"Greetings. I'm J.D, reporter. I mean you no harm."

The tentacle flopped to the floor and rolled, the gesture almost playful. He smiled. It had the air of a puppy rolling around on its back. It thrashed about for a few moments before tiring of its little game. As J.D. gazed in wonder and delight, the tendril reared up lazily and dipped towards him. Tentatively, he reached out a hand, touching the strange appendage. It was warm and slick. He could feel the pulse of a thunderous heart through its skin. The tentacle did not draw away from him. It pushed at his hand, nuzzling it. More of the mint-smelling fluid seeped from its pore, coating his hand. He smiled, a sense of triumph filling him.

"See?" He shouted back to his friends. "What did I tell you? Nothing to worry about. First contact has been made. By me." He punched the air for emphasis.

He was about to become famous for being more than just a reporter. He was the first man to make contact with another life form, Earth's first ambassador to another race.

Murray and Quigs might as well just retire now. They can't beat this.

He smiled as images of their crestfallen, jealousy suffused faces filled his mind. The tentacle shook in unison, as if the owner of the limb was as amused.

Boy, am I glad I took this job today.

The tentacle continued to tremble. J.D. smiled, glad the creature seemed to appreciate the concept of humour. Another moaning sound came from above.

Aye, aye. Big Momma has awoken.

Maybe it was trying to communicate back. J.D. looked up to the sky, craning his neck for a better view. The stick-men tumbled from the portal, stretching out their arms as they hit the air. Thermal currents caught membranous wings, steadying them. He watched in wonder as the shapes glided gracefully above him. They looked human enough, but making out their features was still difficult. They would land soon. Then he could establish contact. Two alien races for the price of one and he was the man about to speak to them.

He shook his head, amused at the thought that this could be the end of the world. What a genuinely stupid idea that was. He didn't feel any danger at all, although his hand felt a little hot and irritated. Maybe he was allergic to the secretions oozing from the tentacles. Making a mental note to be more careful, he rubbed his hand on his jean, wincing a little at the sharp stinging pain. The skin of his hand felt loose and hot. J.D. frowned, deciding when this was over he would wash his hands in cool soothing water.

The pain increased. He hissed a little, looking down at the affected hand.

The skin on the back loosened from the rubbing. It dangled like an old glove, bubbling and falling away to the ground, like the discarded skin of a snake. He raised his hand, dumbfounded and in shock. Muscle and vein uncoiled, unhinging from bone, jarred loose by movement. There was no blood, only a bloody ooze. His breath hitched and came in short gasps as he stared at the smoking, skeletal remains of his hand. Even the bone was beginning to bubble and rot. He felt no more pain, as even the nerves untangled and slithered away, utterly destroyed by the fluid.

The tentacle in front of him stopped quivering. J.D, frozen by terror, watched as the skin bulged and split open to reveal an interior lined with dripping teeth. The tentacle reared forward. J.D. held his hands up in supplication. His disbelief at how badly events had shifted outweighed his fear.

"But, but I thought you were frie—"

The toothy maw closed in around his head, silencing him. The tendril flattened around his skull, squeezing and pulsating. Corrosive sap exuded from the pink-orange skin, lazily crawling down his back, rotting away his shirt, eating into the flesh below. J.D. thrashed as the teeth cut into him, shredding his head and face into scraps. He tried to scream, but his mouth flooded with the taste of mint. The fluid ran down his gullet, liquefying his insides, turning organs into a paste. He died within seconds of the fluid reaching his heart, his organs bursting. The teeth ground through his skull and into the soft meat of his brain. J.D's rapidly deteriorating body went limp, sagging to the floor, headless and oozing. Tentacles fell onto his body in a frenzy, supping noisily at the liquid, tearing into what flesh remained, cracking open bone to get at the marrow. Nothing remained of J.D. They had consumed his clothes, the microphone, even the grass and earth beneath him.

Mac lost his nerve at the very moment the tentacle engulfed his friend's head. He grabbed the camera and Earl's arm.

"We're going. Now!"

Earl looked at him, his head jerking spasmodically. His eyes were large, glassy and hectic. His throat jerked as he swallowed convulsively.

"Come on!"

The long-haired sound engineer didn't move. He looked back at the portal, at the thousands of black shapes now streaming through. The air, stinking of mint and the vaguely sweet smell of corruption, now filled with unearthly shrieks and whoops.

One of the bat-like men swooped down, hovering over Mullen. The heavy-set farmer looked up the creature, clasping his hands together in a gesture of prayer. His lips continued to move.

Earl and Mac heard his babbling even over the din of the bat-men.

"Yea, though I walk through the shadow of the Valley of Death..."

The bat-man spread its arms in mock benediction. It looked directly at Earl, its gleaming black face contorted in a grin of triumph. Earl stared in horrified fascination at the creature. Its head was rough and bumpy, coral like growths erupting from the skin of its cheeks and eyebrows. Its mouth jutted out from each side of its face, too large for the regular sized head. Its eyes burned a sulphur yellow. Mullen continued with his babbling prayer, staring up at the creature, rocking from side to side on the balls of his feet.

The creature bellowed. Earl jumped at the sight of its red mouth, filled with needle sharp teeth all the way to its throat. The creature gripped the farmer, sinking its clawed feet into the praying man's shoulders, tearing through the heavy body warmer. Mullen screamed as the talons slid easily through flesh, striking bone. With a smooth, fluid motion, the bat-man took to the air, carrying its kicking, screaming, bleeding prize with it.

Earl broke. He turned and ran, Mac following alongside him, their equipment now discarded. The noise above them intensified, a sonic carpet of beating wings and high-pitched screams. They reached the van, Mac jamming shaking hands into his pockets, frantically searching for the keys.

"Come on, Mac, Get the door open!" Earl's voice shook with panic.

The beating of wings grew louder with every breath.

"Hurry the fuck up, man."

The sound was almost on top of them.

"Come on, *Mac!*"

Mac found the keys, unlocked the door and hurled himself into the van, slamming the door shut behind him. He dove for the passenger side, hand outstretched to open the door for his friend. Earl looked through the glass at him, his eyes wide with shock. He opened his mouth to scream. Blood sprayed from him, coating the window with a haze of red. He gave Mac one last imploring look before his jaw widened. The crack of bone was deafening even in the confines of the van. A blood slicked orange tentacle burst from Earl's open mouth. The sound-man's eyes rolled back into his head as he died. His limp body slammed against the door, spilling more blood on the glass before being pulled away with tremendous speed.

Mac sat up, jamming a fist into his mouth, tears spilling down his cheeks. The sky darkened with dark wheeling shapes—the bat-men, thousands of them, spinning and soaring in crazy glee, as if they had not flown free in an eternity. One of them landed in the road in front of the van. Mac wiped his eyes furiously. He wanted to see it, the thing that had invaded his world. The bat-man stood tall and proud. This one was different than the one that had taken the farmer—slat thin, the curves of its ribcage showing through black skin. The creature's eyes bulged prominently as if it was being throttled. The mouth was smaller, but still filled with an impossible multitude of teeth. A long, pink tongue flicked from the mouth, licking dry lips. It seemed to beckon Mac forward, daring him to do his worst.

Grief and rage mingled with terror. Mac jammed a key into the ignition, twisting it viciously. The engine roared to life. He looked into the wing mirror. The field behind him was now a roiling carpet of tentacles and mist. A groan filled the air, silencing the screams of the flying bat-men. He felt the low rumble vibrate through the steering wheel.

The ground shook and there was a subsonic thump as something impossibly large hit the Earth. He caught a glimpse of a massive, gelid shape amongst a thousand thrashing limbs, a baleful glowing eye shining through the coils. Steam boiled from the shadowy presence, almost totally obscuring it. Mac watched as paint began to peel from the bonnet of the van, the metal beneath rusting. The glass of the windscreen warped. Within moments, it would crack or melt, leaving Mac helpless and exposed. An overpowering stench of wild mint filled the cabin.

The bat creature up ahead continued to beckon him. The ground shook as the larger *thing* smashed its tentacles against the floor and roared, announcing its presence to this new world. Blood seeped from Mac's nose again. His mind retreated from the chaos. He had to get out of here.

He floored the accelerator. The van leapt forward. The bat-man only had time to let out a surprised squeal as the van barrelled into it, its delicate frame bursting like rotten fruit. Mac felt a slight jump as the van's tires squashed the creature into the dirt. He howled, his sanity broken, his mind on autopilot as he careened down the driveway of Mullen's Farm. The van jerked violently at a sharp bend in the road, the wheel losing purchase. Mac yelled and spun out of control, plunging head long into an old oak. He flew through the weakened glass of the windscreen, his unbelted body smashing into the tree head first.

A bat-man, the same type as the one now lying dead, tire tracks bisecting it, found the body. It drooled at the appetizing smell of the corpse. Its dim mind sensed there were more pickings like this one, alive and fresh, beyond this place. It crouched low, nuzzling the cooling flesh cautiously before taking a tentative bite.

The presence within the mist stilled itself, taking stock of its surroundings. It, its brethren and other denizens of the realm they had left behind, had been aware of this world for eons, but had never been able to traverse into it. Instead, they had been trapped on the other side of reality, only able to observe this universe. Hungry. Angry.

There had been other portals over the ages, some small enough to allow lesser creatures through. Gateways opened by dark magi and witches in this realm, unaware of what lay beyond their tiny little world, only concerned with wealth, power and prestige. The Omniverse was a chaotic place, peace and harmony now in tatters after the Gods had left it, to fight wars eternal.

The Presence and its brethren were now free, and this universe, the Universe Primal, would fall to them. There would be blood and feasting for evermore. Who could stop them now? The Gods had abandoned the Omniverse, Archon Morbius had vanished, and Lucifer was nothing but a petty trickster, a con-artist who dreamt big, taking advantage of the lack of competition. He and his miserable court in Hell were about to receive a shock.

The Presence was amused by this. It would be a pleasure to lay waste to Hell, to raze it from the shores of Styx to the banks of the river Mersey. But first, there were other considerations. This world, this Earth, had to be dealt with. An easy task and one that would be most pleasurable.

The Presence roared its triumph and the Apocalypse began.

LEGALLY DEAD

PASTOR JOHN LOOKED UP as the door slid open. He adjusted his dog collar, clasped his hands together and puffed out his chest. The gesture emphasised his considerable size. The new muscle grafts had taken well and responded to exercise much better than his original muscles ever did. Total bodily muscle replacement was an expensive indulgence, but it did not matter. As a member of the Ecclesiastical Body for the Assessment of the Worker Castes, he was entitled to complete and free health care as well as restorative surgery. It was only right and fair for a God-fearing, hardworking Alpha like himself to be able to call on such scarce resources, unlike the sad specimen that now shuffled into his office.

The pastor looked down at his data-pad, scrolling through the details of the D-70 form.

Yet another standard claimant. Routine and dull. John Joseph Jeffries, Gamma Caste, thirty eight years old, unemployed for a number of years. He had no discernible skills, had left school at an early age and worked in a variety of menial jobs, mostly within the viz-call centre sector. With the advent of A.I. calling, there was no need for human operated call centres any more. Yet another industry had been fully automated, leaving a surplus of jobless lower castes behind, and the Clergy rushed off their feet, processing the inevitable D-70 forms and having to administer the Last Rites to the unfortunate claimants. Business was very good, at least for the Ecclesiastical Body.

The previous week's presentation at the Clergy AGM had been the crowning glory of his career to date. He had been singled out for praise by High Plantagenet Maximus himself. Pastor John had taken a sloppy, underperforming Worker Caste Sector House and turned it into an exemplar of their trade. D-70 forms poured in by the dozen, the claimants processed quickly and cleanly, and what little holdings the claimants left behind, as well as the state benefits they would have taken in the old days, went directly to the coffers of the Unified Church. John had allowed himself a small measure of pride at that. Not too much pride of course. That would be unseemly for a man of the cloth.

He motioned to Jeffries to sit down, trying not to grimace at the smell emanating from the man. He reeked of old dirt, cheap alcohol, cheaper food and the desperation of grinding, hopeless poverty. The poor soul. The D-70 is a blessing for the destitute who have already been through so much suffering.

"Mr Jeffries', the pastor said, his voice deep and clear, friendly even. It was all part of an act designed to keep the claimant at ease. He tried his best to cultivate a warm approachable persona. His face was that of a kindly old uncle, with bright, twinkly, mischievous eyes and an authoritarian Roman nose. He wore his modest head of hair swept back, giving him a streamlined look. John had toyed with the idea of a full scalp transplant, but decided against it. He was far too busy to worry about trivial things like hairstyles and so forth. There were too many desperate members of his flock who needed his help.

Mr Jeffries hugged himself. It was a gesture Pastor John had seen many times before. A comforting act rather than a warming one. Besides, he always kept the office warm. He personally loathed the cold. And, of course, heating cost him nothing. He was a Clergy member.

"Do you understand why you're here, Mr Jeffries?"

The claimant kept silent, nodding vigorously.

"And do you understand the purpose of the D-70 form that you were sent?" Again, the small man nodded. He rocked gently, humming to himself.

"Given that you fully understand the nature of the form and the procedures, I'm delighted to advise you that we can go ahead with your termination. In just under an hour, you will be legally dead." Pastor John smiled with brimming enthusiasm. "How do you feel?"

Jeffries looked him in the eye, fear on his pallid face.

"Scared, to be honest, Pastor," he said, his voice thin and reedy. His accent implied that he was local. The forms had confirmed it. He was a Deritender, born and raised in an area that had seen better days. If John remembered his history correctly, Deritend had been at the centre of the Smiler Insurrection, the first act that had led the world to this very point in history. John counted his blessings. This could have been much worse. The man could have been a Small Heathen. They were notorious for violence and obstinacy. Jeffries would be an easy and painless job.

"There's no need to be afraid, Mr Jeffries." Reassurance suffused his voice.

"Termination is a very painless procedure these days. We pride ourselves on that. Why, in the New Khanates, they don't even wait until you are legally dead. Your organs would be removed as you still breathe. Death is a very painful process in the less civilised areas of the world, especially the areas that have rejected the Good News."

Jeffries still looked terrified. This one was going to take a bit more convincing. He decided on another approach.

"Count yourself lucky that you are Worker Caste, not a Carnivallier, or even worse, a Travellier. Vagrants, thieves and wastrels. They are not even chipped! Do you have any idea what life must be like for those poor souls? No access to anything that would make life meaningful. Healthcare, education, a place to live? All those poor devils have is arduous existence on the road, reduced to begging for credits for those distasteful creature shows they perform. They surely are the most polluted of souls. Casteless and Godless!"

Jeffries gulped, a rather comical effect. John noted the prospective D70's sudden paleness. It made him smile inwardly. His story had had the desired effect. The mere mention of the Carnivalliers and polluted casteless beings was more than enough to scare the sheep back into belief. A firm hand was needed with the lower castes these days. Mollycoddling the Deltas, Gammas and Epsilons would only give them ideas above their station and upset the natural order of things. And upset the lucrative supply of organs.

"Do you have any living relatives? If you have, you could be D-70 exempt. The Church frown upon D-70ing family men. It distresses the flock, as well as depletes them. We're only just starting to get numbers back on track after the Genocide Cataclysm. If you are alone and unemployed, that places such an incredible burden on the state. Legal death is more than just an option. It's a patriotic duty."

Jeffries shook his head. Pastor John knew that he was alone. The Delta had never married and his parents had been killed by a Khanate fanatic fourteen years ago, right before the Grand Inquisition had sent Holy Fire missiles to cleanse the old countries of the old Mid-East. The Distronium Holy Fire Warheads were far less indiscriminate than the fission bombs of old. The Distronic radiation they unleashed destroyed only flesh, leaving buildings and infrastructure intact. That one act was enough to convince the remaining Khanate holdouts to behave and not overreach themselves. There were so few people left in the Mid-East after the Cataclysm. There were so few human beings left at all.

Jeffries began to twitch as the enormity of what was about to occur dawned on him. A pathetic whimpering came from the back of his throat. The pastor ignored it. He was immune to distress—another medical innovation all pastors had benefited from; the complete removal of empathy from the mind. It was a necessary step. Pastors now had the corrective surgery done as soon as they joined the Seminary. In the past, too many had broken under the strain of having the power of life and death concentrated in their hands. The older ones, like John, had taken elective surgery once the new mandate had been passed by the High Plantagenet and the P.F.

"I can see that you are keen to meet our Lord. If there's nothing else to discuss, let's get on with the Last Rites. Is there any particular foundation which you would like your organs to go to?"

Jeffries remained mute. By law, that meant the Plantagenet Foundation had first call on the organs. The Church could bid if it had need of the organs.

The P.F. or Plantagenet Foundation to give them their full name, usually won. After all, they were the wealthiest and highest of the new western world elites and the real power in Britannia. Not even the Church, as powerful as it was, would dare move against them. It had been the Foundation that had sown the seed for the New Society, way back in the Old Times. The world had not been ready for their radical reshaping of the human race back then. Childish ideas, such as democracy and freedom, had held sway in those more innocent days. The Foundation had held back, making minor adjustments where it could, waiting for the right time. The Smiler Insurrection provided the perfect cover. The Genocide Cataclysm helped cement the new ideal. The Plantagenet Foundation steeped forward to bring order from chaos.

The higher echelon members of the Foundation claimed descent from the former British Royal Family stretching right back to the days of House Plantagenet. They claimed the right to rule by virtue of royal blood, and rule they did. The Council of The West administered the territories. The important decisions were in the hands of the High Plantagenet himself. His word was final. The destiny of the human race now lay in the hands of twelve men and women, all scions of wealthy families. Never again would ordinary lower castes be allowed to make the important decisions. Such things were beyond the comprehension of Deltas and Gammas. The Founders would have been proud of the paradise that was being forged from the ashes of a devastated world.

"You do us a great service, Mr Jeffries. There may be a day when a child of the Plantagenets—say Brother Minister Bush's younger son, or maybe Sir Evan Travis' daughter—will have need of an organ. Imagine the honour you would be covering yourself in, if it was one of your organs donated!"

Jeffries nodded and mumbled something indistinct about great honours and service from a throat full of tears.

Pastor John stood, beaming with delight, still ignoring the man's distress. It wouldn't be long for him now. The pastor picked up his data-pad and programmed in the Last Rites, also discretely sending a signal to the Inquisitor detachment stationed in the D-70 room.

"Come, my boy. Prepare to be received into our Lord's Paradise. All your sins are now forgiven."

Mr Jeffries nodded and silently wiped away a tear. Pastor John gripped his shoulder. The suffering of this world would soon be over, and he would awake in the presence of the Lord God.

The call came through, hours after Jeffries had been dispatched to meet God. Officially, at least. Pastor John stood by the glass window looking out onto Brummagem, the second city of Brittania. Separated from the capital Londinium, by the harsh Mercian Wastes, the city still remained impressive. Gleaming skyscrapers dwarfed the few remaining Old Time buildings, those few decrepit monuments still left standing after the Genocide Cataclysm. The sun shone through a red haze, a peculiar effect left by the use of ancient atomic weapons, and other pollutants that had come through the strange phenomena known as Er-Gates.

The Pastor had been a very small child during the war, his memories of that dark time hidden by a veil of thick, greasy smoke. That suited him. Those were the Old Times. He was a man of this new and wondrous world, where God's light shined only on those He favoured. Those nations who had rejected His teachings for their own perverse and polytheistic ways were gone, mouldering bones indented with the marks of the Vastatus, or mounds of ash from the unleashing of God's Holy Fire.

One day, all of those mutant-filled lands would be reclaimed by the F.P. and the United Church. Pastor John looked forward to a time when he could step onto the newly cleansed earth of what had once been a place known as India, and begin to play his part in the building of a new outpost for his God. It was his destiny, his calling. This death watch that he had been on for most of his career was just a prelude, as well as a way of building his power and wealth. One day, he would be a Legate, then a Prelate, maybe even rise to the office of High Plantagenet himself—if Maximus, the old bastard, ever got round to dying, that is. The thought renewed him, filling him with vigour and an eagerness for the work ahead.

The intercom on his desk chimed, interrupting his reverie. He pulled himself away from the view and strode back, pressing a button on the small comm. Magda's honey and lemon voice floated through the speaker grille. There was a hint of trepidation, a quiver of fear in her voice. He liked that. He crossed his legs, mindful of the stirrings in his trousers, then after a second thought, uncrossed them and allowed his manhood to salute Magda freely. There was something about the sound of fear that quickened his pulse, paced his breath.

"Priority call, Excellency. Alpha One. Coming through to your screen now."

Shit! Alpha One.

He felt a chill of fear. Alpha One—the designation of the Council. What could they want from him? He racked his brains trying to find something, anything that he might have done wrong. A chime sounded from the wall, repeating and insistent. Without looking up, he spun in the direction of the featureless white wall behind him, and dropped to his knees in the correct submissive posture. There was a click and a buzz as the large view screen came to life.

"Pastor John."

There was a low chuckle from the direction of the screen.

"The rising star of West Mercia. How pleasing to see you. You look well...John!"

It was the High Plantagenet himself. John recognised the sound of his master's voice. There was a strength and authority to it, but beneath the veneer of civility and power, the Pastor detected a hint of something else, a primal and animalistic quality. The High Plantagenet spoke without any preamble or pleasantry, a chill of malicious amusement in his voice.

"The Tristakozene 1782 trials. You've been hiding the results from me, haven't you? And here was me, your Lord and Master, thinking we were friends. Naughty."

John frowned with consternation. He was sure that his contacts had suppressed that little bit of information. Thinking furiously, he replied back.

"I only held the information back for a brief time, my Lord. I wanted to be sure of what we were dealing with before presenting my findings to you." His voice took on an obsequious wheedling tone. He was powerless to prevent it, such was his fear of Maximus. "I am pleased to report, however, that the new batch not only helps to prolong life, but it also keeps organs fresh and viable long after the D-70 subject is dead." He smiled nervously, his grin sick.

"There's a slight inaccuracy there, John. Right there. Everything else I'm happy with. Rejuvenation, long life, healthy organs, yadda-yadda-yadda. My problem, bearing in mind that my problems are your problems, is that the D-70s aren't dying, are they? Even with seventy per cent of their organs being taken, they are not dying."

The High Plantagenet purred in bemusement. "We have a means for true immortality within our reach. After all these years of trying. Why would you want to hide that from me?"

John knew fully well why he had supressed the information. If true immortality could be achieved, then the Alphas would no longer need organ transplants to extend their life spans. In one fell swoop, the D-70 program would be over. As would be the pastors. His plush lifestyle would be taken away, along with his Caste Privileges. He couldn't allow that to happen. Not to him or his fellow pastors. He thought carefully about what to say next.

"That's not strictly true, my Liege. The D70s survive after death. That much is fact. They may also have a form of immortality. Weapons tests have indicated that they cannot be killed, at least by conventional methods. My team are in the middle of other tests to determine a way to kill them."

Maximus grunted. "And they can't die? This gets better and better, my friend. So again, why the cover up? What seems to be the problem?"

"They change, my Lord. Mentally, they become aberrations. And physically, there are changes. Certain areas of the body atrophy and decompose. Mostly around the head and neck. They function, they live, but they have no faces. The flesh simply falls off."

The High Plantagenet laughed again. It was a cruel, cold sound.

"My dear Pastor, I'm not concerned about lower castes and their fates. That is the price we pay for progress. What I want is immortality. For you, for me, for all the Alphas and some of the Betas. You are going to get it for me. Understood?"

Stunned, John rocked a little, trying to grasp the implications of the statements. The High Plantagenet tutted.

"Do I have to spell this out to you? I'm moving you up in the world. From tomorrow, you will no longer be a pastor. You will be a Legate Director. You will have funds, a team of the best researchers, doctor-men and a facility at your disposal. Not to mention a rise in salary, Healthcare Plus, and as much Tristokozene 100 as you desire."

John frowned.

"I almost hesitate to ask, but why me?"

"Because, my dear Pastor John, you get things done. You're my rising star. There is no one better to manage this task. If I left it to Tremain, Cameron or Clegg, it would take centuries. They are efficient but not the brightest of men. Besides, men always work better when the threat of death hangs over their heads. Find me the path to eternal life or you die. It's as simple as that."

John felt a curious mix of emotions, on the one hand, pride at being promoted and on the other, fear for his life if he failed. He had been noticed at last. If he performed this task well, the possibilities would be endless. It was worth the risk of execution. The decision came easily.

"I accept, my liege."

"Good. A transport will collect you in the morning. From here, you will be taken to the very outskirts of the Ikneld Forest. Your facility, along with a contingent of Inquisitors will be waiting for you. The doctor-man in charge is highly rated; Emilius Range. He is aware that you are coming."

John smiled triumphantly. Doctor Emilius Range. He had struck gold. The man was a genius from a long line of geniuses. The search for immortality would be a short one. There were some loose ends to be tidied up, however. He looked up at the screen.

"What's to be done with the D70s?"

"Dispose of them', Maximus said. He sounded distracted.

"But...but they can't die anymore. Not in the usual sense, anyway. And it will take months to complete the final tests'

"Then round them up and ship them off somewhere. Or would you prefer I came up to Brummagem and did the job for you?"

The High Plantagenet was beginning to sound annoyed and the sound of threat was evident in his voice. John bit his tongue. Maximus was capricious with those who served him well, let alone those who upset him. The Coventry Crater stood as a stark reminder to those who upset the High Plantagenet. Legate March had been an idiot, a good hearted idiot, but an idiot nonetheless. As he became older he started to show signs of independence, going against the Council and Maximus. The final straw came when he dared to question the appalling conditions of the Epsilons. Years of good, dedicated service had been cast away in that one single moment. The High Plantagenet had sent him to Coventry for retirement and not long after dispatched a Star Wormwood projectile. Thirty thousand souls including the Legate had found their way to the arms of the Lord and the population of Britannia had learnt an object lesson. Do not annoy, upset or irritate High Plantagenet Maximus.

John pondered the question as quickly as he could, aware that his leader was awaiting his counsel. Sending the D70s away made sense. At least, they would be out of the public eye. But where? The outlying colonies were out of the question. For starters, he would be heading there. He didn't want a load of skull-faced mutants on his doorstep. The Mercian Wastes perhaps? No one with any sense lived in the expanse between the forest and Brummagem City. It would be an ideal dumping ground, however, the logistics would be a problem. A drop off in the wastes would mean sacrificing a whole transport and it's Inquisitorial Guard. There was no room for survivors on this mission. John was a fantastic liar, but even he would have trouble coming up with an explanation to the Prelate Council for the loss of men and materials. If the High Plantagenet approved it however...

Yes, he decided. That would be the best course of action. Dump the overflow of used D70s in the Wastes. They would not trouble anyone out there. Maybe they would even find a way to die.

"I have an idea, my Liege, but it will need approval from you and a high level of secrecy."

"Consider it done. There will be an official decree with you within the hour. The Ministry of Dissimulation will give you a secrecy blanket on this. Now go and enjoy your last day as a pastor."

John beamed with satisfaction.

"My eternal thanks, my Lord."

"Thanks are not necessary. Only results. We will speak soon, my servant." There was a click and a hiss as the screen shut down. The former pastor rose, his knees screaming their relief. His face split in a huge smile, his eyes twinkling with excitement. Everything followed to plan. God was truly with him.

The working day rounded to a satisfying close. Pastor John relaxed into the form-fitting sofa nestled in the corner of his office. Another ten souls had been despatched to St Peter's gates, one of them a former pastor himself. He had to retire on health grounds and as such would become a burden to society. The pastor had accepted his fate with an air of resignation, knowing that there was nothing to be done. Retirement, or D80 as it was now known, was a rare phenomenon, especially amongst the pastoral branch of the Clergy, who were always fitted with the best organs available.

The retired pastor's wealth and holdings would be a fine addition to the Vatican Coffers; after Pastor John took his cut, of course. Some creative book keeping would see a nice swell in his credit account.

Technically, it was illegal, but all of the Clergy and the Ruling Castes, right up to the level of High Plantagenet did it. The job pastors did was stressful, despite the empathy suppression. A little extra reward made it worthwhile.

The D70 problem had also been taken care of. By the end of the week, the Mercian Wastes would have some new residents. It had been a very good day at the office.

The door to his office opened and a tall, strikingly good-looking woman strode in, bearing a tray with a bottle of fine champagne, another perk of high office. Perks were his by right. The woman set the tray down on a small table next to where John sat, and poured the champagne into his glass. She smiled at him, brushing her raven-black hair away from her face. The effect set the Pastor's heart galloping.

"Thank you, Magda, my child. Will you be joining me?"

Magda shook her head. She was beautiful. All Clergy secretaries had to conform to the Pontificate standards of beauty, and Magda was no exception. Her pouty lips were accentuated by the lipstick she wore and her flawless body. The swell of her breasts, hugged by the little black dress, was enough to make even the Plantaganet Maximus have sinful thoughts. Not that he was celibate behind closed doors of course. The Clergy had their needs too, and with bodily renewal came a resurgence of urges that had lessened as their flesh had grown weaker and older.

"Is my schedule cleared for tomorrow?"

She nodded, casting her cool blue eyes over her Secreteriat data-pad.

"I've taken the liberty of clearing everything, Your Grace, including your meeting with the Sahota Brothers Chemical Conglomerate of Spa."

John frowned slightly at that. The Sahota Brothers were another loose end that needed to be tied up. He owed them money for his black market supply of Kozy. The brothers could make life very difficult for him if that bit of information got into the wrong hands. Tremain owed him a favour. It was time to collect.

He smiled at Magda.

"Send a comm. to Chief Inquisitor Tremain. I want a meeting with him tonight." Magda looked at him, mild curiosity on her face.

"I gather you have some things that need to be discussed?"

The Pastor threw his head and roared with laughter. Magda remained stone-faced, her eyes like chips of blue ice.

"Plenty my dear, but it's all extremely dull. Nothing for you to worry your pretty little head over."

There was no need to tell her about his promotion yet. He would be needing a new secretary, one that fitted his new station, but there was still fun to be had with this one. Maybe Tremain would appreciate her as a gift, along with payment for the Sahota affair. Knowing the head Inquisitor's taste for inflicting pain, she wouldn't last long. Still, as a plaything, Magda would be a pleasant diversion for him.

She bowed her head and turned to walk away. The pastor eyed her figure appreciatively, noting the taut muscle of her calves, the elegant movement of her coltish legs. A spark of heat pulsed through his groin.

All work and no play makes John a very dull boy indeed.

"My child, stay and keep me company. It's been a long day and I'm weary from the trauma of having to tend to those more unfortunate than ourselves."

Magda turned around and regarded the pastor. John mentally undressed her, his eyes crawling over her frame. She shivered visibly. John savoured the moment. He grinned like a wolf, enjoying the emotional distress she was showing. This was true power. The girl loathed him, that was plain to see, but there was nothing she could do. He became aroused by her helplessness. John could take her, at any time. It would be a death sentence to refuse him. The pastor's word was law. Refusing would be tantamount to blasphemy, an offence punishable by death. One quick call to the Torquemada and Magda would soon pay the price. Death at the hands of this most specialised branch of the Inquisitors would not be easy or quick.

She unzipped her dress, letting the paper thin garment fall to the floor. John, scenting victory, beckoned to her, his leer satanic. He let her push him back into the sofa and unfasten his bulging trousers.

What a triumphant day this was turning out to be for this servant of the Lord.

Pastor John lay back, his chest heaving. Sweat bathed him, more than usual, but the girl had been more vigorous than ever. She had torn at him with an animal lust that had overwhelmed and inflamed him, so much so that he had taken the Lord's name in vain more than once. It didn't matter. A few *Heil Marias* would make things right between him and his God. He had no need to fear the Lord's wrath.

His nerves still twitched with the throes of orgasm. The sensation sent a thrill of delight through him. There would most definitely be a repeat performance, after some wine and some stilted, dull conversation with the alluring but vacuous secretary.

An ice cold glass pressed into his hand. He sat up and sipped the champagne gratefully. Magda looked at him, her eyes cool and hooded. There was a weariness about her that was quite unusual. Like all of her colleagues, she was normally a vivacious if airheaded young lady. Today however, there seemed to be a spark of intensity, mixed with something else. Hatred perhaps?

"What's troubling you, my child?" He took a long draught, draining his glass. Champagne was meant to be savoured, but this first drink was needed to quench his thirst. The girl refilled the empty glass and stood in front of him, pulling her dress back on. There would be no repeat performance for the moment anyway. Trying not to let his disappointment show, John looked up at her oval face, framed by her luscious crown of black hair.

For a moment, he caught a look of utter disdain in her features. Who could that be directed at? Not him, surely! He was a pastor, universally loved by all and especially by God. There could be no earthly reason to hate him. He sipped his drink a little more slowly. Magda smiled, the look of hate melting into her usual bright charm.

"I have been your secretary for a long time, Pastor." John shivered with delight at the sound of her voice. He nodded in acknowledgement.

"I've dealt with your schedules, ensured the smooth running of the office, made your life easier so that you can continue to function, even with the great burden that your calling entails." John nodded again, unsure of the direction that this conversation seemed to be taking. He was beginning to feel a little light headed.

"I've also helped you reconfigure the accounts, so you can get your cut. I've doctored progress reports to the Council, The Grand Inquisitor, even the High Plantagenet himself. I've helped you to change the records of Workers, and Pastor Barnabas, in order to hit our D70 quotas for the month. And I know about the Tristakozene preservative. I know what it can do people."

John sat up now, disconcerted. What was the silly little girl getting at? He tried to pacify her.

"I know all this too, Magda, my dear. If your conscience bothers you, seek answers from the Lord. It's all in God's plan."

Her face changed. The usual detached yet flirtatious veneer disappeared, transforming into something cold and deadly. She raised her right hand. Astonished, Pastor John realised that she was holding an old-style snub-nosed pistol.

"My dear girl," he said, keeping his voice smooth and controlled. "Where in the name of God did you get that? You know, small projectile weapons are banned."

Magda nodded.

"Banned and treated as such a low-level threat that no one scans for them anymore."

Alarm turned to full blown fear. What in the name of the Lord had gotten into the girl? He made as if to get up. Magda levelled the gun at his head. There was no mistaking her look. It spoke of only one thing: murder.

"Please don't move. I'll kill you if I have to, but I'd much rather stick with the plan."

John froze, then shifted back into the impression his body had left in the memory foam sofa.

"Can I ask what you intend to do?" His voice fell, timid, not his normal, booming, preacher's tones.

She laughed coldly.

"Nothing yet. Please help yourself to some more champagne. I insist. If you don't, it won't end well for you."

Her eyes were steely. Pastor John believed she would make good on her threat. And drinking champagne seemed a pleasant enough activity. Could this be some strange sexual fetish? A power play perhaps? Some women did have strange kinks these days. Comforted by that thought, he reached for his glass. Magda shook her head.

"Not the glass. The bottle. Down in one. I know you can do it. I was in Vienna, remember?"

He nodded, despite the fact he had actually blacked out in Vienna. There was no point trying to explain that to the girl. She was on the edge. One wrong word might send a bullet flying through his skull, blasting his brain onto the wall behind him. He grasped the bottle by the neck and looked Magda in the eye.

"Bottoms up, my dear."

The bottle tilted to his lips and he drank deeply, opening his throat and letting the expensive fizz flow down his gullet. Within moments, it was empty. He put the bottle back on the table, feeling himself warm with the flush of alcohol.

I'm going to be very drunk in a moment, John though, a bit incoherently. All that alcohol in such a short space of time was bound to affect him quickly.

"Well done. You've finished it now. I guess I owe you an explanation." Still keeping the gun trained on him, Magda pulled up a chair.

"Davitts." She said the name tonelessly. John looked her in sedate confusion.

"You have no memory of a man called Davitts? Mordechai Davitts? A D70 you condemned twenty years ago?"

John shrugged. There had been so many over the years, they just melted into one long, faceless stream of lost souls needing to be guided back to the Lord. The room grew warmer. His cheeks felt as if they were on fire. He stifled a giggle and a burp.

Magda kicked out a long leg. Her pointy shoe connected with the pastor's shin with such force that there was an audible crack. The pastor shouted as pain flared up his leg, bright and hot.

"You heathen bitch!!" He spat the words out, then clenched his teeth against the roaring pain. His shin might have fractured. No matter, he could get a new one. But the pain was a nuisance.

"Mordechai Davitts was my brother. You altered his records to make it look as if he had no family and then D70d him. In the process, you took the huge sum of money that he'd inherited from our father. The money he was planning to split between us when I could finally get to Britannia legally."

Horror surged through Pastor John's young veins. This couldn't be happening. He had covered his tracks perfectly, forging records when required, D70ing people when he could. He had even indulged in old fashioned murder at times. How could he have missed this? He cursed. The room was hot now. Sweat sprang from his forehead.

"I thought you were..."

"*Alpha*? High Caste? A true child of God? Trust me, Pastor. I am definitely not Alpha, not after what they did to us, all of us, after the Genocide Cataclysm. How they ushered it in through their own greed and stupidity! How they left the rest of us out there to die at the hands of the Vastatus or due to Distronic radiation! How they plan to use the people who have been left behind as their source of immortality, an immortality that not one single one of you Alphas deserves!"

His ears began to roar, and a sharp pain cut deep into his left arm. An iron band clenched around his chest. His lungs felt like a pair of bellows being squeezed in a vice.

"Magda. I'm sorry. Please, you have to believe me. In the Name of our Lord, I am so sorry." She laughed, a humourless and bitter bark. John took a huge whooping breath, trying to squeeze oxygen into his unresponsive lungs.

"Please help me," he squeaked.

"You are beyond help, Pastor. You, the Church, the High Castes, the Foundation, even Maximus himself—your time is running out. The end is coming soon. For you all!"

Pastor John gasped as the band around his chest tightened.

"What have you done, bitch?" His face was on fire. His pulse boomed in his ear with every expansion and contraction.

"You're having a heart attack." She grinned wickedly. "A little something I added to the champagne. I could call for medical help, but that would mean you getting retired on medical grounds. Another D80 in a week. What would the High Plantagenet make of that? One of his best operatives: defective. Alternatively, I do nothing and you die from the heart attack."

She laughed again. Pastor John could feel the life slowly being crushed out of him.

"I'll leave it with you." She stood and pressed an emergency medical comm. into his hand.

"It's a direct line to Medco. I'll let you decide what's best. You'd better decide quickly though. You're going an awful shade of blue."

A cruel smile twisted her face. She stood, secreted the gun away and looked down on him. John's eyesight began to dim, but there was no mistaking the look of contempt on her face.

"All these years, I've waited for my chance. Killing you just doesn't seem as satisfying as I had hoped it would be. I'll have to keep on killing, right into the very heart of this stinking empire. Maybe cutting the High Plantagenet's throat will do it."

John tried to speak, tried to scream his hatred for her. A harsh croak spilled from his blue lips.

"Goodbye, Pastor John. God Bless."

With that, she left, her mocking laughter echoing around the office.

Pastor John reached through the overwhelming pressure and pain, feeling the ice of death tingling in his fingertips, his scalp, and through his penis. He pressed the emergency comm. button. Maybe retirement wouldn't be as painful as this.

He collapsed face-first onto the floor, his heart slowing down as it reached the end. The stone floor was soothing, the cold marble taking the edge off his soaring sense of overheating. A tear fell from his right eye. As his vision darkened, he found himself wishing for reincarnation, just to be able to avenge himself against the Davitt's bitch. The thought comforted him as he crashed into the dark.

He smiled and the lights went out.

GOD BLESS GEORGE A ROMERO

Introduction by Doctor P. Das

The following account was found amongst some papers during the Great British Reconstruction of 2025. There have been many documentaries and stories written after the fact, but genuine 'on the ground' accounts of the period known to many as the 'Apocalypse Wars' have been hard to locate.

The author remains unknown, one of millions who succumbed to the catastrophe that nearly destroyed us. The hints and clues scattered within the text indicate that the writer was an ordinary member of society. He seems to have been unfortunate enough to have been left behind during the wave of botched evacuations known as the Conservative Folly. Students of history will remember this as one of the worst examples of government mismanagement of the crisis, almost on a par with the Delhi Disaster and the Retreat of the Africas.

The account is genuine, of that there is no doubt. The British Midlands was badly hit by the Dead, and, until recent times, was one of Europe's white zones. It provides a fascinating, albeit brief, insight into the horrors of small town England during the Days of the Dead. It is my hope that many valuable lessons from this account can be learned. My only wish is that we could find a name for the poor soul who endured such horror in the last days of his life. It would be a fitting epitaph for him.

Dr. P Das, Professor of Modern History, New Birmingham City University, 6th April, 2026.

Tuesday

They never tell you just how boring the days can be in the zombie films. Now don't get me wrong; I used to love all the old zombie flicks, especially the George A. Romero ones. Fucking hated the remakes though. Bags of overblown Hollywood shit in my opinion, but there you go. You've got to have an opinion and I'm no exception. The films make out that life in the Zombie Apocalypse is all guns, shopping malls, death defying stunts and last minute escapes with the Deaders nipping at your heels.

The reality? No electricity, no gas, and no way to entertain yourself. Even a Sherman Tank is boring these days. No internet, you see, and trying to get to a shop, unarmed, just for a couple of jazz mags is a very risky undertaking.

That's why I'm writing this. Helps pass the time and keeps cabin fever at bay. To be honest, I don't think anyone'll survive long enough to read it. We are so royally screwed. There's no 'Blitz Spirit' pulling us together this time. Not when your enemy's trying to dismember and eat you. The Nazis may have been rabid, anti-semitic, cross-dressing perverts, but at least when you shot one, they stayed dead.

I suppose I should try and write something of use, like those nutty Zombie Survival Guides that were all the rage when the shit started flying. Fat fucking load of good they were. More people died following those useless books than survived. A guide book on surviving Cthulhu would have been of more use. Come to think of it, a Heston Blumenthal cook book would have been more use. At least I could make my potted meals a bit more interesting.

Maybe I should go for a documentary type of thing—like Kerouac, but with walking dead dudes. It wouldn't be set on the road either. The roads are now chock full of Deaders and abandoned cars. Even if they weren't, there's no vehicles worth taking out here. The army took all the good ones and what was left was torched. All that's left are burnt out wrecks. Or Minis.

If you're a survivor reading this, there's no point in telling you how it all fell apart in a matter of weeks. You'll have lived it. The government legged it to Canada or some other Commonwealth bolt hole. Us plebs got left behind, an all-you-can-eat buffet of the less wealthy and connected. I hope every single one of those elitist bastards has gone through a dead digestive system. It's the least they deserve. 'We're in this together.' Yeah right. Whatever you say, Prime Minister.

The Royal family deserve some credit. They toughed it out, stuck with us. Fair play to them for that. I'm not sure if they all survived, but I hope they did.

[*Editor's Note: The Queen passed away of natural causes, but the remaining Royal Family did survive. The members of the British Cabinet, however, still remain unaccounted for, but given how bad the situation in the former Commonwealth was, and still is, it is highly unlikely that any of them survived.*]

Anyway there's no point in being bitter. I'm here, and lucky to be alive after the massacre at the evacuation point. I saw the Army truck carrying my wife and daughter break free of the zombie horde and get away to freedom. I'll try and find them once I find a way out of this town.

Head north. That's where the young army bloke said they were headed. There's more open space up North, less chance of being mobbed by a herd. You can take the fight to them easier if you're not hemmed in by buildings. You can also avoid them a lot easier as well.

I was queuing for the last ride out of town when the fences came down. I shat myself, to be honest. Literally as well as figuratively. Those fences were meant to be unbreakable. Then again, the Titanic was meant to unsinkable and look how that turned out. Loads dead and James Cameron's worst film came out of it. If, by some chance, George A. Romero's still alive and he's reading this, please don't make the same mistake as Cameron. Film this as one of your grim satirical pieces, not a saccharine piece of shit. And make sure the actor who plays me isn't fat.

So the fences came down. Me and Young Army Bloke looked at each other, utterly terrified. Over the panicked shouting and screaming, you could hear them; the moans of the dead, the buzzing of a million flies. A noxious stink settled over the former car park. We were all familiar with this smell, a miasma of rotting flesh, blood and death.

I could feel myself getting squeezed by the frenzied crowd, trying to get away from the broken teeth, the clawing, grabbing hands. Something warm hit me in the face; blood. I tasted its metallic tang, but I couldn't tell who or where it came from. There was a lot of blood flying about, along with bits of flesh, some from the dead, some not. My sanity was on a knife edge. The noise was overwhelming—moans, screams, crying, praying.

My nerve broke at that moment. It was like a switch that had been flipped. Nothing particular sparked it off. My head just went, and I began lashing out, kicking and punching, trying to find space. An older man in front of me began to gasp, clutching his right arm. His face was going greyer by the second, lips flapping open and closed for air. He fell and I saw a gap, took the chance and ran. My feet stomped in to the man's fleshy gut, but I had a feeling he was almost dead anyway. Everything was a bit of a haze after that moment. Just memories of running, hands reaching for me, more screaming that could have been my own. I can't even remember getting back to the small block of flats that had been my family's home for the last month. Were the keys already in my pocket or did someone give them to me? There's a dim and distant memory; a hand outstretched with a bundle of keys. The keys are flecked with blood. The memory disappears back into my subconscious.

I must have locked up at some point, and the army was kind enough to leave the shutters pulled down on the ground floor flats, barbed wire atop the high brick walls they built around this place. They did well fortifying these places. High walls all around, wrought iron gates front and back. I'm safe enough here. I just shut all the blinds, and have hunkered down here ever since, opening the blinds to let enough daylight in for me to write this and read one of the grand collection of cheap and nasty paperbacks left behind by the previous owner.

I'm trying to keep some sort of routine but without any timepiece, it's a bit difficult. It's like the old caveman days; go to bed when it's dark, wake up when dawn breaks.

It looks quiet out there today. Think a supply run's in order. The small off-licence around the corner might still have some good stuff left. No one really looted, mainly because no one had the time. The Deader thing hit the South Midlands really quickly. We were unprepared.

Most people thought this thing would just be confined to the cities and stay out of the sticks. Boy, did we get a rude awakening on that one.

I'll have a peek out of the back windows. The path out back leads onto a main road and the shop's just across the way. If there's not too many Deaders about, I might be able to sneak out and back in, without being noticed. I'll give it a go. If this is the last thing I ever write, and if it does get read, then it's been interesting. And George A. Romero, God Bless you. You may have got it really wrong in your films, but I've got a lot of love for you.

I made it. Holy shit, I made it! It was nerve wracking though. I was right on the money about isolated stragglers, but it was still a lofty proposition going out on a run armed only with crowbars and cleavers. No guns. I never got the chance to steal Young Army Bloke's one before he was torn to shreds.

I opened the gate and had a quick peek. There were a couple of Deaders hanging around outside Papa John's Pizza. Young lads, by the look of them and their shredded clothes. This was going to be easy! All I had to do was close the gate as quietly as I could—there was no need to lock it. They aren't that clever at opening things like doors and gates. The gates closed. I kept the crowbar gripped tightly in my right hand, and walked out onto the street, alert and looking around in every possible direction. The adrenaline was pumping away now. My senses cleared in anticipation.

The sun was bright and warm. It could have been a normal day under different circumstances. The hoody dead were the only zombies close by. I could see others at the top of the road about a mile away, milling about in that dozy disinterested fashion that only dead people can pull off without looking stupid.

If I made this nice and quick they'd never notice. I tried to slow my breathing down, using some old yoga technique picked up from a book. It made no difference whatsoever. My heart thumped in my chest like a jackhammer on steroids; my skin crawled as adrenaline flooded my system and the muscles in my neck and shoulders tensed. The world seemed clearer, brighter, more defined. I was buzzing. I was undefeatable. I was ready to kick some rotten arse. I flew into them, my targets locked. The taller one of the two looked deader than the other. His skin was pure grey, flecked with old dried blood. He looked at me and I swear I heard a creaking of long dead tendons scraping as the thing turned its head. Poor sucker was missing its lower jaw, so he wasn't a great threat. Nothing to bite with.

I smashed the curved end of the crowbar into his forehead, tearing away the loose rotten flesh. His head caved in with a crunch and a splat. Treacly, half-congealed blood rolled down its face. The thing backed off.

Not wasting any more time, I swung again. The whole top of the creature's head buckled inward, a slop of brain and bone falling onto the warm pavement. It groaned and pitched forward face first.

One down, one to go.

The other shuffled towards me. She was a girl, probably not much older than thirteen, when she'd had her abdomen scooped empty. Her raggedy, blood-stiffened top was bowed inward, no supporting flesh behind the material. She still looked fairly fresh. Maybe she was one of the unlucky ones from the evacuation point.

Again, the crowbar hurtled through the air, ripping into her forehead. The crowbar jerked as I wrenched it back towards me, tearing skin and bone away from her head. Her forehead came away with a rending sound, the flap of skin hanging down and obscuring her face. Blood, less congealed than the other one's, pattered onto the floor like raindrops. Spinning the crowbar round, I jabbed it viciously into the gaping hole in her head, spearing her brain. She swayed for a moment and then toppled without a sound.

There was no time to be hanging about mourning these people. I had to get my stuff and go. I risked another glance around me. The road now seemed totally empty. The unreality of my situation hit me. I was the only living thing on a street that had once bustled with people doing normal, everyday things; buying pizzas, visiting the bookies, going to the off-licence for beer and fags.

My eyes began to fill, but I pushed the impulse to cry into a deep corner of my soul. This was no time to be blubbing like a kid lost in the street. If I didn't make this quick, then I'd be joining the Deaders. The lot at the top of the street were still milling about, but they wouldn't be doing that for long if they saw me. It would only take one to spot me and make his move. The rest would follow his lead.

Without thinking, I kicked the door as hard as I could. It flew open with a crash that reverberated up and down the silent street. My friends from up the road were bound to have heard that. You had to be profoundly deaf not to, even if you were dead. The next few moments were like an insane version of Supermarket Sweep. I grabbed a wire basket, shoved in everything I could get my hands on and sprinted across the road, taking a quick glimpse to my left.

The horde seemed oblivious. They still milled around on the horizon, disinterested in me and my little expedition. Finally, a bit of luck. I don't believe in guardian angels or any of that shite. The fact that the dead have risen and started to eat the living had kind of put the kibosh on the whole 'Higher Power looking out for the Believers' thing.

I made it back in, threw the series of bolts that kept the gate locked and went inside, trembling from the adrenaline rush and almost insanely happy.

The shopping's been put away, I've eaten, and now the dark is beginning to sweep in. You don't realise what true night looks like until all the power's gone. The streetlamps are just ornaments now. Even the flickering light of a candle seems puny against the night. The day's worn me out. Staying alive has become a lot more tiring these days. It puts everything that went before into its true perspective. No more work, financial or relationship worries. The only thing I have left to do is survive. And that drains more than your body. It takes it out on your soul.

Wednesday

The morning has finally arrived. I didn't sleep well. Every now and again I'd come around in a soupy stupor, convinced that I could hear a car and gunshots outside. My body was too exhausted to respond to the simple task of getting up and having a look. I drifted back off, only to come around yet again to the sound of civilisation. By the time I'd dragged myself out of bed to have a look, whoever it was, had gone. I crawled back into bed and just lay there, hearing stretched to breaking point, but there were no more sounds. The thought kept bouncing around my head, round and round like an irritating carousel. What if I'm not alone? Are there any other holdouts out there? Where are they?

I must have dropped off again. When I finally woke up, a thin sliver of light came through the curtains. Alert and semi-refreshed, I got up and wandered around the top floor flats checking the streets for any signs of activity. There seem to be more Deaders today. They're still pretty spaced out, not a huge cluster fuck of them like there were during the evacuation massacre.

That doesn't really reassure me though. Just where the fuck did this lot appear from? If more of them start appearing, it's going to make getting out and about more difficult. I might have to chance a trip outside to see if there's anywhere safer, or maybe a car that hasn't been junked. One fuck of a tall order, I know, but options have to remain open at a time like this.

Looking out of my flat window, I saw something odd. A Deader lay on the road, thrashing about. It was a bit hard to tell from this distance, but it looked like someone's run him over. His abdomen was concave. There was a red puddle around the creature's middle and loops of grey stuff, almost like thick, grey, silly string strewn across the road. If I didn't know any better I'd have said that someone had mown that poor fucker down. He kept trying to sit up, but the damage was too much. He flopped back down and raised a ruined hand in the air, as if he was trying to catch the attention of a passer-by. Two or three other Dead shuffled past it. They weren't interested. The meat has to be fresh and alive, not grey and maggot ridden. Maybe, just maybe, those sounds I heard last night were real. Mulling on that, I moved away from the window, sat down and started to write.

Loneliness does strange things to the mind. I've been alone for over a week now. No contact with any living being. I'm excited by the thought that there could be others like me, trapped and alone. The excitement fades as reality bites. A thought enters my head; the Dawn of the Dead motorcycle gang. What if these survivors are looting, thieving, redneck bastards?

Considering the tint of my skin, would it really be a good idea to reveal myself? They might not be like that, but these days, there's no telling. It's not as if I can pick up the phone and call some hotline to report a racist incident now. Not that that shit was any good when the world was normal.

It might be better to stay out of sight just for now. See if these guys—or even ladies—make themselves known. Play it by ear, see what they're about and go from there. If they're good guys, cool.

If not, then I'll either have to avoid them, moving from this spot, or I'll have to find a way to take them down, individually. Fuck it, even if they're good guys, I might have to play it like that.

Being the hero counts for fuck all in a world as fucked up as this. To be fair, it didn't count for much in the old world. Heroes were distinctly thin on the ground back then.

Sometimes you have to do what's right to survive and every now and then, I keep getting a horrible feeling. Did I do something bad to end up in the safety of these flats? The whole evacuation saga is still jumbled up in my mind. The only clear image I keep getting is keys stained with blood, and the high piercing scream of a man in agony. My mind keeps slamming a shutter down when I push too hard. Am I hiding something from myself? That's a question I can't answer. Maybe it's one that I don't want to answer.

I spent a long time just lying there on the rickety, moth-eaten sofa after breakfast. The silence had descended again. No cars, no loud music, not even a dog bark. Just the blood rushing through my ears, that hissing noise that I only ever noticed on the margins of sleep or drunkenness. That noise used to comfort me once. Now it's a reminder of how alone I am. There's nothing to hold my attention, to stop my mind from going to Defcon Four. I got up a few times. The creaks and groans of the building settling had transformed into something more sinister. At one point, I swear I heard the dry rustling of air being pulled into dead lungs.

I forced my brain to think about more pleasant noises—the lads on a Friday, the roar of a football crowd, the moans and groans of lovemaking—but those thoughts made me gloomy. If I carried on like this, I'd go mad within a few days.

I can't stop the dread though. The dread that maybe I am the last one standing in a town of the dead and that the silence will eventually kill me.

Sometime, in the darkest depths of night, I'm roused into a half awake state. I'm sure I can hear a dog barking outside. My mind's playing tricks on me. You see, our dead friends are quite partial to dogs, as well as cats, horses. Giraffes. The dirty fuckers eat anything basically. I bet they'd even go for a Pot Noodle if someone jammed one into their dirty, leprous faces.

The dog's barking is getting more frantic by the second. I lie there in a soupy, half-conscious state. Even if I could move, what could I do? It's dark, as in arse-hole dark. There's Deaders out there. As much as I love dogs, I'm not going to risk it.

Eventually, as I knew they would, the barks turned to furious cries and howls of pain, which, though mercifully short, stay with me long after the world becomes silent. The dog's screams of agony propel themselves around the confines of my skull, only dimming as I fall back into the arms of sleep. Before the night takes me, I decide, in that strange groggy way that you do before you finally fall asleep, that I'm going to kill myself tomorrow.

Thursday

I'm sure that the squished Deader is my local M.P. I've been watching him for about ten minutes now. He's trying to sit up again and his intact but very pale face has struck a chord in me. The only way to confirm it is to go outside and have a closer look, but that's not an option at the moment. If it is him, I'll smash his head to a pulp. Horrible little bastard, he was. Never did anything for us back in the day except claim ridiculous expenses and make up ridiculous policies. They all did.

Anger begins to boil up. I push it away, burying it deep down. Anger clouds your judgement, leads to mistakes. I come away from the window and settled back on the sofa, gently drifting on a cloud of nothing but the blood in my head. It's only later I realise that there is absolutely no sign of the dog from the night before. Either I imagined it, or those boys are hungrier than I thought.

Either way, I'm not comforted. I'm not comforted at all.

The roar of an engine and the crack of gunshots woke me up. I wiped my face and bolted to the window, nearly collapsing when I saw what was outside. There were three men in the streets blasting away at the Dead, clearing the street out. I could see them, mouthing words to each other, but I was too far away to get anything they were saying.

I knew at once what they were all about, though. One of them was dressed in an S.S. uniform, probably nicked from the local costume shop. This guy had longish hair. I couldn't make out his features clearly, but that didn't matter. His sartorial taste told me what I needed to know.

The other two were dressed up in regulation bovver boy gear, head shaved down to the skin, MA-1 flight jackets and cherry-red Doc Marten boots. The white laces, denoting fascist sympathies, left no room for doubt. I groaned inwardly. God was having a laugh. The only human company I'd had any chance of getting to know, and they were all fucking fascists. Thanks a fucking bunch, God, or whatever the hell you are. I was close to tears. This wasn't fair.

The taller of the two skins looked directly at my window, gesticulating wildly with his pistol. I ducked away from the curtain that instant, convinced that he'd seen me. I stood there trembling for a few minutes, my heart jumping as I heard the clanging of the gates. When I looked again, Tall Skin was kicking the gate for all he was worth. Nazi Man walked up to him, grabbed his shoulder and pulling him away, leading to a full on argument—at least that's what it looked like—in the street. They screamed into each other's faces. I only caught a few words but I'm guessing that they've put two and two together. Why else would the gates be locked from the inside?

My heart leapt into my mouth. I realised that I hadn't locked the back gate, only bolted it. The Dead wouldn't be able to figure the bolts out, but these twats would. And if they got in—

I looked out of the window. Tall Skin and Nazi Man had calmed down and seemed to be having a polite discussion. There was no sign of Baby Skin. He was either in the van or he was poking around, looking for a way in. I knew what I had to do. Grabbing the key, I made my way downstairs, as quick and as quiet as I could. Getting out of the ground floor level wasn't easy. They were still at the front gate. If they'd looked through the frosted glass panels of the front security door they'd have seen me. I hugged the wall, gripping my trusty crowbar, and shuffled to the back door, out of sight around a bend. I stood there for a few moments, waiting for the shaking of my legs to subside.

Once more in control, I opened the back door. The gate seemed clear. Maybe Baby was back at the van. Just to be sure, I moved into the overgrown grass lining the path, and crept along. Anyone standing at the gate would have a clear view of the door but nothing else.

There was a snort and a splat. A large, glistening gob of phlegm flew through the railings. That was Baby accounted for. Pushing myself up against the wall, I gripped my crowbar, still trembling with fear and trying my best not to breathe to fast. I had to move quickly. If he raised the alarm, I was dead. A pale, thin hand groped for the deadbolt.

Resisting the urge to smash his hand off, I waited. The bolts were being thrown in steady succession. Time slowed down at that point. I got into position, raising the crowbar. The gate squeaked open and Baby bounded in, so focused on the back door that he didn't even notice me. The crowbar swung. I put every bit of strength into that blow. The boys head crunched and he flopped to the floor. No time to lose. I shut the gate, threw the bolts, and locked it with my keys. Baby lay face down on the gravel path. Blood seeped from the cut on the back of his head.

Dragging him out of sight, I placed him under the huge bush that held court in the middle of the grass. You remember what I was saying about survival and having to do what you have to, to stay alive? I did it. I took the Stanley knife I had in my pocket and brought out the blade. I agonised over this, I really did. Baby looked barely out of his teens. His chest was rising and falling, a bit unsteadily. He was still alive. If he stayed that way, he would tell his mates and that would more than likely be the end of me.

I took a deep breath and pushed the carpet knife's blade into his throat, jerking it across. The boy's eyes flew open and his hands went to his throat. Blood fountained out, spraying my face and the grass, as the boy bucked and writhed. He looked at me with accusing eyes. There was a moaning in the air. Took me awhile to realise that it was me, not a deader at the gate. That's when the realisation hit me. I had to get Baby inside and finish the job. If I left him out here, the scent of blood and fresh flesh would bring the horde to me.

In a frenzy, I grabbed his boots and dragged him inside, slamming the door behind me. The flat to the left was still out of view of the main front door. I always left this one unlocked. It served as a spare weapons cache, and another place to stay if I got fed up of being upstairs.

I dragged Baby Skin into the darkened flat, leaving a snail's trail of blood. The choking sounds were becoming less frequent now, but I wanted this over and done with.

"I'm sorry," I whispered, and knelt down on the floor.

It took me ages to take off his head. By the time I had finished, I was bathed in blood and bits of gristle and meat. In a fog, I stripped my bloody clothing and left it on the floor of the flat. Stood for an age just looking at the headless body, a sick, fetid feeling inside me. Is this what Deaders feel when they've turned? There was no way back from this. I'd killed this kid to survive. Can anyone ever come back from that without being changed?

I'm not sure that I want to know the answer to that.

Friday

I couldn't bring myself to write any more yesterday. After sluicing myself down with freezing water, I cracked open a good bottle of Glenfiddich and curled up on the sofa, trying to drink the demons away. I'm not so sure it worked, but it certainly helped me sleep. I think it's the only thing that'll help me sleep these days. I'm kind of glad in a way that everyone I know is most likely dead. Life's a fucking bitch right now without the added strain of being accused of alcoholism. The dead are on my door step, eating anything that moves. The only humans I've seen in weeks, probably months, are gun toting, looting, neo-nazi bastards. And, to add to all this cosmic fun, I decapitated a young lad, no more than seventeen years old, just to save my own worthless hide.

Compared to this litany of horror and total disaster, being an alcoholic is small fry, wouldn't you say? These justifications, and more, begin as soon as the bottle is opened and continue on, long beyond the point where coherent and logical thought has been smashed into the wall by a tide of piss-warm whisky. I pass out where I fall down, on the floor, mouth agape.

When I wake up, I'm still glued to the mohair. I'm sure that my cheek now has the carpet pattern engraved into it, but I could not give a flying fuck at this point. This morning has that horrible grainy film feel to it. Colours, or at least the colours I can see from my comfy spot on the floor, look washed out, and the thin sliver of light coming through the gap in the curtain is like a razor slicing into my eyes. My tongue feels too big for my throat; my mouth is so parched that for a second I can't even open my mouth. A silver bolt of pain smashes through my liver like an enraged rhino.

It's been a long time since I had a hangover. I'd sworn off the booze before this thing kicked off. Done pretty well too. There's no one around to castigate or keep chewing my ear off about the demon drink and the other ten million clichés about alcohol, so there's no need to worry anymore. I'm about to fall off the wagon with a resounding crash. After everything that I've seen and done, I think I deserve a drink.

With a slow, Deader-like movement, I sat up, grimacing as the world decided to spin around at light speed. An acid belch wormed up from my gut. Jesus, I thought to myself. Hangovers really are the worst feeling ever. Until you have another drink. There was a horrible second where I reached for the bottle and nearly tipped it over. I gripped it as if it was the most precious thing in the world, and to me at that moment it was. A few hefty slugs later, I felt semi-normal. Well, at least I thought I did. I was probably as smashed as I was last night, but I didn't care. Yesterday's incident had pushed me closer to an edge that I was now precariously walking along.

I'm a killer. Another image comes swimming into my half sober mind; the crowbar swinging and hurtling towards flesh and bone, but this time it wasn't the boy. The hair was too sparse and grey. The image melted away, and I tried to make sense of this. Drink? A nightmare? Something that I'd done and had buried away in some fetid little storeroom in the back of my mind.

A shotgun blast came from outside, pulling me into the present. It was muffled, almost as if it was in the distance, and it definitely wasn't coming from the side street. I stood up a little too fast. The world began to grey out at the edges again. Another hit from the bottle sorted that out. I got to the rear flat and looked out onto the main street.

Lanky and Nazi were by the gate. The blast I heard must have been one of them taking pot-shots at the few Deaders skulking about on the other side of the road. I almost smiled until the realisation hit me that these two twats were drawing a lot of attention to themselves. With dawning horror, I also realised something else: in my haste to get Baby out of sight, I'd left a smeary trail of blood that lead from the spot where I'd hit him, onto the grass and right to my back door.

They'd obviously seen it because the pair of them were intent on smashing the gate in. Fuck! Fuck, fuck, fuck! More Deaders were beginning to appear, drawn by the commotion and the scent of living flesh. The gate swung open, almost off its hinges, and they stormed in, not bothering to shut the gate behind them. The blasts I heard must have been them shooting at the lock.

So much for my nice little redoubt. Kicking myself for being careless, I sobered up in an instant. They'd be on me very soon. I had to get armed and make a final stand. Panicked, I ran back to my flat and started gathering up weapons, including the pistol I had robbed from Baby Skin. Now, I've never fired a gun in my life, but I had to learn quickly. My life depended on it.

The downstairs door crashed open. I heard them clattering into the hallway. In their rage they'd obviously abandoned stealth. Closing my apartment door as quietly as I could, I cocked the gun and waited. They'd obviously found the body.

The air was torn apart by vile screams, insults and vivid descriptions of what they were going to do to the killer. It sounded like there were a hoard of them down there. Furniture was being smashed. There was a tinkling of glass, then a whump sound which really made me nervous.

If that was what I thought it was, then I was right-royally fucked. The footsteps thumped up the stairs. I held the gun in front of me. My arms trembled slightly, both from shock and the hangover. Sweat began to run freely into my eyes. I could just about make out their footsteps over the sound of my own heart trying to claw its way out of me. The footsteps went silent. For a second, I heard an all too familiar wailing and moaning from downstairs. We had guests to this little party and they would need to be fed. I almost laughed. The sanity that I had tried so hard to cling to was vanishing rapidly. I tensed.

The door flew open with a resounding boom, splinters of wood flying into my face. Without thinking, I pulled the trigger. The figure in the doorway jerked once and fell heavily. Through the smoke I could see it was Lanky. There was a huge hole in his head.

Lucky shot! I grinned and pulled the trigger a second time as Nazi flew in like a dervish firing in all directions, but nowhere near me. Maybe he was so mad he couldn't aim straight. He hit me with a force of a truck and we both smashed to the floor.

"Bastard, bastard, Paki bastard," he hissed at me. Spit flew from his jabbering mouth onto my face, the smell of it making me feel sick. He drew his arm back, fist clenched. Without thinking, I jabbed my thumb into his right eye, pushing as hard I could until I was rewarded with a squishy *pubph!*

He fell back, screaming, raising his hand to his wounded face. Freshets of blood ran down his right cheek. I just lost it then. Snarling, I dragged him into the small living room and threw all the deadbolts, aware that the moaning noises were getting louder.

Nazi tried to stand but it was too much for him. The long haired scruff sank to his knees. I picked up the large machete by the sofa and stood in front of him. He snuffled and whimpered.

A blast of memory surfaces, unbidden and unwelcome and I'm catapulted back to another time.

We're running—me and Wells, the caretaker—running from the car park. A Deader horde is close behind us. I've got a crowbar in hand, its weight comforting, but much use against a major horde. Wells lags behind me. I can hear his wheezing, his pleas. He wants me to slow down, he can't keep up. I slow to a jog, my heart leaping into my throat as I see the horde behind us. They may be slow but they're gaining ground. Wells falls to his knees, his chest expanding and contracting. I look down on him. He looks up at me, and mutters thanks.

He's slowing me, a dead weight. He's going to get us both killed. It's got to be me or him. Maybe he'll keep them distracted. There's a brief moment of hesitation before I swing the crow bar down on his head. He falls forward, tries to get up, but I hit him square in the jaw. His face takes on a peculiar, lop-sided look. He reached out to me, eyes pleading. I see the keys, stained with his blood, snatch them from him and run....

The truth has knocked the wind out of me. I return to reality. Nazi is weaving about in front of me, a red trail dripping from his mashed eye socket. He must have got away when I had that blank moment.

"Got ya, Paki," he shouts, triumph in his voice. There's a thumping at the door. I guess the guests have arrived. I look down at my stomach, frowning at the blossoming red stain. The long haired lunatic waves a knife of his own, leering at me. It's not very big. The damage will only be a flesh wound. I laugh at him, the wooden handle of the machete smooth in my hand.

"Afraid not," I say.

I'm very calm, considering I've been stabbed. Maybe because the end's coming? It's all spiralled out of control so quickly. New world, new rules, I guess. I'm not going to survive this, so I go for broke and I lash out with the machete, still smiling, still calm. The huge blade passes through Nazi's neck. He looks puzzled, blood dribbling down his chin. I pull the knife out and move closer, pushing it deep into his gut, jerking it from side to side. He groans and falls onto me. There's a sting of pain as he stabs me in the side and twists the knife. The sting blossoms into fire and we both scream and fall to the floor. I push him away and he rolls onto his back, choking and twitching. The banging on the door gets louder. It's a heavy wooden fire door. It should hold a little while longer. Hell, I'll be dead pretty soon anyway and they'll sense it and go back to the aimless wandering they did before.

Nazi's breathing becomes strained. Not surprising, really. I manage to untangle most of him with the machete. His internal workings are now a jumbled, slick pile on the floor next to him. There'll be no rising, not for him. I've decided to take the fucker's head off. It's the least I can do. This cunt and his stupid friends ruined everything. There's no way on Earth I'm letting him come back. I hold my wound with one hand and bring the machete down on Nazi's neck with the other.

This is my last entry. I've managed to keep it together and coherent for some reason that I've now forgotten. I'm forgetting a lot of stuff as death approaches. I wonder if this is normal, or whether it's all part of the process. Pretty soon, it won't matter anyway.

The whisky's all gone now. My vision's starting to darken, bit by bit. I must be nearly there. It's getting harder to hold the pen. I can smell my own blood in the air, rich, tangy. The smell of the dead now seeps under the door which is starting to buckle. There must be a lot of them in that hallway, all pushing up against each other, vying to be the first to taste fresh meat. Had I not been so badly injured, I'd be really upset. Fuck it. I think it was always meant to happen this way. It was either this, starvation or insanity. This is the lesser of all those evils, even though I didn't actually choose it.

It's nearly time to go. I can feel bits shutting down inside. My eyes are heavier and the door has started to splinter and crack. This is almost like the ending of a George A. Romero flick. No one wins, no one loses. The status quo remains. Good old George. God bless him. I wonder if that was my MP smeared across the road. I never did get to—

THE WORLD STOPS
WHEN THE SMILING MEN CRY

"MALKY."

He ignored the whisper, not wanting to draw attention to himself. He was too exposed. All exits had been covered by the Smiling Men. The only way to escape was to stay incognito, to blend in with the Saturday shopping crowd and pray that Lady Luck was feeling generous. He made a show of being engrossed in the information screens around the square that played the same message over and over again. Michael's Mantra, they called it—Hope Brings Unity. Be Hopeful, Be Unified, Behave! The litany had not changed since the day Brother Michael, Sister Penelope and the Arch-Pastors had taken their 'social revolution' and twisted it into something terrifying.

"Malky".

Again the insistent whisper. He did not turn to look. There was no need. He knew the nasally, London inflected voice anywhere. Malky sighed.

So much for discretion, Asghar. Fucking idiot.

Malky walked backwards a few paces until he was level with the man. He spoke out of the corner of his mouth, his voice low, tone partly exasperated, part menacing.

"You do know the meaning of the word 'inconspicuous', don't you?"

He watched Asghar nod from the periphery of his vision, the man's long, sallow face serious.

"Course I do. I'm a journalist, aren't I?"

Yes you are, Malky though sourly. *Not a very good one, though.*

"So how's whispering my name in public inconspicuous then? There's ears everywhere. You should know that, Mr Journalist."

Asghar looked down at the cracked and dirty pavement, suitably admonished. Malky softened a little. The journalist looked chastened enough. He turned his head.

"Codename."

Asghar nodded. "Yes, Malak. We'll stick with that."

Malak. Arabic for 'angel'. Close enough to his real name and his nickname to be used without arousing suspicion. Maybe that's why Denver had chosen it. Malky certainly did not regard himself as an angel. Society would not either. He had done terrible things to undeserving people. The time for penitence was here.

"Why are you here anyway?" He kept his tone friendly. Asghar smiled. Somehow, the expression didn't soften his features. The smile accentuated his nose, transforming him into a leering, bearded clown. Malky hid his distaste.

"Denver sent me. He's had word that Arch-Pastor Michael and Sister Penelope are coming here to address the protestors."

Malky raised his eyebrows in surprise. Emotional displays were so rare from him these days. Only a mention of his former employers could raise even a flicker of feeling from him.

"Interesting. Why would Arch-Pastor Michael come here? He spends most of his time ignoring the rest of the country in favour of the capital shit-hole. Why come to Brum?"

Asghar looked at him, his expression overeager. "Denver says that he's come to explain the Approved Music Act and the Arch-Pastor Agreement. Hoping that people will calm down over it."

Fat chance, Malky thought sourly. Of all the intrusive edicts passed by Arch-Pastor Michael and his second-in-command, Sister Penelope, the Approved Music Act had hit a collective nerve. Music was there to be listened to, to be used as a balm or a stimulant. It was not there to be subjected to the whims of rulers who felt threatened by its messages.

The Act had been Sister Penelope's brainchild, the result of much consultation with the Social Justice League of Britain and North America. Unacceptably masculine or aggressive music was to be banned outright. Punks, rappers, and even classical music lovers who still listened to the great artists of old, such as Oasis, would have their favourite entertainment wiped out. Riots had erupted within minutes of the announcement.

Malky was not surprised. Sports, books, games—all of the arts had fallen under the scrutiny of the Social Justice League and their poster children. The world was becoming duller, more joyless and more dangerous even than it had been under the stewardship of Call-Me-Dave and the 'Eton Rifles'. They, at the very least, had an excuse for being dull. Cyborgs often were. It was a side effect from having had their flesh replaced with machinery. At the very least, the Social Justice League had outlawed most Cyborg Enhancement and decommissioned Call-Me-Dave and the Eton Rifles.

Small mercies indeed.

"This could be our chance to take them out."

Malky shot Asghar a warning glance. If one person heard the sedition, they would both be dead. The S.J.L. did not take too kindly to brown people whispering treasonous words, despite their avowed anti-racist stance. It had been a ploy, a means to take power before revealing their true intentions. The people had felt betrayed and the Resistance was growing.

Asghar looked away. Malky looked at his watch, then back at the throng of people gathering in front of the old Council Offices. Placards decorated the gathering. Various sound systems blasted out banned hits in defiance of the law. A mock-up dummy of Sister Penelope, uncannily accurate right down to the red hair, was held aloft. Malky grinned.

She's not going to like that.

The Lady was notoriously sensitive and thin-skinned. Mocking her and her appearance would have serious repercussions for the poor effigy-maker. Penelope was known to exact punishment herself. She wasn't very forgiving, despite the sweetness of her demeanour and her ageless, wrinkle-free looks.

The atmosphere began to change. The party mood from a few moments ago gave way to an edgy silence.

"Heads up, As. They're about to move in."

Asghar looked around nervously. Malky pushed his way to the front of the crowd, leaving the nervy journalist behind.

Right on time, he noted. He hated being right about this, but he had created the situation. A line of trucks rumbled in from the far left side of the square, stopping with a hiss of air brakes. Doors opened. The hushed air gave way to the stomp of booted feet and an awed gasp. Malky looked over, moving back a little so as not to be seen.

And there they are. My children. His heart jumped as the vehicles continued to disgorge large, black-uniformed figures. They lined up, marching forward in unison, face masks pulled down. He knew what was behind those masks. He also knew what to expect. Shock and awe, they had called the effect. How right the planners were.

The massive figures stopped a few feet away from the outer edge of the protest. People moved back, muttering nervously to themselves. Most of them had seen this unfold on television. To experience it in real life was more frightening. One of the black-clad giants stepped forward. He stopped, his arms hanging down at his sides. He raised his hands, gripping the black helmet. His companions did the same, the effect unsettling. As one, the figures pulled their masks off. The crowd gasped in collective horror as the Smiling Men revealed themselves.

Malky, sickened by the sight, forced himself to remain rooted to the spot. This was his doing, his creation. He had to see what he had created, how it was being put to use.

The lead Smiling Man stepped forward another pace. A camera drone appeared from nowhere, hovering around the Smiling Man. There were more gasps as the Vid-Screens around the square blazed to life, all of them showing the Smiling man in full, glorious colour. Malky stifled an acidic burp, gazing in rapt attention as he studied the thing he had helped to create. The creature's pallid skin stood out in stark contrast to the ebony of his uniform. Like his fellows, he was completely bald. There was not one hair on his head and face. His eyes were covered by a fusion of sunglasses and binoculars that protruded from his face. The high definition image on the screen showed the fine tracery of scars around the equipment. His pale skin was smooth, wrinkle free.

The magick still works then. Wonder who they got to take over from Grimoire after I killed him?

He would ask Denver when he returned to Deritend. The Smiling Man dropped the helmet, the sound of it hitting the floor, startling some small children in the crowd. They should have been terrified by now anyway. The pallid visage, dark goggles and smooth skin was made even more frightening by the wide toothy grin worn on the faces of all of the Smiling Men. The smiles were fixed in place by surgery, brainwashing, a combination of drugs and, of course, Grimioire's *majicks*. What had originally been an attempt to give a friendly face to law enforcement was now a travesty of life and humour—pallid, soulless clowns who could only smile for eternity but never laugh, nor even speak naturally.

A vocoder and loudspeaker was buried in the throats of each one of them. They didn't even break their smiles to speak. Technology had taken care of communication.

The leader surveyed the crowd. Malky recognised the tactic. He had programmed that into them. He was scanning for weak spots, potential entry points for the squad. Standard tactics. Someone tugged his jacket. Irritated, he turned. Asghar hopped from one foot to the other, agitated.

"We'd better go, man. Word is, more units are heading this way. They're going to block off all the exits, kettle us in."

Malky nodded.

"I know. Standard Pacification Program Nineteen-seventy-three. A *Garuda* should be on its way too."

"So why are we still here? You're wanted and I'm not exactly Mr Popular with the S.J.L. at the minute."

Malky sighed, looking down at the floor. How could he explain his self-loathing to the young journalist? What possible turn of phrase could make him understand that Malky had to see his creations in action? He had created this. Others, such as Grimoire, Range and Call-Me-Dave, had expanded on his work. Arch-Pastor Michael and the S.J.L. had taken it further, after breaking their promises to stop the Smiling Man Project.

But the final responsibility lay with him—Malkit 'Malky' Singh— gifted cyber-surgeon, activist, last of the Great Magi, and a butcher. He felt the weight of the lives ruined by his work. It was a never ending lodestone of shame that he carried on his shoulders. Witnessing what his 'children' could do would remind him of the utter failure that his own hubris and blind adherence to ideology had led him to. He gave Asghar a penetrating stare. The journalist shifted, uncomfortable with his gaze.

"You go. I'll make my own way back. Go on. Get out of here. Tell Denver that the plan still goes ahead tonight. I just need to see something first." Asghar, relieved at being given permission to go, made as if to speak. A look from Malky silenced him. He nodded, pushing his glasses up the bridge of his nose.

"Good luck. See you later."

The journalist melted into the crowd. Malky sighed with relief. It was one less thing to worry about. Now he could enjoy the show. He made his way back to the front of the crowd.

The protestors waited. The air of expectation was heavy, laced with the metallic sting of fear. The lead Smiling Man opened his arms in a welcoming gesture.

"DEAR CITIZENS". The voice was harsh and metallic with an odd inflection. It was a sing-song voice, emphasis being put on the wrong words, as if the creature had never been taught to speak properly. "THIS GATHERING IS UNAUTHORISED. IT DISTURBS THE PEACE, HARMONY AND UNITY THAT WE STRIVE TO ATTAIN EACH AND EVERY DAY. YOUR CONCERNS HAVE BEEN NOTED BY THE AUTHORITIES. PLEASE DISPERSE IN AN ORDERLY AND GOOD HUMOURED MANNER."

The enhanced voice echoed around the square.

No one moved. The leader scanned the crowd again.

"PLEASE   DISPERSE.   FORCE   IS   UNPLEASANT   AND UNHARMONIOUS. WE HAVE NO WISH TO HURT YOU. HOWEVER YOU ARE BREAKING EDICT ELEVEN STROKE THREE OBLIQUE ONE. UNAUTHORISED GATHERING LEADING TO DISRUPTION OF HARMONY AND UNITY."

Malky smiled despite himself. That was a new edict. It had the hallmarks of Arch-Pastor Michael all over it—vague appeals to harmony and unity but little else. The Eton Rifles had never bothered with such niceties. In their day, The Smiling Men would have marched in, breaking up the protest with a minimum of fuss and a maximum of force.

The silence held for a few moments. A lone voice broke it.

"Fuck off, you freaks!" The crowd, finding its courage from this one dissenter, began to murmur in agreement. An object flew from the throng, striking the leader in the chest. He didn't flinch. Smiling Men felt no pain. The pain receptors in their brains had been switched off, or rather burnt out. The leader looked down at the projectile, then looked back up. Without a sound, he bent down and grabbed his discarded helmet. He scanned the crowd one last time. There was no emotion on that face. It was a blank, null and void.

As one, the Smiling Men put their helmets back on.

Malky swallowed, his throat dry. He knew what was coming next.

In unison, The Smiling Men pulled extendable batons from their belts and primed them. A low-level humming filled the air as the battery packs engaged, transforming the batons into portable cattle prods. The crowd, frenzied now, began to hurl placards and other projectiles at the ranks of the Smiling Men. The creatures held firm. Not one of them moved.

Malky made a fist and bit into the meat at the side with anguish.

The Smiling Men moved forward, graceful and poised. Their marching gathered momentum and pace as they charged into the crowd.

Screams, dull thuds and an obscene crackling filled the air. Malky watched in horror, his eyes watering as the stench of cooking meat filled the air. The Smiling Men were not pacifying the crowd. They were char broiling them. The batons had been set to maximum. One touch was enough to kill instantly. His brain froze as he watched Smiling Men jab their batons into their victims, leaving them pressed against bare flesh and skin.

Greasy smoke began to fill the air as several protestors burst into flame. The Smiling Men waded through the dead and dying in complete silence. He saw a young boy, only about twelve, being hoisted from his feet. His captor forced the baton into the boy's mouth with ease, flicking a switch. The boy shrieked as arcs of electricity rippled across him. The Smiling Man stood still, even as the boy's corpse began to smoulder. Only when flame burst from the dead child's nose, ears and eyes, did he let go. He dropped the body and went off in search of another victim.

Sickened, Malky turned, pushing his way through the crowd. Faces of all colours filled his vision, mostly drawn and pale with shock. A few looked on in glee, enjoying the spectacle of mass carnage. Rage boiled inside him. He looked for a likely target, someone to vent his anger against. A young skin-headed boy, dressed in the brown shirt and sash of the S.J.L. Leader Guard stood to his right. The young man was almost salivating, his eyes half closed in orgiastic delight.

Malky pulled the switchblade from his pocket, opening it. The boy didn't notice him until the moment the knife plunged into his gut. His expression turned to one of bewilderment, then shock as Malky jerked the knife upwards, only stopping when the blade scraped against his sternum. The boy croaked, blood spilling from his lips. Malky stepped aside, letting him crumple to the floor to join the thick, greasy coils of intestine that had fallen from the wound.

He moved faster, pushing people out of the way. The switchblade, still sticky with the boy's blood, he closed and put away. His rage subsided for the moment, the kill taking the edge of it. The crowd thinned as he reached the main road. Malky looked down at himself. Amazingly, there was no blood on him. A miracle.

He turned left, walking up the main street towards the hover-bus stop. A roar filled the sky. He looked up. A dark shape blotted out the sun for a moment. He squinted, trying to get a clearer view. It was a *Garuda*, Mark II, by the looks of the fin section. The markings told him who the owner was. It was Arch-Pastor Michael's personal heli-plane.

Malky stopped, considering his options. This could be a golden opportunity to kill the Brother. He dismissed this out of hand. There was no way of getting close to him. To even attempt assassination here would be suicide.

No. It was better to stick to the original plan. Putting his head down, he hurried to the hover-bus and got on, paying his credits and heading to the back of the bus. A few more people got on in silence. Their pallor, and the vomit stains down their fronts told him all he needed know.

Malky squeezed the corners of his eyes, trying to stop the tears.

He failed.

The bus pulled away, leaving behind a street full of thick greasy smoke.

Denver sat in a darkened corner of the old, creaking warehouse. A plump spider skittered across his foot before shambling off into the dark and the dust. He watched it disappear with envy.

Being able to vanish. How I wish that I could vanish so easily.

Vanishing was nearly impossible in the world today. Along with C.C.T.V, bank cards for currency, and G.P.S. fixing in communication devices, there were also the Chips, another innovation floated by the Eton Rifles and put into practice by Arch-Pastor Michael. The chip, a subcutaneous tracker no larger than a pinhead, enabled the S.J.L, the Smiling Men—even the Arch-Pastors—to be able to watch citizens permanently. The signals were relayed to various points around the country —Counting Stations, as they were known. A central point for receiving the information would only be more vulnerable, easy to knock out. Denver gave the S.J.L. credit for their security. He also gave Malak credit for his cyber-surgery. None of the Resistance members possessed their chips anymore. Malak had removed Denver's personally and taught the doctor-men how to remove the others. The rest of the population would have to wait, just for the time being. Things were about to change.

A door creaked open at the far side of the warehouse. A large figure sauntered in, briefly silhouetted against the light of the sun before it closed the door behind it. Denver squinted, trying to make out the features. It couldn't be a Smiling Man. The figure was too broad. He opened a drawer and pulled out an ancient projectile weapon. The Smith and Wesson may have been old, but it still worked. Denver knew this with some regret and sadness. The Leader of the Guard cadre he had shot had left him with no choice. The knowledge did not make him feel any better.

"Den?"

He smiled. The deep voice, warm and pleasant, was recognisable. The Old Coventry twang made it even more so.

"Out the back, Barrington. How is it out there?"

"Fucking diabolical. The Smilers are out everywhere bashing people."

Denver grinned, cheered by this thought. The plan was working well. With mass protests erupting all over the city and Arch-Pastor Michael on the scene, the Smiling Men would be pushed to their limits. There were too few of them, and reinforcements from London and Manchester would not be able to reach them in time.

Barrington stepped into the light. His youthful face broke into his trademark smile. He shook Denver's outstretched hand, his huge brown paw engulfing the older man's. Denver bade him to sit, which he did, perching his powerful frame precariously on an old, beaten office chair. The chair creaked and groaned under the weight of all that muscle.

The young man had been a cage fighter and mixed martial artist once, before Sister Penelope had brought in the edict banning 'aggressively masculine sports and entertainments'. He had gone from being a star earning a good living, to a young, angry man fighting to survive. Joining the resistance had been a logical step for men like Barrington—disenfranchised and cast out by a system that claimed to represent them, only to spit in their faces when power was attained.

Denver knew the truth of this. He had, after all, been part of the S.J.L.—idealistic, anti-racist, anti-everything. He had joined the movement hoping for change under the near-fascist regime of Call-Me-Dave and his cyborg cronies. When the change came and Arch-Pastor Michael swept to power with all the promises of hope, unity and equality for all, Denver had been right there, at the heart of it all. He had witnessed history in the making, the culmination of years of hard work and struggle. Now, he wondered what it had all been for.

The S.J.L. had become as fascistic as its predecessors, passing nonsensical edicts that flew in the face of human nature, micro-managing every aspect of the lives of the citizenry—even entering into unholy alliance with unsavoury shadowy groups such as the Plantagenet Foundation, Leader Guard and the Inquisitors. He had helped spawn a monster. It was time to kill the monster off once and for all.

He looked at Barrington, pulling himself back into the present. There was little point in dragging up the past. What was done was done. It was time to fix things.

"My boys are all ready, Den. As soon as Malky gets back, we'll get moving." Denver nodded, scratching the end of his nose in silent contemplation. He noticed Barrington staring at him intently.

"Nerves, my friend, nerves. We've planned this moment for so long and now it comes to us. Things have a habit of rolling around quickly."

Barrington nodded in agreement. "They do. But the chance is here now, in our laps. If we can take the Smiling Men out, then Arch-Pastor Michael is helpless. He'll have to listen to us."

Denver saw the sense in that statement. Barrington did as well. He was not the only one feeling betrayed by the S.J.L's about face.

"He will indeed. The Edicts will be rolled back, the P.F, Leader Guard and The Arch-Pastors will be rounded up and shipped off. Maybe we can even get the Collider shut down once and for all as well."

Barrington smiled again.

"Told ya. Let's have a bit of optimism around here."

The two men lapsed back into silence, each one studying the plans for the final act.

Malky crossed the piece of scrub with haste. The old, ramshackle warehouse was still there. He felt relieved. After the horror of the Square, he felt on edge, tense, expecting everything to blow up in his face. He reached a door with a keypad on it, carefully entering his code. Malky took one last look around the waste ground, which had been known as a 'bomb peck' in the days before the S.J.L. and the Eton Rifles.

The hairs on his neck rose. He paused before entering the building, scanning the area. The bomb peck was hidden from the main road by old tattered billboards on three side, and by the river Rhea on the fourth. No sane person would try to wade through the Rhea. The water was a filthy gold and brown sludge so toxic that it killed within minutes. It was not a pleasant way to go. He had seen someone fall in once, by accident. The girl had been knocked over during a scuffle with some S.J.L. activists and pitched face-forward into the sludge. She had surfaced once, but by then it had been too late. Her face had been obliterated, running like tallow down her front. He could still hear the choked gargles as liquid remains ran down her throat.

He looked up at the sky. All clear. There was not a heli-plane or camera drone in sight. The sky was a brilliant azure, a rarity these days. Most days it was a sullen lead blanket, morbid and oppressive. The feeling of being watched intensified. Someone or something was definitely watching him.

Cut it out, for fucks sake. He was getting paranoid, or at least more paranoid than normal. Shaking the feeling off, he stepped into the cool, dusty darkness of the warehouse. Once inside, he could prepare a *magick* to flush out anyone in hiding, if indeed there was. He was still a Grand Magus, after all. The Last of the Magicians.

"The wanderer returns."

Malky shook hands with a grinning Barrington, settling down on a seat next to the huge man. Denver looked more serious than normal. His lined face looked drawn, haggard. His white hair stuck out at crazy angles as if he had been tugging at it in frustration. He had the look of a man who hadn't slept in days.

"Good to have you back, Malak." Malky smiled at this. Denver was the only one who insisted on calling him by his codename at all time. They all had one. Barrington was 'Zulu', a reference to the days when football wasn't outlawed and football fighting was still indulged. Denver was known as 'Moses', a prosaic reference to him leading his people to the Promised Land. Malky had picked that one himself.

"We're still go for tonight", Denver said. His voice was cracked and tired. "Barrington says that the Smilers are spread out too thinly. The Small Heath Apex is ours for the taking. We can get in, insert the program and be out before anyone spots us."

Malky nodded, satisfied. "You got the disk?"

Denver nodded, patting his trouser pocket. Malky grimaced. For a man who prided himself on security, the disk wasn't very secure.

"You do know how important that disk is don't you Den?" The older man nodded. "So why keep it in your trouser pocket?"

"Easy access, my friend. Besides, this is Deritend. Our turf. Who can get to us here? The local Smilers are all out in the city, the S.J.L. cadres are awaiting their glorious leader. No one can touch us here."

Barrington murmured in agreement.

"I'd still feel better if it was secure—" Malky stopped abruptly, looking around. "Where's Asghar?" The other two shook their heads.

"Not seen him", Barrington said.

"I told him to come back here. He should be back by now." The feeling of paranoia and dread he had felt earlier returned, more intense and ferocious than before. Something was wrong. Asghar would never risk being on the streets for too long. The journalist was timid by nature. His instinct would have been to get to safety quickly, and safety these days meant Deritend.

"What's wrong?" Barrington was now alert, concerned at the look of haunted fear on his friend's face. Malky put a finger to his lips. The men fell silent. Denver switched off the small desktop lamp, plunging the warehouse into a semi-gloom.

They sat and waited, senses stretched to their limits. Paper rustled, followed by a squeal. Malky looked into the dark. It sounded like a rat. The warehouse became silent once more.

"What's got into you?" Denver's whisper was strained. He heard nothing. Malky glared, his finger still pressed to his face. He gestured for the others to get up.

"We have to go. Now."

The warehouse shook as fists pounded on the door.

The men froze, looking at each other. Fear lined their already strained faces. The banging continued, growing heaver, more insistent. The walls wouldn't stand for long. They were made from sheets of corrugated iron, not designed for a sustained onslaught. Light seeped through fractures in the structure as the walls began to buckle inwards.

Malky looked around frantically, searching for any possible exits. There was no time for a ritual, not even a quick one, such as the Suite of Concealment. They were trapped. The only options left were to bluff it out or fight it out. There was no middle ground.

The main door blew open. Sunlight flooded in, blinding the three men momentarily. Malky gripped Barrington's arms, tugging him back. They all shielded their faces from the flying shrapnel.

Nothing moved.

The smell of cordite, sweat and expectant fear filled the air. Shapes moved around in the sun-drenched day beyond the remains of the door.

"What do we do now?" It was Denver. His voice was reedy and thin.

"Nothing. Yet." Malky looked across at Barrington. The big man was relaxed, his arms hanging loose by his sides. His face was blank, his mind running through all possible strategies.

"Let's see what happens."

It was the only course of action left to them.

Two figures appeared at the savagely tattered remains of the door—one tall and thin, the other shorter, slightly rounded. They stepped through the door. The taller of the two opened its arms in a gesture of welcome.

"Mr Denver. It's been too long." It was a young voice, the Northern inflections soft and friendly. Behind the two figures, a bulkier mass obscured the daylight. The men hissed. It was a Smiling Man. The shape was unmistakable.

Denver stepped forward as the figures drew closer.

"Arch-Pastor Michael. Sister Penelope. This is a surprise."

Arch-Pastor Michael laughed. "31-10. Lights please. I do hate talking to people in the dark."

The Smiling Man marched smoothly past its masters, and stood before them. A crystal blue column of light blazed from its skin, bathing the interior of the warehouse in a cold glow. Denver and Barrington watched, open mouthed.

"You never said that they could that", Barrington whispered.

Malky chuckled softly. "You never asked me if they could."

Arch-Pastor Michael spoke a little louder, cutting them both off.

"That's better. Would you agree, my lady?"

Sister Penelope stepped forward laughing, a lunatic screech devoid of any joy or amusement. She was younger than Michael, her pleasant, round face adorned with a short-cropped and vividly red hairstyle. She was dressed in a neutral blue singlet and trouser, the cloth cut in such a way as to disguise her curves. Arch-Pastor Michael was thinner, taller, long faced. He had the disaffected air of a student trying to stay awake during a lecture. His dirty blond hair was neatly combed and parted. He wore the same type of outfit as Sister Penelope, a black sash cutting across his midriff. They were every inch the poster children they had been groomed to be.

The Smiling Man, 31-10, took up a guard position by Arch-Pastor Michael's right side. It was helmetless and goggle less. Its eyes were wide, staring in perpetual awe. The grin was fixed firmly in position, a permanent legacy of its creator's intention and an incantation that paralysed the muscles totally.

Malky stared at the thing in horror and recognition.

"Ah, Dr Singh. I brought someone special with me. I'm sure you recognise 31-10?" Malky nodded, speechless. Barrington nudged him.

"What's going on?" Malky shook his head.

"I'll explain later."

Denver moved closer to the pair. 31-10 swivelled on his heels and put up a hand.

"PLEASE REMAIN WHERE YOU ARE. ANY FURTHER MOVMENT WILL BE CLASSED AS A THREAT AND DEALT WITH ACCORDINGLY."

Denver nodded his understanding.

"How did you find us? More to the point, how did you sneak in?"

Sister Penelope laughed again. It was such a cruel sound from so attractive a face. "Stealth *Garuda*. First edition prototype. *Michael* and I thought we'd give it a test run. It works beautifully, don't you think?"

Denver had to agree. They had no inkling that a *Garuda* had landed until the doors had been blown away. He frowned. The Lady had only half answered the question. Before he could speak, Sister Penelope held up a small delicate hand.

"Your friend Asghar. He was most forthcoming. We picked him up not long ago. It's amazing how an amnesty, as well as a generous stipend and job offer turns people's heads."

Malky reeled in shock.

The little Judas bastard.

No wonder he had been so eager to leave the demonstration. Barrington squeezed his fists. He had vetted the journalist himself, despite his own misgivings.

"I should have killed the little fucker when I had a chance."

Penelope laughed melodically, a mock look of disappointment on her face.

"Now, now Barrington. There's no need for vicious attitudes. We're all friends here. We want to work with you to provide peace, hope and unity for the citizens. Why do you still insist on fighting us? What is wrong with you people?"

Denver bowed his head. He whispered.

"Because you betrayed us."

"I'm sorry. What?" Sister Penelope cocked her head. "Speak up little man. I can't hear you". Denver looked up and turned around, a sad smile on his face. He gestured to his friends before turning back.

"Maybe you'll hear this." He screamed and charged forward, barrelling into Sister Penelope. She squawked as she hit the floor hard. 31-10 spun around, marching towards the smaller man. Denver pulled a sheath knife from his tunic and leapt towards the fallen Lady. 31-10 caught him by his head and flung him into a wall. He hit the metal with a crunch, groaning as he slid down the wall into a crumpled heap.

31-10 moved towards the battered and broken Denver, pulling a long, black tube from his belt. Denver squirmed, trying to sit up. The Smiling Man pointed the object and pressed a button on the hilt. Flame roared from the end, engulfing Denver. He shrieked as the fire ate into his clothes, licking eagerly at his skin. 31-10 did not relent, keeping the steady flow of flame going. Denver tried to stand. He reached out, burning skin and sizzling fat falling from his arms. The Smiling Man stood statue-like, watching dispassionately as the man burnt to death.

Denver groaned and collapsed into a spitting, bubbling heap. Only then did the Smiling Man stop the flame. Denver sighed and curled as his life ebbed away. The fire stiffened and cured his cooking tendons.

Arch-Pastor Michael, helping Sister Penelope to her feet, admired the gruesome spectacle, the ghost of a smile on his face. He sniffed deeply, savouring the aroma of burnt cloth and roasted flesh. His eyes shone.

Barrington roared, charging forward. Malky stood, frozen in horror and disbelief. Thick, cloying smoke filled the atmosphere. 31-10 spun smartly as Barrington smashed into him. The Smiling Man did not flinch, rooted to the spot as the former cage fighter bounced off him, hitting the ground.

Barrington leapt to his feet, swinging a huge brown fist toward the side of 31-10's head. The Smiling Man caught the blow with an open palm. Barrington groaned as his knuckles popped. He shuffled backwards, dismissing the pain, one thought in his mind. He was going to take the freak down, no matter the cost to himself. He steadied himself momentarily before launching a high roundhouse kick. His boot made contact. 31-10 rocked a little but stood firm. He looked at his assailant, his face expressionless, save for the perpetual sick grin.

"CEASE AND DESIST YOUR ATTACK. YOUR EFFORTS ARE FUTILE. CONTINUED ASSAULT WILL RESULT IN TERMINATION." The soulless voice, amplified by the vocoder, echoed around the cavernous space. Barrington paused.

"I'd listen to him, if I were you. Smiling Men don't make empty threats." Arch-Pastor Michael smiled brightly. His face was flushed, he was aroused by the violence. Confused, Barrington looked back at Malky. His friend nodded slightly. Breathing hard from his exertions, the cage fighter stepped back, regarding 31-10 warily. The Smiling Man did not respond. Barrington jabbed a finger at the creature.

"Ok. Truce."

The Smiling Man looked away for a brief second. In an instant, 31-10 moved forward with impossible speed. Barrington, unprepared, raised his arms to ward off the attack but it was too late. He shrieked as The Smiling Man speared his left eye with a finger, bursting the delicate orb. The cage fighter fell back, clutching his eyes. Blood seeped out from the gaps between his fingers. He collapsed to his knees.

"ASSAILANT INCAPACITATED."

Malky rushed to his friend's side, crouching down.

"I'm ok." Barrington's voice sounded dreamy, shocked. Malky looked up at the Smiling Man.

"Why?" He demanded. "Why do that?" The Smiling Man looked up at the ceiling, considering his response. None was forthcoming. Arch-Pastor Michael snickered.

"New programming, Doctor Singh. People fear mutilation more than death these days. It's not enough to kill your enemies. If you're prepared to do that little bit extra, you're truly feared."

Malky stood, his face full of hatred.

"This isn't how it was supposed to be."

Sister Penelope giggled again. She wrapped an arm loosely around Arch-Pastor Michael's shoulders, giving the scientist a mocking look.

"You can't be that naïve, can you? The Smiling Men were never going to be the peacekeeping force you envisioned. Look at him. Does that look like the face of peace and harmony?"

Malky glanced at 31-10.

He shook his head. She was right. How could it be? The pale skin, all pigmentation leeched from it to bring uniformity. This was the Social Justice League's racial policy in all its glory. Harmony through homogenisation.

He could make out the fine traces of blue veins under the almost-transparent flesh; the eyes, fixed and staring, wide open in an expression of shock; the smile, designed to be friendly and welcoming, but in practice sinister and threatening. A Smiling Man could never be an instrument of peace, not in the way he had planned. They were tools of intimidation and control, nothing more, nothing less. He saw this now, had seen it from the moment the first Smiling Man had emerged from its healing cocoon.

The memory burned him, shame and self-loathing erupting from deep within. His excitement had ebbed away in the face of the creature he had helped to create. He had found a way to extend the lives of terminally ill people and give them new meaning and a task for their new lives. As the first Smiling Man had stood before him, healed from the surgery and from the rites and rituals performed by Grimoire, his own naivety and good intentions had sickened him. He had been used, his cyber-surgeon skills twisted and warped to create a shell. Grimoire's magic had transformed the minds of his 'children', changed them from living, thinking people, into soulless, amoral monsters.

He took a step towards 31-10. The Smiling Man remained still. He moved closer until he was stood directly in front of him. Malky raised a shaking hand and lightly touched the Smiling Man's cheek. He shivered at the coldness of the skin. It felt like the face of a corpse.

"31-10", he whispered. "You were the first."

Again, the Smiling Man did not respond. Malky knew that the creature wouldn't. All past memories were locked away deep inside the creature's mind, all emotions pushed away by the *magicks* wrought by strange and twisted Grimoire, supplemented by Malky's own technical and surgical skill. The Smiling Man remained still, statuesque. Malky withdrew his hand, studying 31-10's face. It was a face he had known all his life. This was Arch-Pastor Michael's gift to him, a final way of twisting the knife. What better way to break him than to bring his first victim to the party? His first subject, who had volunteered so willingly, knowing that there was nothing left to lose, that his last moments on Earth would be filled with agony and fear as the cancer ate away at him. His first subject, a man who believed in his skills as salvation.

Malky gazed into the face of 31-10. A tear rolled own his cheek.

31-10, the first of the Smiling Men.

31-10, his crowning achievement.

31-10, his own flesh and blood.

He gazed into the slack, dead face of his elder brother.

"This can end, you know", he whispered.

31-10 remained inscrutable. He had never been much of a talker in his normal life. At least that was one thing that Malky had not taken from him.

"How? Your disk? The one that was on Denver when we burned him? Asghar told us about that plan too. He has certainly earned his reward today."

The mockery in Sister Penelope's voice was scathing. Malky ignored her, even though she was correct. The disk had contained a program, a virus developed by himself, with help from Denver and other members of the Resistance. It was to have been introduced into the collective consciousness of the Smiling Man, stripping away the dark conditioning, dragging the memories of who they once were back into the light. The Smiling Men program would have collapsed as the creatures remembered their *lives*. The S.J.L. would not have been able to maintain control.

It didn't matter. The disk had been important, yes. But there was another way, one that was a little slower, but would have the desired effect.

Some incantations, some *mugicks,* took time and ritual. The rites had to be followed with precision. Others, however, were effective as phrases. They did not require any special preparations, merely a mouth to utter them and a voice to give them shape.

Malky smiled.

He had been holding onto this magick for a long time now, ever since he had devised it and, under the cover of secrecy, implanted it. It would take time for this to spread but it would work. He *knew* it would work. Belief and power were essential to it working.

"31-10. Listen to me very carefully. I'm going to tell you something."

Arch-Pastor Michael shuffled over. His eyes narrowed.

"What are you doing?"

Malky's smile grew wider. "I'm giving my brother some much-needed wisdom. It took me awhile to learn it, so I thought I'd share it with him." He gazed up at the monster, fondness in his eyes. "We shared a lot through our lives, you know."

Arch-Pastor Michael pointed a finger at him.

"Stop this. Stop this right now and I'll make you sure your death is easy and painless."

Malky laughed. "I'm a dead man anyway. I have been for a long time now. I couldn't just lay down. Not until this was over. 31-10!"

The Smiling Man looked down, his attention fully on the man who was once his little brother.

"Wisdom. This is wisdom that must spread. Understand?" Curiously, the creature nodded. It recognised the voice as that of its creator, rather than a blood relation, but that recognition was enough. Malky inhaled, held his breath for a moment then spoke loudly and clearly.

"The World Stops When the Smiling Man Cries!"

A soft throbbing began to rise, as if from all around them. They all looked around questioningly. All except 31-10 and Malky.

"Remember and repeat. The World stops When the Smiling Man cries."

The throbbing became heavier, more insistent

"31-10! REPEAT! THE...WORLD STOPS...WHEN...THE...SMILING...MAN CRIES!"

The deep pulsing became a subsonic thud. 31-10 staggered back as it hit him. He paused for a moment and looked at his brother.

Eventually, the Smiling Man straightened. Looking ahead, he spoke haltingly at first, his words gaining strength and power with each utterance.

"THE. WORLD. STOPS WHEN THE SMILING MAN CRIES. THE WORLD STOPS WHEN THE SMILING CRIES, THE WORLD STOPS WHEN THE SMILING MAN...."

Malky threw his head back and laughed, a good, clean, unburdened sound.

Arch-Pastor Michal and Sister Penelope glared at each other in bewilderment.

31-10 did not stop. He continued to repeat the phrase in his lilting mechanical voice.

The pain had subsided to a dull rotten ache. He could feel the remains of his eye pressing against his palm. The air was tangy with his own blood. Jumbled thought caroused through his mind—his first pint, an away day to a grim Northern town surrounded by friends, all watching each other's backs—riots, the inorganic yet soft features of Call-Me-Dave expounding on his vision for the country and the world.

Gently, Barrington pressed his hand to the ruin of his left eye, gritting his teeth against the sheet of agony running through him. He breathed deeply, reaching to the breathing exercises taught to him from a young age in various *dojos* around Birmingham. His mind became focused, calmer. He looked around. Malky and the Smiling Man were locked in a gaze. Was he seeing things? The Smiling Man had an expression on his pallid face. The staring eyes did not seem as wide as they had been. The look had softened. What did that phrase mean? Why was he repeating again and again like a stick record?

Barrington got to his feet. It didn't matter, not for the present anyway. There was still a fight to be had. The chances of surviving this were slim, but he wouldn't go down on his knees. True to his codename, he would fight it out like a Zulu, like a warrior, head held high. For the moment however, he would observe, analyse the situation. When the moment presented itself, he would be ready.

Arch-Pastor Michael seethed inside. This charade had gone on for long enough. Denver was dead. The Resistance was now leaderless. Their figurehead was now a charred, greasy mess on the floor. It was time to finish this. He felt a keen sense of disappointment. Bringing 31-10 with him was a deliberate ploy, a means to knock Singh off balance. He had hoped that being confronted with his own handiwork, with his own *brother*, would have shattered Singh's sanity. The man was more resilient that he had thought and resilience meant danger—danger to him, to Sister Penelope, to the Brave New World that he intended to create. Hope and Unity could only be achieved with a cowed populace, too frightened to step out of line. The Smiling Men were his means to achieve this end. And that was why Singh had to die, here and now. He was the only one who knew the weak points of the Smiling Men project. And he was the Last of the Magi.

Michael reached into his tunic, slyly.

Singh was too distracted by the mad Smiling Man to notice. He wondered what the meaningless phrase, repeated over and again by 31-10, actually meant. It sounded empty, cod-philosophy made up by a dead man walking. Unless—. A horrible thought gripped Michael. Could it be a *magick*? That was impossible. Even a man of limited magical knowledge such as himself, knew that *magicks* took too long, were too complex to be distilled into a single word or phrase. If Singh had discovered how to do this, he could become the most powerful man on Earth. Michal shook his head. This was not happening. Not now, not ever.

Carefully, he pulled the knife from his tunic and held it behind his back. Sister Penelope glanced and nodded as she mirrored his action. As one, they moved forward.

Malky waited. It was working. The hard glare of 31-10's eyes were beginning to soften. The spell coded into the phrase 'The World Stops When the Smiling Man Cries' was beginning to unravel the mental blocks put in place by Grimoire. He had no idea how long the process would take. It was untried, untested. No matter.

The die was cast. He would have to wait. He noticed movement from the corner of his eye. It was Arch-Pastor Michael and Sister Penelope—the new dictators, architects of a bleak and humourless future.

"What did you say to him?" Sister Penelope drawled, the mockery dripping from her voice. "Is that from your childhood? A stupid little nursery rhyme? A phrase from a song you both listened to as children? Were you hoping to stir a memory, get our friend onside?"

Malky looked down at his boots, smiling. What could he possibly say to this child in a woman's body? They drew closer. He turned to face them. They looked tense, Michael especially so. Malky shrugged.

Without warning, Michael sprang forward thrusting his arm out. Malky *oofed*, his breath slammed from his body as the skinny fist made contact and twisted. He heard a *rip* as the Arch-Pastor pulled his hand up, unzipping him with the keen blade. Agony flared throughout his abdomen. The knife cut through his stomach, the wound opening up like a bloody mouth. Blood pattered to the floor. Shocked, Malky simply stared, his mouth wide open. Sister Penelope screeched, swinging her arm in an arc. There was a gristly tearing as her knife plunged into his neck. He pulled away, slapping a hand onto the ugly rent in the side of his throat.

The murderers stepped back, breathing hard, both grinning, flushed with the thrill of taking another's life. Malky staggered backward, blood jetting from his neck, intestines uncoiling and hanging from his front. He whimpered as he fell into the arms of Barrington.

"Malak!" Barrington eased him to the floor, cradling the dying man. Malky looked at him, his eyes fogging over as his life poured from his ruined body. "Stay with me, man. Look at me, look at me!"

Malky mouth moved. He gurgled, blood pouring over his lips.

"Try not to talk, ok?"

The blood became deeper, richer, flowing more freely. Barrington watched helplessly as the light in Malky's eyes faded. He gurgled once more and went limp.

31-10 watched the scene, trying to make sense of the images that blossomed in his mind. He saw the man on the floor as a young boy throwing a ball, mouthing words that he couldn't hear. The image distorted, twisting and fading into a red, tinged with black. Screams shattered the air around him, heat crisping the hairs in his nostrils. He was strapped to a table, thrashing around. The air was suffocation, thick with the stench of shit and blood. Winged creatures flew high above, eyes glowing, ragged wings flapping frantically. A word came to him unbidden: *Hell.*

31-10 shuddered involuntarily. Another image flashed before his eyes—a man in a white coat, middle aged, eyes magnified by thick glasses, his round, jowly face mournful as he delivered a verdict.

"Three months, maybe more if you look after yourself."

Needles of shock and grief pricked him as the information sank in. On the heels of this, he saw the man on the floor again. They were sat in a white sterile looking room. The man on the floor—Mal?— spoke in hushed yet hopeful tones.

"It'll work, bro. I'm telling you. This will work."

More images rushed forth. They came thick and fast, too fast. 31-10 staggered at the onslaught. It was too much. He saw a baby, knowing instinctively that it was this Mal—two boys in school uniforms posing self-consciously for the camera; the thrill of pride as Mal stood on stage, dressed for an occasion that he could not yet fathom, being handed a roll of paper; faces that he recognised—mother, father, cousins, uncles, aunts, friends.

31-10's life unfolded before him, the realisation of who and what he was shocking his system. He began to tremble violently, clutching at his head. Too much! It was too much. He threw his head back, his agonised roar flat and metallic as it burst from his vocoder.

The two Arch-Pastors jumped, startled at the outburst from the Smiling Man. Michael and Penelope dropped their knives in surprise. Barrington saw his opening and took it. Gently laying his dead friend down, he leapt from his crouching position, barrelling onto Michael. The thinner man did not stand a chance, crying out as a rib snapped from the sheer force of Barrington's heavy body smashing into his. The men fell to the floor, Barrington astride Michael's chest. He said nothing. Words were inadequate for the loathing that he felt for this man—loathing at the broken promises, the lives destroyed, the principles shattered. The Arch-Pastor whimpered and began to plead, his voice high and whining.

"If you let me go, we can forget about all this. You can be rich. Yeah, rich and powerful. Come on, man. Just think about it."

The wheedling tone of his voice made Barrington sick, increasing his disgust for this creature, this creature who had the blood of thousands on his soft, young hands.

This creature who had cynically promised the world to the downtrodden and disposed, left behind in the wake of the Cyber-Despot, Call-Me-Dave.

This creature, unrepentant to the last, looking for ways to save his skin.

Barrington shook his head and wrapped his strong hands around Michael's throat, squeezing with all his considerable strength. The Arch-Pastor thrashed around beneath him, his face changing from white to purple in seconds. His eyes bulged, his tongue lolled, drool running down the side of his face, turning red as the hands squeezed relentlessly. Barrington increased his grip, not stopping even as bone crunched and disintegrated. The Arch-Pastor stopped moving, the life draining from him. Still, Barrington did not let go. Fury blinded him. He continued, the dead man's neck feeling rubbery, full of splintered bone.

Someone shrieked behind him.

The sound barely registered.

Sister Penelope watched as the black man murdered her counterpart. She made no move to help him. This was expedient. The coon could do the hard work of removing the Arch Pastor. With Michael gone, she could now be the sole ruler of Britain, no power sharing needed.

Michael may have shared her vision, but he just didn't go far enough. He was weak, indecisive at times and worst of all, he was male. He wouldn't have understood the need to subjugate the Male Species. He would have fought her. This nigger had done her a favour. Michael was gone and she didn't even have to lift a finger. All that remained now was to kill him. There would be no witnesses left. She would be free to concoct any story and the public, stupid sheep that they were, would believe her. She could even spin this to show her own heroism, taking down the big, strong darkie that was guilty of the killing of the Nation's beloved Arch-Pastor.

She looked around, her eyes lighting up as she spied the flame baton discarded by 31-10. Scooping it up, she took a moment to familiarise herself with the controls. The *black* had his back to her, still intent on throttling a corpse.

Perfect.

He wouldn't know what hit him and by the time he figured it out, it would be too late. He would be cooking.

She raised the baton, aiming it at the broad expanse of Barrington's back.

Goodbye, you black bas —

She screamed as a hand gripped her hair, yanking her backwards. The baton clattered to the floor. Sister Penelope struggled as she was lifted up. She kicked her legs uselessly.

"Let me go!"

"NEGATIVE. REQUEST DENIED."

31-10? As if in reply, she was jerked upwards again with such force that her scalp tore slightly. A thin trickle of blood ran down the centre of her forehead.

"31-10, what are you doing? Let me go!"

"NEGATIVE. YOU MURDERED THE ONE KNOWN AS MALKIT SINGH. MY BROTHER."

In spite of the pain and terror, Sister Penelope felt confused. How could this be? All past memories were wiped away. How could 31-10 know this?

"I...I...I REMEMBER."

The Smiling Man let her drop, then spun her around. She looked up at him, dwarfed by his sheer bulk.

"31-10", she pleaded. "Please. Stop this. We can fix you. We can fix all those unwanted memories."

The Smiling Man shook his head. The normally blank eyes were suffused with anger. The smile, as always, remained untouched. It always would. Only *magick* could correct that and the last of the true magicians was now dead. Sister Penelope swallowed, her throat now dry with a crippling terror. 31-10 placed a hand on each side of her head.

"I REMEMBER BECAUSE THE WORLD STOPS WHEN THE SMILING MAN CRIES. DO YOU NOT SEE? THE WORLD WILL STOP WHEN THE SMILING MEN CRY."

Sister Penelope cried out as 31-10 squeezed his hands together, the pressure vice-like. She tried to pull the hands apart but it was no use. 31-10 was too strong. Her skull began to crack under the immense force. Her jaw popped and dislocated. She struggled furiously as her cheekbones caved in. Her left eye *plubped* from the socket, to hang against her cheek. For a few seconds, the world looked insanely upside down, seen through that eye. 31-10 flexed his muscles. Sister Penelope's head, unable to withstand more, splintered open with a wet, sucking sound.

Before she died, with her good eye she noticed a solitary tear running down 31-10's pallid cheek. It was followed by another, then another, until the tears became a torrent.

The Smiling Man was crying

The world fractured and went dark as 31-10 crushed the life from her.

The silence was oppressive. The smell of death was heavy in the air. Smiling Man and Fighting Man looked around at the carnage, then at each other. 31-10 had scooped up his brother's body. He couldn't remember why, not yet anyway, but he didn't want to leave his brother's corpse behind. There was something that he needed to do with it. The knowledge would come. Even now, gaps were being filled. He could feel a warm wave, coursing through his nervous system, the blocks and programming being soothed and removed.

Barrington sighed with sadness. His two closest allies and friends were gone, and he was now half blind. It was not a victorious day. The Arch-Pastor and the bitch queen were now dead, but others would be there to fill in the gaps. The S.J.L. was too big to remain leaderless for long. Everything now depended on 31-10 and the effect of the mysterious phrase.

"YOU REQUIRE MEDICAL ASSISTANCE. I WILL TAKE YOU WHEREVER YOU NEED TO GO."

Barrington nodded his thanks.

Where would he go? That was the question. Would he even need to hide? The one witness to the killing of Sister Penelope was now his ally, at least nominally. There was no trail leading anyone to his door.

No, he wouldn't run and hide. There was too much to be done here. The Resistance still needed him. He would remain here in Birmingham. There were plenty of safe houses across the city. He could lie low for a short time, have his injuries attended to and then get back to work. The Resistance would not die, not on his watch. He owed it to Malky and Denver. And he also had a score to settle with the traitorous journalist Asghar.

First things first.

"Maybe it would be better to burn this place down?"

31-10 nodded. "AGREED. DESTRUCTION OF FORENSIC MATERIAL IS A DESIRABLE OUTCOME. THERE MUST BE NO POSSIBILITY OF EITHER OF US BEING EXPOSED."

It made sense for both him and the Smiler.

"What will you do now?"

"I HAVE BUT ONE TASK. THE SMILING MEN MUST CRY AND THIS WORLD MUST STOP. WHEN THAT FUNCTION IS COMPLETE, I WILL LEAVE." 31-10 nodded, satisfied with his own answer.

Barrington paused, stifling the question he had. He didn't want to offend the creature. Besides which, he was tired and in pain. The answers to all his questions would reveal themselves in the fullness of time.

See, Malky? Even I can be philosophical when I want to be.

He smiled. 31-10 looked at him, head cocked in a gesture of curiosity. "YOU ARE AMUSED?"

Barrington waved the question away. "Doesn't matter. Come on, let's get destroying, and get out of here. There's a lot to do."

The Smiling Man nodded again. This time, the gesture was more natural, more fluid. Whatever Malky had done, it was working. If all the Smiling Men were exposed to this, there would be chaos. The government would no longer be able to enforce their edicts. Maybe that had been Malky's plan all along. It would be fitting if his brother was the catalyst for this.

He looked at the creature. The world wouldn't stop when the Smiling Men cried. It would merely change. And that was all they could hope for.

DENOUEMENT: BLOOD AND SULPHUR

DARROW WAS BORED NOW. His lunch break was over, his cigarette break welcome but too long. It was time to go back to work. Cameron had been with the prisoner, Null, for two hours straight. He knew he should relieve his superior. Darrow walked hurriedly through the grey, featureless corridors, his internal radar honed from months of repetition and a great sense of direction.

Darrow rounded the corner. The guards were no longer outside Interrogation Room 31-10. Pulling out his gun, he moved stealthily but quickly, his danger sense on fire. He put his hand on the door knob and readied himself.

One, two…

The door swung open. Darrow flattened himself against the wall, gun raised, butt end first. Anyone walking out of the interrogation room was getting brained first, questioned later. No one came. Confused, he crept through the door into the sparse room.

"Ah, Mr Darrow."

It was Null. The man looked at him, beaming. He glowed with health; radiated it, in fact. Cameron sat across from him, silent and unmoving.

"Boss?" Darrow tried to keep the note of apprehension from his voice. He failed. Something wasn't right here. Cameron had not responded to him. He sat staring at Null. Darrow could see the ghost of a smile on his face, even sideways on. "Boss, you ok? Where are the guards?"

Null sighed, a happy sound. "The guards are…indisposed, shall we say? And Mr Vale is perfectly ok. I've been keeping him entertained. Haven't I, Cameron?"

Cameron Vale nodded slowly and spoke, "You have." His voice sounded dreamy, thick and far away as if he had been hypnotised.

Darrow raised his gun, pointing it at the strange, foreign man. He moved closer.

"What have you done? Eh? What...the fuck...have...you...done?" He jabbed the gun for emphasis. Null remained unruffled, a look of mock offence on his swarthy features.

"Me? I've done nothing, my friend. As I said, I've merely been keeping Mr Vale entertained." Darrow narrowed his eyes in suspicion as Cameron nodded. He looked almost translucent, as if he was fading from the world. Null leant forward, his voice dropping to a confidential whisper. "I've been telling him stories."

Cameron laughed softly. Null joined him. Darrow stepped back, looking from one to the other as if both were insane. Cameron's laughter began to degrade into sobbing. "Please, no more. No more stories. I can't pay the price anymore. It hurts too much."

Darrow looked at his boss. Pink tears streamed from Cameron's cheeks, becoming thicker and redder. His face, once cool and calm, began to contort in agony. Darrow blinked as Cameron's skin rippled. Something underneath the thin layer moved, frantically. Null put a finger to his lips.

"Sshhh. It'll all be over soon, Cameron. All the hurt, the anger, the frustration. I'm taking that away and more. It won't be the end. You'll be immortalised. You will be a Tale yourself, someday. Would you like that?"

The sobbing man nodded as his tears became thicker and more profuse. Darrow stepped back, unable to process what he was seeing. The gun was still pointed at Null.

"Whatever you're doing, you stop it! Right now!"

Null shook his head, smiling regretfully.

"It can't stop. Not now, not ever. The Tales need to be told, you see."

Darrow clenched his jaw, his anger flaring. "What Tales?"

Null stood, smiling.

"I thought you'd never ask. The Tales, Mr Darrow. The Tales of despair, greed, arrogance. The Tales of the darker parts of this Omniverse, the parts that you and the rest of this miserable existence keep poking with a stick, wanting to see what rears up and shows its fangs to you. The Tales that form part of my punishment for leaving a story incomplete, for having the bad grace to die before finishing."

As Null stretched to his full height, Darrow noticed something odd about the man's left leg. He looked closer, nearly dropping the gun at the sight. Null's left leg was no longer there. Instead, a thick, beige tube of flesh sprouted from his hip, supporting the man. Instead of a foot, the tube curled around and traversed the floor, much like a snake. Darrow followed it with his eyes, his throat closing. The tube was wrapped around Cameron's lower half. It pulsed obscenely with sick life. With every pulse, Cameron diminished, as if it were draining him dry.

Darrow, fighting the urge to vomit, brought the gun back to bear on Null. "Let him go, now."

Null held up his hands. "Impossible. He would die and everything that he was would be wasted. This way he lives on in me and, in a sense, I will live on through him."

Darrow's temper exploded like old sweating dynamite The time for debate was over. He rushed forward, gun raised, ready to smash Null's head in. The deformed man grabbed him by the throat and lifted him effortlessly. Darrow struggled, trying to prise apart the grip. He dropped his gun.

"Stupid child," Null said mildly. "Do you really think you could hurt me? I've lived lifetimes, my friend. I've touched and tasted things that would drive you to insanity if you caught even a glimpse of them. I've travelled this world and others, gathering stories, gathering *khuna aur gandhaka* unending, while you rolled around in your own filth, learning how to live."

He squeezed a little more. Darrow coughed.

"I could kill you now and take your *khuna aur gandhaka*, your blood and sulphur. Who would stop me? *Unit Cabal*? Unlikely. They have tried so many times. The only reason they caught me this time was because it suited my purposes at this time. It won't happen again unless I will it."

Darrow pulled at the hands in desperation. Dark shapes nibbled at the fringes of his consciousness. His head felt large and heavy, his lungs were bursting, screaming for air. Null's voice came to him through a murky echo chamber.

"Would you like to become a *Kahāni ki Khuna aur Gandhaka*?"

Darrow tried to shake his head.

"Of course, you wouldn't understand Hindi. A miserable Little Englander, such as yourself wouldn't bother to learn a 'brown language.' Hindi is the closest analogue to my own native tongue, you see."

Null paused, a stricken look on his face. "Home." he whispered. The moment passed. He turned his attention back to the choking man. "I asked you if you would like to become a *Tale of Blood and Sulphur*? That's the price Cameron and all the others before him have paid. I tell the tale, they give me their blood, their sulphur. Of course, the process kills them. You humans are so fragile. How did you ever crawl from the primordial slime?"

Spots began to dance in front of Darrow's eyes.

"I'm going to kill you now. Null goes free, the Tales will still be told and I can now hide from my enemies in plain sight."

Null increased his grip.

As Darrow blacked out, he noticed Null's face shifting, rearranging to take on the shape of another man. Darrow died, and the last thing he saw was Null's body wearing Cameron's face.

Null threw the limp body into the corner. It landed with a crunch on top of the guards he had dispatched earlier. He turned back to Cameron. The man lay face down on the table. Null hadn't even noticed his passing. No matter. His usefulness had ended. Null had his blood, sulphur and his identity. Cameron Vale, the real Cameron Vale, no longer existed.

He went easy enough.

Null closed his eyes and concentrated. The feeding tube unwrapped itself from the dried husk that had once been Cameron Vale, shrinking back into Null's body. He grimaced, bone cracking, as the tube reformed into a normal, skinny leg. *It never used to hurt before.* Maybe age was finally catching up. Whatever it was, he could muse on it later. He had needed new clothes and a new identity. Cameron closely matched him.

Null stripped the corpse quickly and efficiently, discarding the dried remains into the corner. He dressed, satisfied with the cut and fit of the dead man's clothes. Searching through his pockets, he found Cameron's proof-of-identity and wallet.

Excellent. Time to go.

One thing remained.

One minor detail.

The pile of corpses in the corner. The guards had been unfortunate. One of them had become too curious, poking his head in, to check on Vale. When he saw what was happening, he had called his colleague into the room. Null had been forced to quickly change into his natural state. It was the only way to kill two heavily armed guards quickly. He had felt no pleasure in their deaths. Had they not been so nosey, they would still be alive, and there would have only been two bodies to dispose of.

He thought furiously for minutes, considering and discarding possibilities before coming to a solution. It would be risky. *Unit Cabal* bases had sensors geared for any type of paranormal activity. Using a *majick* would be reckless. He huffed. What was the point of living if one did not take risks?

He straightened up, clasping his hands together, reciting the words as taught to him by a man named Grimoire, a man from a place far in the future. Smoke curled around the bodies. A light wind gusted through the room, increasing in strength as a hole appeared in the floor beneath the corpses. Null concentrated harder, pushing the bodies into the open void. They fell from the world, silently, the hole closing up behind them. There was no trace.

Null threw back his head, laughing. He was free. Free to walk amongst men once more, free of being a refugee, free from the burden of exile. Now he could live, feed and tell the Tales once more, no longer having to worry about Jericho, Stavlakis and the other *Cabalists.*

He had played the Game and won.

Still smiling, Null took one last look around the empty room. He smiled.

The Tales of Blood and Sulphur would continue. And that was all that mattered.

AUTHOR'S NOTE

WELL HERE WE ARE again, dear friends. Another time, another place but the Tales remain the same. Kind of. You are holding (peering at) the third iteration of Tales of Blood And Sulphur. Sadly, the mighty Booktrope, my erstwhile publisher, has fallen. There's not much I can say on that subject. Nor do I wish to. These things happen. It's part of the author journey. A new home has been found. That's all that matters.

Tales is now safely in the steady and safe hands of Messrs. Ralston and Flowers, heads of the Shadow Work Imprint. I'm happy with that.

Once agin, being the fair minded chap that I am, I have included a bonus story in this edition. This being the 'Booktrope Era' version, I felt it was only fair to include a short I wrote for the Forsaken 'Horror Holigans' anthology. Call it a bonus track. If you like. I've kept it separate from the other animals solely because I felt it didn't fit into the established rhythm of Apocalypse Minor. It's clearly a Clay piece dealing with Clay themes but it jars with the current order of stories. The strange thing is that an earlier version of this new story was part of the self published Tales.

'Nothing To Fear In The Dark' was originally known as 'The Guest From Hell'. In its infancy, it dealt with the subject matter as the version you are about to read (nasty TV presenter, enigmatic guest, weary put upon PA), but it was a lot nastier. There were crispy critters, a whole audience of the dead and a ginormous set of disembodied hands (that served no real purpose. I just liked the imagery. The hands will make an appearance one day). The graveyard scenes never happened and Simeon Kalfou, our TV anchor tormentor, was a lot cruder and much nastier. He was also known as Zalman Kolto (again, something I'm saving for later).

Bar these differences, the essence of the story has stayed true. It's a tale of bullying, hubris, external forces coming to aid the helpless and a little commentary on sensationalist chat show presenters, a subset of Humanity I have little time for. As with all my work, I'm proud of this story. It represents J.G. Clay frozen in one moment of time and space, a momento of thoughts and ideas from the past. It also represents, and brings to a close, my time with Booktrope, a time that has gifted me with a bit more knowledge, many more contacts and a whole load of friends.

Anyway, it's time for me to go and explore the Clayverse and see what other terrors are out there for me to report back on. I will return soon.

In the meantime, enjoy the show. Things are about to get a little rough…

NOTHING TO FEAR IN THE DARK

THERE WERE TWO LESSONS that Marnie Klein had learnt early in life. These truisms had been drilled into her by a father who wanted his offspring to live in the light, unafraid of the irrational fears and hatreds of the small minded.

The first; there was nothing to fear in the dark. There never had been. Monsters were the figment of febrile imaginations, attempts to rationalise the unknown, to give a shape and a name to things that were beyond the knowledge of the time. As a child, Marnie had strode fearlessly through horror film nights without flinching, had slept safe in the knowledge that the shape in the corner of her dark bedroom was nothing more than a pile of clothes and that the creaking of the stairs in the depths of night were the sounds of wood settling after the relentless pounding of feet. The dark of night was birthed by the absence of the sun; nothing more, nothing less. The inky black surrounding her as she sat on her father's grave held no surprises. The junkies and glue sniffers had moved on to new haunts. Others with more evil intent had an entire city of victims to choose from. A small forlorn cemetery tucked away in half forgotten area was not a choice hunting ground.

Her head swirled, her mind nowhere near as numb as she wished it to be. Monday was approaching. The dread coalescing in the pit of her stomach was not dissolving under the onslaught of cheap harsh vodka. She raised the half full bottle and swigged with a fierce determination, gagging at the raw potency of the gut rot booze.

The second lesson – perhaps the harshest one under the circumstances – was that the dead do not talk. Her father had been a non-believer, a rational secularist of the highest order, but gentle in his beliefs. He had often shook his head at some of the wilder pronouncements of New Atheists, regarding these men and women as equivalent to the very people they fought against. But he remained wedded to the secular ideal. Dead was dead. There was no afterlife, no pearly gates, no paradise stocked with muscular doe-eyed virgins, no endless repetition of rebirth and resurrection. The dead stayed dead.

This was of little comfort. Marnie needed his counsel now more than ever. The dark clouds of despair and desperation were too heavy for her to bear. She had no one left to confide in. The only child of two deceased parents stuck in a city where genuine friends were rarer than rocking horse shit, Marnie shouldered a great weight on her own. Two large unadulterated vodkas had sowed the seed in her mind; *go to Dad. Maybe, if he sees the state of me, he'll come.* She smiled ruefully, shaking her head at the idiocy of a drunken idea. Dad was gone, mown down by a van driver too intent on making the last drop of the day. Jonathan didn't stand a chance. His thin frame had been pulverised as the vehicle barrelled into him; death had been instant, his face wrecked as it had hit the windscreen, his bones splintered and sundered as his lifeless body slammed into the tarmac of the warm road. In moments of guilt and in the syrupy timeframe of nightmare, her imagination filled in the gaps. She saw her father – friend, idol, teacher – broken, twisted and leaking life onto baked ground; the kindly thin face reduced to a morass of blood greased meat and gristle, lidless eyes rolled upwards, a crazed grin showing through sliced and bruised lips; splintered bone poking through rents in the skin, white and red; organs that had once pulsed with vitality now reduced to thick paste that oozed from a broken carcass.

Her imagination, once a blessing and a boon, had become a curse and a tormentor.

Marnie rubbed her stinging eyes and looked skyward. The night had become stranger recently. The Northern Lights were not so Northern at the moment nor where they a comforting fascination shade of green. Veils of red and orange pulsed and coruscated above her, beautiful and threatening in equal measure. The eeriness of this new phenomenon was heightened by strange groaning sounds that seemed to rumble above from all points on the compass. The religious were in ecstasy, loudly proclaiming the end of days. The rational looked to science; Fukashima, volcanic ash, global warming. Conspiracy theorists and UFO enthusiasts threw down their own takes on the situation from the mildly eccentric to the utterly outrageous.

None of this was relevant or even interesting to Marnie Josephine Klein, twenty eight, raven haired, short-sighted and the P.A to the worst human being on the planet. If the word ended tonight, it would be a blessing. There would be a brief moment of pain followed by blissful nothingness. She would never have to face Martin 'Kaiser' Stark again. The mere thought of the man made her tremble. Two years working for the self-styled 'Kaiser of Chat Show TV' had reduced a strong confident kickboxing woman to a shell frightened of her own shadow and the subject of lunchtime and water cooler conversations. She had never overheard the gossip only speculate. Her colleagues probably wondered why she took the job in the first place and, more to the point, why she stuck with it. These were questions that she often asked herself. She knew why she stayed. Kaiser was vindictive as well as vicious. If she left, he would see to it that she never worked in this town again, maybe even the country. The reputation she had lovingly built up would count for nothing in an instant.

Marnie had toyed with the idea of asking her previous employer to have her back. He had been a horror writer; a little odd and eccentric, a big kid in the body of a forty something man; a science fiction fan who had insisted for a whole week that she address him as 'King Monkey' and had gone into paroxysms of delight when she had procured John Carpenter's autograph through a university acquaintance. The years preceding that particular gig had been great, but working for J.G, as he liked to be called, had been fantastic as well as a little odd. Pride held her back, even during her drunkest or darkest moments. The author had also been quite hurt when she had resigned. Loyalty was a big thing in his eyes. He felt as she was abandoning the family. There was no guarantee that he would welcome her back to the flock with open arms.

No, she was stuck in a nightmare job; well-paid but soul crushing. There was no way out for her, save insanity or suicide. The choices were unappealing. The sky rumbled overhead, a wheezing groan reverberating over the city. In the distance, alarms were triggered by the vibration. She raised her bottle in salute. Someone or something recognised her plight. Almost as if in reply, the firmament moaned again, a softer sadder sound this time that brought a tear to the drunken girl's eyes. Taking a deep breath, she raised the bottle to her lips again, forcing liquid oblivion down a throat bruised from tears and booze. She grimaced, her head shaking as fire detonated within her. The vodka tried to escape but Marnie clenched her teeth swallowing to keep it down. Eventually, the burning and nausea subsided. On the heels came a drowsiness, heavy and profound. Drink, stress and lack of sleep had been threatening to descend on her all week. She tried to fight it, dimly aware of the risks of falling asleep in a graveyard, maybe even being arrested for public drunkenness. Kaiser would have a field day if that were to happen.

It was no use. The fatigue was too strong an opponent and her strength had deserted her. Within moment, her eyelids slid shut, her face became slack and her breathing slowed. As she slid into unconsciousness, she seemed to her father's voice whispering to her.

There is nothing to fear in the dark. There are no monsters. Only Helpers.

She smiled and fell into a deep sleep.

The shadow detached itself from the night and glided towards to the sleeping form. It had no features to speak of, the vaguest suggestion of a humanoid form the only clue as to its origins. Ribbons of red haze, similar to the lights in the sky, shimmered across its gleaming ebony form. The shape paused at the slumbering girl's feet, seemingly studying her. The girl's pain throbbed from her. It could taste the metallic tang of panic and defeat from her dreams. Images flashed through the shape's consciousness; a hard angular face, blue eyes as cold as chips of ice, a stern lined brow topped with sandy immaculately combed hair. The shape seemed to nod its indistinct head in confirmation. Above it, in the firmament, a thin tendril of red haze thickened and writhed.

The shape leant down, scooping the comatose form up effortlessly. The bands of crimson on its surface danced in strange patterns. A low growl rumbled from the sky. The shape nodded twice and emitted a keening throaty sound before disappearing into the undergrowth with its burden.

A half empty vodka lay on its side, forgotten and abandoned on the grave of a dead father.

The canteen buzzed with excitement and activity. Plates clanged and crashed, cash registers beeped continuously and a hundred conversations ebbed and flowed. Crew, guests, audience members, journalists and hangers on sat in tight huddled groups, speculating on the show and whether the prime time evening slot would curb the Kaiser's vicious persona. Some hoped for a tamer version of the man who reduced Geraldo Riviera to tears on his last visit State-side. Others wanted to see the full blooded Kaiser, the man who threatened live on television to punch a well-known and equally vicious Scottish comedian's lights out (rumour had it that there was a scuffle between the two later that same day. Nothing was ever confirmed.). Anticipation was high, given the emotive subject of the premiere edition of *The Kaiser Questions*: 'Should the Religious Right be reined in?' Across the country, internet pundits, religious fanatics, neo-Nazis and trolls were cracking their knuckles, limbering up for the inevitable internet war.

Marnie Klein sat alone in a corner, watching with a dispassionate eye. Her jet black hair was scraped back into a tight pony tail, accentuating her widow's peak. She looked pale yet radiant. Several comments had been passed about a subtle difference in her demeanour, a change that couldn't be defined. Her eyes seemed more verdant than before, her bearing severe and brisk. Early on in the evening, one of the panel guests –a young British Muslim journalist rumoured to be a supporter (and possible financier) of terrorists –bumped into her, nearly spilling his coffee over himself. He glared at her, his teeth grinding in anger and contempt. Marnie returned the compliment, her gaze cold and detached. The journalist, ready to launch into an invective filled rant, stopped dead in his tracks. A sly terror stole over him. He saw something unpleasant in her eyes, an ancient malice at odds with her plain yet pretty look. The journalist looked away and stalked off, muttering about 'kuffar bitches' under his breath. Marne shrugged off the incident as if it had never happened.

She cast her gaze over the throng her mind elsewhere. The weekend had been a mystery to her, a mash up of jumbled images and deep slumber. She had awoken in her own bed on the Sunday, feeling remarkably fresh. Vague memories had assailed her; a bottle of vodka, her father's grave, gnashing despair and, strangest of all, a warm embrace. She had awoken alone. There was no question of a lover. Besides the touch had been one of a good friend not a lover. Even more puzzling was the sense of anticipation and the total ebbing of the debilitating sickening dread that she had been feeling all week. All ennui had gone. She felt more like the old Marnie – alive and excited.

Marnie Klein finished her drink and checked her watch. It was almost time to go to work. His Majesty would require his pre-show skinny latte – boiling hot and loaded with sugar. She had worked for him long enough to know his likes and dislikes. Kaiser Stark did not hold back his opinions. They were given, wanted or not. She stood and made her way over to the counter, scanning the crowd again. There were a few familiar faces, some acknowledgements. She ignored them all, fixating on the Asian journalist. He glared back at her, stroking the goatee beard adorning his chin. Marnie smiled wondering what his response would be if he could see himself through her eyes – gutted and shredded, his clothing scorched rags, his face streaked with thick clots of his own blood, his chest and abdomen an open hollowed out wound. As he moved around to face her fully, she saw tattered intestines, the ragged ends of the organs blackened and charred by some terrible heat. The mulch of ash and flesh slid from the cavity of his stomach and onto his lap before falling to the floor with a meaty *splat*.

This was more than an illusion. She knew this without knowing why. The vision was a premonition, the fulfilment of justice. The journalist was going to die soon in the same manner that he had himself had financed. The Universe was moving and conspiring to punish him for helping to fund death. She felt no distress. It was only fitting that a death monger should die in in the manner of his victim.

Her eye caught another – a university lecturer who had caused a controversy vile enough to get him the sack. He had admitted after months of speculation that he was a white supremacist and firmly believed in a racial hierarchy where white men ruled supreme, the 'coloureds' were subservient and the Jews a dim memory of an extinct race. He didn't look so superior to Marnie. Swastikas had been carved into him, whole chunks of meat and skin carved out down to the bone to form the dreaded symbol. He was drenched in crimson, his face the masterpiece of the body art. His nose had been flayed off to form the centrepiece of the Nazi emblem. Marnie watched, fascinated, as his breath formed air bubble in the blood filled cavities at the centre of his face. His forehead was a deep maroon trench, flecks of skull showing through the gore. Tiring of the spectacle, she had to the counter to order Kaiser's latte.

Ram, the server, beamed at her, his jowly face wobbling with delight as he greeted her with infectious enthusiasm. He was whole and injured. Marnie felt glad. The short chubby cook deserved no harm. He was a peaceful happy man who had endured the trauma of exile from his family, friend and homeland, his only crime being of different creed. Yet he remained gentle and kind. She paid him, shared a little joke and left the canteen ignoring every well-wisher and so-called friend. There was nothing left to say to these people.

"Do you know why they call me the Kaiser, Errol?"

Errol Preston has heard the anecdote a thousand times, maybe even more. Diplomacy and the need for employment ensured his silence however. Directing jobs were like gold dust these days. There was no need to rock the boat. Nodding and agreeing were sensible courses of action.

Kaiser swept his cool blue-eyed gaze over the corpulent harassed looking man.

Fucking slob. Look at you with your cheap shit shoes and hand me down clothes. If this scruffy turd wasn't so useful, I'd have got him the sack years ago. Kaiser paused for effect. Clicking his fingers and jabbing a finger into the director's face. Errol flinched, a shower of dandruff dusting his shoulders. Kaiser swallowed his distaste, his need to release the punchline greater than his physical disgust.

"Because I fucking rule. Unlike the original Kaiser however, I'm going to stay king and don't you forget it. Worldwide, son, worldwide."

Errol remained mute. He was tired. Weeks of unrelenting rehearsals and meeting had sapped his strength. Kaiser was demanding. Everything had to perfect for his new show. This was prime time, a slot guaranteed to propel him even further into the big leagues. Get this right and America would be begging him to come over. Then the fun could really begin. Kaiser enjoyed slaughtering sacred cows and America was full of the bastards. Britain was becoming soft and dull, too many years of nanny states and busy bodies stifling controversial opinions. Except for his. Kaiser had a rare combination of thoughtlessness and charm. It didn't matter what he said, the public seemed to love him. Others before him had tried the same approach and failed. Errol finally found his voice.

"Fifteen minutes to go."

Kaiser shrugged. "And. Do I look nervous? No. I'm just ready to get out there, start tearing a few new arseholes and make a few headlines. I've got the assets, haven't I? The face, the voice and the balls to go big in this game." His smile was disarming and warm, or at least it would be if it reached his eyes. They remained as dead as ever, giving his whole look a chilling effect. The door swung open. Errol looked over his shoulder, grateful for the interruption. Being alone with Kaiser made him anxious. Marnie breezed into the dressing room clutching Kaiser's drink. She glanced at Errol and smiled. He shivered. The grin was deeply unpleasant. It brought to mind a skull's grimace. Without a word, she set the drink down on the dressing table and handed Kaiser a clipboard.

"Tonight's running order as rehearsed. And your drink."

Errol's anxiousness increased. There was something off in Marnie's intonation. She sounded stiff, almost robotic, a million miles away from the nervy almost shrill woman that she had become. Kaiser snatched the board away from her.

"Efficient. It's only taken you two years to get the basics. Better late than never."

Marnie said nothing. She stood, studying Kaiser in fascination as if he were a new insect species. A secretive half smile played over her lips.

"Will you be needing anything else?"

Kaiser shook his head, nearly overcome by an inexplicable urge to run away from this woman. He fought to control his voice, afraid of the tremor that gripped his throat.

"No. Off you pop. Meet me back here after the show. We can make a start on interviews, social media, all that stuff."

The P.A nodded and, wordlessly left. Both men looked at each other, confused and slightly uneasy at Marnie's offhand behaviour. Her normal mode was 'sickeningly fawning and apologetic'. What had happened?

Kaiser resolved to find that out once tonight's show was over. He would break her down until he got to the truth.

Marnie moved swiftly down the corridor, propelled by a force that she didn't quite understand. She knew that there was someone coming, someone that she had to meet, but she unsure of who it was. She rounded the corner and headed towards a service corridor, well away from prying eye. The presence that drew her in shone like a beacon.

There is nothing to fear in the dark. The thought comforted her.

A huge shape filled the end of the corridor. The lights blinked on and off. She made a mental note to tell maintenance. The shape moved towards he, extended both hands. Into the light stepped, a giant of a man. He towered over her, his bulk filling her field of vision. The man was bald, his ebony tight skin shining in the flickering light. His face was benign and scholarly, his eyes brown and kindly yet heavy with forbidden knowledge. He smiled, his brilliant white a stark contrast against the purple black of skin. There was a flash of gold in that smile. That did not surprise her. His dark suit looked very expensive. A gold tooth felt and looked right. The crisp white shirt was open at the collar, the lack of a tie giving him a smart yet controlled casual style.

Marnie had never met this man before but a deep part of her knew him. He was a familiar presence. She held her hands out and gripped his huge hands. He held her considerably smaller hands in a gentle deft grip.

"Miss Klein." The voice was a pleasant deep rumble that emanated from the depths of his chest instead of his throat. She smiled. "A pleasure, *mon cheri*. This is an unpleasant task but one that must be performed, I regret to say. This *man*, this Kaiser, had been in our sights for some time. Echoes of the pain he had caused reverberate outwards, a ripple effect that disrupts and distorts all that it touches."

She nodded despite not fully understanding him. She knew in some sense that this man, this ebony giant had come to help her, to rid her of the man who had made her life a misery but she could not fathom how he had known who she was and how to find her. He smiled, a benevolent grin.

"One day, Miss Klein. One day. Suffice it to say that we heard your cry for help. When we realised the cause of your distress, our appetite for retribution increased. We had to assist you."

They lapsed into silence. The air around the couple hummed and fizzed with energy. It made Marnie's skin crawl, the sensation pleasant. She frowned.

"What will you do to him? I saw-"

"Saw what?"

"His injuries. The manner of his death."

The behemoth threw his head back, his booming laughter echoing up and down the deserted corridor. The laughter finished within seconds and his face became serious.

"We should have realised. You have a sensitive, a slight one, but the talent is there nonetheless. Fascinating. We won't kill him. We are merely going to strip him of his assets."

Marnie opened her mouth. The man put a finger on her lips to silence her.

"Sshhh. So many questions but not enough time to answer them. All will be revealed in time. You will know when and where. I will leave with this. My name is Simeon. Simeon Kalfu. I'm your Helper. There are other names for my kind depending on the Summoning and the intent behind it. Intention is the key. Now, I must attend to the business at hand."

Simeon released her hands and stepped back. His form wavered for a brief second. Marnie blinked her eyes. In that brief moment, he seemed to elongate, his limbs stretching and elongating, his fingers growing, tipped with wicked looking talons. His eyes burned red, the colour of the New Northern Lights. The moment passed. He was Simeon again.

"Please try not to interfere. We wish no harm to come to you. You are an innocent. Mr Stark is not. Goodbye, Miss Klein. For now."

Without another word, he pushed past her and made his way to the studio, leaving her alone, confused and a little afraid. The lights stopped flickering and regained their former luminescence.

"Marnie, have you seen Kaiser?"

Errol rushed to her, breathless and sweating. She shook her head.

"Fuck's sake", he spat through gritted teeth. "I've got execs screaming at me left right and centre, journalists wanting to know what the fuck was going on with him and his ex-wife on the phone bleating about how he's going to make his maintenance payments. Now where the fuck is he?"

Marnie regarded him with a twinge of pity. Errol's reputation was on the line too. The show had been a live train wreck. It had started out so promisingly. Kaiser had used all the tricks of his trade – vitriol, invective and a healthy dose of sarcasm all served up with his customary charm and wit. Little by little, it all went wrong. Kaiser became confused and distracted, mixing up the names of the guests. He had begun to pace the stage, ignoring the panel of guest. His attention was focused on the audience and on one man in particular. A giant of a black man three rows from the front. Marnie had smirked in recognition. Simeon Kalfu did not acknowledge her. He fixed Kaiser with a benign and bland stare.

The host's behaviour had become even more bizarre. He had begun to twitch, pointing at the man, ranting at him. Errol, frantic, bellowed at his host, all fear and timidity forgotten as Kaiser melted down on stage. In the end, Kaiser, the King of Chat, stormed off set and had not been seen since. Neither had Simeon. His seat was empty.

"I'll check his dressing room." Exasperation filtered through Errol's voice.

Marnie watched him walk away, knowing that he would not find him. Not in his dressing room at least. She also knew that wherever he was, Simeon would be close by.

Kaiser jumped out of the Jag and shambled through the cemetery gates, not even stopping to lock the car. He looked terrible.

His clothes were rumpled and sweat stained, his eyes hollow frantic and red rimmed. He exuded a stink, the sweaty funk of fear and madness. That man. What was he? Why had he done?

As he walked through the graveyard, he tried to piece together events from the jumble in his mind. The show had started well enough. He had brought his 'A-game' to the proceedings. But slowly and inexorably, it had begun to unravel. He became aware of someone watching. Eyes bored into the back of his head. Figures flitted by in the periphery of his vision, too quick for him to recognise. Smells began to assail him – the odour of roasted flesh, blood and shit. As his control slipped, he began to seek out the starer. They had to be in the audience. Whoever it was behind him. He turned, furiously scanning the crowd, his gaze zeroing in a heavy muscled black man. Kaiser brought the full force of his glare to bear on the man who did not even flinch. Then the world lurched into insanity. As he watched, the man began to *change*. Facial features became sagging and droopy, melting and running like warm wax. The thick stream of bloody flesh flowed over the man's white shirt reducing it to a butcher's apron in seconds.

Kaiser mumbled to himself as shock and terror battened him. His bowels voided, the warm shit running down his legs and the cries of disgust from the audience barely registering. He was too transfixed by the transformation. The man's clothes begin to ripple as the body beneath tore open and melted. Fabric tore, the sound deafening to Kaiser's overwhelmed senses, as the man's limbs elongated. Joints creaked as they reformed into impossible angles. A small frightened voice in the back of his mind jabbered at him, urging him to run. His legs would not respond, even when the travesty of a human being raised its face and looked at him. A black void, shot through with veins of red shifting light looked back at the terrified host. Deep within the void, something moved. His eyes strained, trying to make sense of it. The amorphous shape shifted too quickly for his brain. All he could see were teeth – wailing gnashing teeth of various sizes and shapes – and deep red eyes. The creature began to quiver. Deep mocking laughter issued from the hole in the man's face. As its true face came into view, Kaiser's last vestige of sanity snapped. He fled, walking briskly at first before running screaming from the studio. Kaiser did not look back. He could feel the creature's hot breath on his neck, the reek of carrion enveloping him.

Still screaming, he dove into his car and screeched away into the night. The memory of the drive eluded him. He paid no attention to the route following a voice within directing him to this cemetery on the edge of the city. The voice soothed him, assuring him safety.

He stopped walking looking groggily around him. The graveyard did not seem familiar. He had never been here before. Why had the voices directed him here? He turned in a slow circle. There were people here; mute, unmoving, stood by graves and tombs as if they were guarding them. The sense of unease returned. An odour, reminiscent of burnt pork tickled his quivering nostrils. It came from behind him. Kaiser squeezed his eyes shut, willing himself not to turn. His body disobeyed; his feet shuffled him around in a semi-circle. The smell thickened, the savoury tang of roasted flesh mixed in with the astringent choking fumes of petrol. His breath hitched in his throat as bile rose in his throat.

His eyelids, the disobedient bastards, slowly opened. He howled at the sight before him.

Two of the burnt corpses might have been children. They were small in stature. Beyond that, identification was near impossible. Fire had erased their facial feature. Each of the corpses wore lipless grins, bone white teeth gleaming in the burnt ruins. The taller one inclined its head forward. Kaiser gagged as a long thin white worm uncurled from the gaping hole where a nose had once been. The worm dropped the floor with a sick wet sound. The children giggled, their laughter carefree and happy, the true sound of childhood.

"Jesus, no", Kaiser spat through clenched teeth.

A voice rich dark with a hint of the Caribbean came from behind him.

"Jesus would never intercede, my friend. Not for one so tainted."

Kaiser spun around, trembling with fear and fatigue, but relieved that he didn't have to stare at the charred horrors anymore. His eyes widened, his lips drew back in a snarl.

"You!"

The giant man stepped out from behind a gravestone and opened his arms as if he was receiving rapturous applause. Kaiser's eyes alighted on the gravestone. The inscription stood out, even in the gloomy half-light of the red tinged night. He rubbed the bridge of his nose as he registered the name on the stone: JONATHAN KLEIN.

That can't be anything to do with the dozy bitch. Can it?

The giant walked steadily down the short incline and stood before him, filling his sight.

"Simeon Kalfu at your service."

Even in the extremity of his terror, Kaiser felt the rage boil within, the rage that had sustained him for most of his life and had propelled him to the height of his profession.

"Who are you? What is all this?"

Simeon chuckled.

"Retribution most divine, Mr Stark. You've been on our radar for some time. Actually, not just ours. There's a whole host of entities who have shown an interest in you. We're just glad that we got to you first."

Stark frowned, his fear lost in confusion.

"Entities? What are you, Intelligence? CIA, MI5, MOSSAD? Who have I pissed off this time? Is this some attempt to freak–."

Simeon held up a hand.

"Enough, Mr Stark. If it makes you feel a bit more important, then yes, those particular organisations were beginning to tire of you, as were a host of other more uncivilised groups. No, we are something else entirely."

Kaiser's fury simmered. His equilibrium was returning, a legacy of his self-discipline. This freak show was a ploy, a way to keep him off balance and destroy his career. It wouldn't work. As long as he had his face, his voice and his bollocks, they would never destroy him. Simeon favoured him with a sly secretive smile.

"Fuck this. I'm going."

The giant shook his head.

"Regretfully not. We can't allow you to leave. Not until retribution is extracted."

Kaiser snorted.

"Try and stop me, you black bastard."

He turned to leave.

The charred dead had company. His mind lurched again towards madness. A small crowd of people barred his escape route back to the car. His bladder ached to be voided, even though it was empty. His eyes bulged, drinking every detail, every wound of the hideous gathering. The smell of rot was overwhelming.

"I don't have to", Simeon intoned lifelessly. "My friends here have done the job for me. I'm sure you recognise some of them but let me give you an introduction."

Kaiser bit his lip, wincing as the taste of copper flooded his mouth.

"I know the burnt ones will be difficult to recognise but I'm sure the names will strike a chord. May I present Mrs Annalise Roy and her two children Cody and Shannon?"

Kaiser's hand flew to his mouth. The burnt corpses – hairless, skin crisp and flaked with dreadful lipless grins – moved forward with awful vigour. He groaned and put a hand to his mouth as recognition dawned on him. His mind jabbered the details at him.

Annalise Roy-her two children Cody and Shanice-killed in a house fire set by Annalise's ex-husband. The children had been DNA tested on his early morning hit 'The Kaiser Show'. Mad with rage and jealousy, the ex-husband had burnt the house down in a fit of rage on discovering that the children weren't his.

The burnt things that were once human stirred, as if in acknowledgement. One of the children giggled. Kaiser heaved, bile bubbling at the back of his throat. He shook his head slowly.

"I wasn't responsible. It was that psycho bastard husband of hers."

Simeon growled.

"What about Anjem Saif Kadhari?"

At the sound of his name, a slim young man with olive skin –a light smattering of beard growth adorning his baby face – stepped forward, beaming with pleasure.

Anjem Saif Kadhari-a Saudi Arabian asylum seeker. Appeared on the Kaiser Show. Was outed as an illegal immigrant and deported all because of Kaiser's anti-illegals campaign. Kadhari nodded at him, his head wobbling as the movement threatened to dislodge it. Kaiser saw the deep yawning wound in the boy's throat, the cigarette burns on his face, the bruises that mottled his neckline.

An older man, dressed in a plain suit and tie stood at Kadhari's shoulder. He glowered at the chat show host, his hatred palpable.

Sir Alan Delany – a crusading politician, man of the people. Brought down low by Kaiser's own personal crusade against him. Disgraced after revelations of his infidelity, he had killed himself. The kindly looking man glowered at him, the burn mark of the rope livid against the fish belly white of his neck. Hid head canted to the left, his neck obviously broken.

"Not my fault, not my fault, not my fault."

Simeon laughed again, indulgently.

"I have a surprise guest for you. You cannot absolve yourself of blame for this one." The silence of the night was shattered by an ululating wail. The crowd of the dead parted to make way for one last guest on this cavalcade of horror. A large beetle-like shape crawled towards him on all fours, leaving a trail of blood and fluid on the ground like a snail's trail. Soft looking pieces of organ fell from the ruptured frame of the thing. The stink was incredible

"Jesus, fuck, no." Kaiser backpedalled as the horror scuttled towards him, cackling insanely. Strong hands held him firm.

"Look! Look at what you caused."

The creature stopped and reared up on smashed crooked legs; white shards of bone poked through torn and sheared muscle. Its torso gaped obscenely, the freight of organs within pulverised to paste and scraps. He choked as the odour of bile, excrement and freshly opened veins overwhelmed him. The creature looked at him and cackled again, the one remaining eye flickering insanely from left to right. Its face was a ruin, the jaw unhinged and hanging, its shredded tongue lolling obscenely. Remarkably, its hair – black and curly – remained undamaged, save for a few matted clots of brain and bone that stuck like adornments

Kaiser swallowed again. "What. Who did you say this was?"

"The name doesn't ring a bell? Lilith Le Grande, your former Personal Assistant? Lilith Le Grande, the woman you ground into the dust? Lilith Le Grande, the girl who was so traumatised by the end of your affair that she threw herself in front of a lorry?"

Tears began to stream down Kaiser's face. The crooked twisted monstrosity once known as Lilith, looked up at him. Its single bloodshot eye ceased rolling and fixed on him. He saw love in that ruined gaze, a love that had destroyed a beautiful young woman and given rise to the reeking thing before him. The smashed horror uttered a queer choking sound, halfway between a laugh and a sob before turning and crawling away, its head hanging in pain and shame. He felt Simeon at his shoulder.

"Marnie Klein was almost the next victim of your utter disregard for anyone else. That could not be allowed to happen. She has a special place in the Omniverse, unrealised by herself and almost strangled by you. She will grow once you have been removed."

"You're going to kill me", Kaiser said tonelessly.

Simeon sighed. "A pointless exercise. There is no value in killing you. The end would be too swift and Hell would lay claim to you. No, we need you alive. That will give us time enough to perfect a *magick* strong enough to dissolve Hell's claim on you." Kaiser turned away from the gaggle of dead flesh. He looked up at Simeon.

"So what? What are you going to do?"

The large black man gazed down at the floor for a few moments. He began to quiver, imperceptibly at first. Kaiser watched in horrified fascination as the man's scalp began to writhe and pulsate. Simeon looked back up, the change upon him. His handsome features began to liquefy, the skin sloughing like a snake's. His dark brown eyes remained unchanged, the glint of warmth obscene in the river of melting meat. Kaiser's legs became weak as he observed the change up close. Simeon's skull grinned at him, his face now glistening ropes of blood and mucus that coated his shirt. The rest of his head remained untouched, adding to the bizarreness of the spectacle. Incredibly, Simeon spoke, his words clear and articulate despite the lack of lips and tongue.

"I'm going to asset-strip you." The bone of Simeon's grinning white visage began to crack and flake. Bone became dust, falling from the ever growing void. "Your face, voice and balls are important to you. I'm going to relieve you of them."

Kaiser tried to back pedal. The faceless horror grabbed his arm in a vice-like grip and squeezed. He screamed as his radius and ulna shattered like dry twigs. Jagged bone erupted from the skin, opening gaping bleeding wounds.

"Look at me!" Simeon commanded. Kaiser obeyed despite his desperation. He stared into the red streaked void, suddenly aware of how similar they were to the New Northern Lights. Was he the cause of the strange new phenomena? With surprising regret, Kaiser realised that he would never find out. Death seemed inevitable.

There was a stirring in the dark space of Simeon's head. Something muscular and thick uncurled itself in the inky depths and slithered towards him. Kaiser began to thrash madly, screaming 'no' over and over again, an entreaty to the thing that called itself Simeon Kalfu. It was too late in the day. Three dripping tentacles uncoiled themselves from the black hole in Simeon's head and reared above the terrified man. Each thick appendage terminated in a strange fleshy flower-like organ which opened and closed sleepily. Hooked incisors lined the 'flowers', daubed in shining saliva.

Kaiser prayed silently.

Simeon giggled.

In unison, the tentacles whipped towards him, fastening themselves to different areas. He felt blind panic as one gripped his face and squeezed. Agony lanced through his forehead and jaw as the teeth punctured his skin. Another clutched his throat, biting into the soft meat and hooking around his larynx. The last one tore open the front of his trousers and boxer short. Kaiser felt the wind tickling his scrotum briefly, then pure torment as the appendage swallowed his genitals whole. He felt a momentary warmth and slickness before the mouth clamped down and the teeth penetrated his manhood. He couldn't scream. The tentacle on his face blocked his airways. The pain became all-consuming, expanding and blooming until all he felt was torture. Beyond the haze, he heard a deep voice. It sounded underwater, bubbling but still coherent.

"Goodnight, Mr Stark. God bless."

The tentacles wrenched away from him and the pain devoured him.

Marnie felt the call two weeks later and let it guide her to a small coffee shop in the city centre. She ordered a cappuccino from the friendly but tired looking Italian gentleman behind the counter and decided to take it outside. The day was warm enough and she had taken up smoking again, despite being unemployed. Everyone had a vice these days. It was part of being alive.

She sat, watching people of all nationalities go about their business some happy, some sad, others psychotic. The strange talent that Simeon had recognised was beginning to bloom. At times, it could be overwhelming. For the moment, Marnie avoided crowded places. The onslaught of emotions had caused fainting and bleeding from the ears and nose.

A copy of 'The Guardian' had been left on the table. Curious, she unfolded the paper, scanning the front page. Kaiser had been relegated to a piece at the foot of the page. An eminent American plastic surgeon proclaimed his facial reconstruction impossible. There wasn't enough left to build upon. Kaiser would have to remain under care for the rest of his life, a faceless horror bereft of communication thanks to the removal of his larynx and devoid of his manhood. His eyes had been severely damaged leaving him totally blind. A small part of her felt pity for the man now locked inside his head forever unable to interact with the world around him. In those moments, she let herself remember his bullying, his scorn and his anger towards her. The pity evaporated in seconds.

In the days after the police had found him, she had been questioned. All standard procedure of course. A hideous mutilating attack on a celebrity had to be investigated. The eyes of the people and the media were on the police. They had to be seen to be doing something. She had been told on good authority that one of the policeman who found him – a veteran officer who had been one of the first on the scene during 7/7 had copiously vomited and resigned on the spot. She could understand why. Marnie had seen his injured long before they had been inflicted. She had foreseen them that last terrible night.

Marnie inhaled and exhaled deeply. There was no point in mulling over Kaiser's fate. He had got what he deserved. It was time to rebuild. She put the paper down and sipped on her coffee.

"Is this seat taken?"

The voice, so rich and familiar brought a smile to her lips.

"Be my guest."

Simeon sat down, displaying a surprising grace and poise for a man so large. He clasped his hands in front of him, looking at her expectantly.

"Would you like a drink?"

He shook his head.

"Not for the moment."

The pair lapsed into a comfortable silence for a moment, both sizing each other. Simeon broke the silence.

"We have a job offer for you."

Marnie cocked her head to the left slightly, a trait that she had since childhood. Simeon took this as encouragement.

"I can't discuss it too much here, however, I can tell you that the pay is very good, there are plenty of benefits and you'll never have to work with the likes of Kaiser again."

She smiled, finished her drink and gave the dark man a level stare.

"I'm interested. But I'd like to add some terms."

"Name them."

"One, I want to know exactly what happened to Kaiser."

"Why?"

"Curiosity."

Simeon nodded stroking his chin thoughtfully. "And the second?"

"Who you really are?"

He laughed, a happy relieved sound.

"Is that all you require? Such simple terms, Miss Klein. I'm sure they can be accommodated."

"That's what I wanted to hear."

Silence descended again, broken momentarily by two Sikh gentlemen chatting loudly to each other in Punjabi. That never failed to amuse Marnie. She had known a few Sikh families growing up. They were good hearted people and larger than life. Loud volume was a way of life for them, no holds barred communication but without malice. The two men laughed heartily as they walked away. She watched them.

"What am I getting into, Simeon?" She turned her head back. His face –distinguished and handsome – was sombre.

"Are you afraid?"

She nodded. "A little, yeah."

"A little fear is a good thing but take care not to be lost in your fear. Remember your father's advice."

She nodded in agreement, repeating the phrase to herself. It seemed to have more potency now. Things had changed, maybe beyond recognition, but there was nothing to fear in the dark nor would there be. At least, she hoped that there never would be.

The look on Simeon's face said otherwise. She finished her drink and the pair headed out into the warm August day.

ACKNOWLEDGMENTS

There's some big thanks that need to be given. I may have written the book, but there has been a herd of people behind me contributing in ways beyond measure.

Firstly, a huge thank you to my Forsaken team for helping me hammer this collection into a gleaming shiny tower of malevolence. Chris Nelson and Michael-Israel Jarvis – your editing and proofreading skills have helped to reshape the ragtag bunch of stories I had into something fresh, new and dangerous. Thanks, guys. (By the way Michael. Oasis *do* rock. That's my final word on the matter). Massive gratitude to Ashley Ruggirello for the awesome cover art -it's an artistic dark gem.

A quick shout out to the Dons of Shadow Work Publishing, Duncan Ralston and Thomas Flowers III, for taking a bereft and bedraggled Clay and giving him a new home with some fantastic and talented house mates. Hopefully, this won't be a one shot deal, more of a 'supergroup' type of affair.

Next up, *family* and friends – the two most important words beginning with 'f'. You're too numerous to list individually, (even though that would bump up my word count astronomically), but you know who you are. Peace, people.

A quick special thanks to my English teachers – Miranda Watson, Anita Tanner and Carole Hansford – for actively encouraging my insanity.

And last, but no means least, a humoungously large thank you to my lovely wife, Rachel, and my fantastic step-daughter Molly. Thank you for the faith, the support and the cups of tea. Always appreciated.

One more special and heartfelt thank you has to be said, and that one goes out to you, dear reader of mine. Thank you for taking the time to delve into the dark world of J.G Clay. Please feel free to visit anytime. I'll be waiting…..

ABOUT THE AUTHOR

J.G Clay was born in Leamington Spa, Warwickshire in 1973. A life-long horror and science fiction fan, he has written for his own amusement since his teenage years, taking time off to do the usual things that adolescent boys do and growing up disgracefully. Now in his forties, he has returned to his passion for the dark, the weird and the twisted.

Off duty, he has a passion for music, films and Birmingham City FC. He can also hold down a half decent bassline.

J.G lives with his wife and step-daughter in Rothwell, Northamptonshire – the heart of the English countryside.

For more delicious dark fiction,
visit www.jgclayhorror.com
and www.shadowwork.com.

78356602R00141

Made in the USA
Columbia, SC
15 October 2017